THE SEAM
SECRETS BENEATH THE NORTH POLE

THE SEAM

Secrets Beneath the North Pole

Deborah A. Wilson

Published by Arctic Meridian Press

First edition

ISBN: 979-8-9946743-0-7

Cover design by Adam Fyda
Interior design and formatting by Daniel Pyle
Copyediting by Dan Hanks
Author photo copyright © 2026 by Chuck Slay

Printed in the United States of America

To my beloved family, steadfast friends, trusted colleagues, and cherished clients—this work is humbly dedicated.

Each of you, in your own way, has shaped my journey with your presence, wisdom, encouragement, and love. Some of you have walked beside me for many years, while others appeared only for a season; yet all of you have left an imprint upon my life. It is through your prayers, patience, and unwavering support that this book has found its form.

To name you all would be impossible, and perhaps unnecessary—for you know who you are. In moments of joy and struggle, you have reminded me that no one travels alone. Your contributions, spoken and unspoken, have been threads woven into the fabric of this work.

May this dedication stand as a tribute to the immeasurable value of every relationship God has entrusted to me, and as a quiet testimony to the power of community in nurturing both faith and creativity.

ACKNOWLEDGMENTS

First and foremost, I give thanks to the Creator, the source of all inspiration and the giver of every good gift. Without His guidance, grace, and sustaining hand, this work would never have been conceived nor completed. To Him belongs the glory for the talent and vision He has entrusted to me.

I am deeply grateful for the many people God has placed in my life across the years—family, friends, mentors, and encouragers—each of whom has contributed in quiet yet meaningful ways to this journey. Their faith, patience, and support have been constant reminders of His provision.

With special affection, I remember and thank Mrs. B. Price, my college English teacher, who first impressed upon me the power of reading and the art of writing. Her influence awakened in me the discipline and joy of words, a gift that has carried me to this moment.

To all who have walked alongside me, knowingly or unknowingly shaping my path, I offer my sincerest gratitude. This book is as much yours as it is mine.

PROLOGUE

The year was 1922 and the world above the Arctic Circle lay in a silence older than memory could recall. Here, night and day were not separate states but strange companions, entangled in a twilight haze that lingered without end. The heavens glowed faintly, their horizons blurred by veils of cloud and refracted light. At odd hours, slivers of dawn writhed against the sky like restless spirits, only to vanish behind curtains of drifting frost.

The sea, bound in armor, groaned under the weight of ice thicker than cathedrals. Floes drifted like slow-moving fortresses, colliding with the patient inevitability of centuries. A gale wandered across the frozen expanse, dragging sheets of snow into spirals that hovered in the air, dancing like living breath. Even the wind here sounded ancient, carrying with it the voices of explorers long claimed by the white abyss. To step into this desolation was to step outside of time itself.

And yet, through that wasteland of frost and shadow came a vessel no man had built. Its form slipped across the frozen surface as if ice and sea alike made way for it. No rivets or seams marred its skin; the exterior gleamed with an uncanny sheen that reflected not the pale moonlight but a hidden radiance from within. To glimpse it—even for a heartbeat—would have been to know instinctively that it did not belong to the world of men. But no human eye beheld its passage.

When at last it came to rest amid a broad snowfield, it did so with a deliberate calm, as if its arrival were meant for silence alone. No echo rang; no groan of pressure cracked the ice. Sound itself seemed banished, leaving only the faint hiss of falling snow. Then, with measured inevitability, a panel in its side dissolved into nothingness, and six figures emerged. They came at twilight, when the line between heaven and earth dissolved into a veil of ice and light.

The six figures advanced across the desolation, taller than any seafarer or hunter who had dared these brutal frontiers. Their cloaks, heavy with frost, shimmered faintly as though spun from the daybreaks themselves. The storm clawed at them, shrieking with a thousand frozen teeth, yet it could not master them. The cold retreated like a beggar denied at a king's gate. Their strides pressed deep into the snow, yet they moved with impossible grace, as if the earth itself bent to bear them forward. Each step echoed with gravity, not weight, as though time itself paused to reckon their passing.

At their head walked the tallest. He halted, and the wilderness hushed. His eyes swept the horizon where sky and ice folded into one another, and the brilliance of the snow seemed to dim before his gaze. No breath clouded the air around him. The stillness of his presence commanded more than silence—it commanded obedience.

To his right walked one whose cloak carried the glow of hidden fire, her steps softening the snow instead of crushing it. Mercy clung to her like a second mantle, and the storm faltered at her passing. Beside her strode one broad of shoulder, his cloak rimed in darker frost, his every motion carved from judgment itself. Behind them walked two alike, their hoods drawn low, their forms luminous in outline. When they turned toward each other, even slightly, light coursed between them as though they spoke in a language the earth itself could not translate.

The last lingered at the rear, a shadow within radiance. His cloak brushed the snow without marking it. He moved half within this world and half beyond it, the air around him thinning, trembling, as though reality strained to contain his shape.

Together they crossed the unbroken wilderness, six beings where no life should stand, their silence heavier than thunder. And though no word was spoken, the land itself seemed to understand: this was no passage of mortals, but of heralds. They had not come to be seen. They had come to begin.

The tall ones formed a circle. At first, no words passed among them. Instead, they lifted their faces toward the heavens. Above them, the dawn shivered into arcs of color—emerald, gold, and violet bending as though answering a call. For a moment, the lights of the sky seemed alive, swaying not by chance but by will. At last, the tallest one raised his hand. His voice, when it came, was neither loud nor strained, but carried effortlessly across the snow, each syllable striking with the weight of command.

"This is the appointed place," he said, his tone calm, unstoppable. The words lingered like frost on stone. "But not the appointed hour."

They continued talking amongst themselves, but their speech was carried away by the wind.

They bowed their heads, as if preparing for prayer, and continued speaking to each other in a manner that earth beings could not understand. From beneath their cloaks came faint glimmers, delicate lines of light etched into fabric or skin—it was impossible to tell which. Each glow pulsed in rhythm, as though responding to a heartbeat shared among them.

For a long while, they stood in silence, listening. But it was not the ice, nor the wind, nor the sky to which they attended. Their attention reached elsewhere—downward, inward, to a presence hidden beneath the crust of snow and stone, or perhaps to a voice that echoed from beyond the realm of earth itself. Then, with a motion so seamless it seemed rehearsed for centuries, they turned as one and approached the heart of the snowfield. The tallest bent, pressing his palm against the ground. At once, the ice groaned as if woken from slumber. A crack tore open, not jagged like broken ice but deliberate, shaped by design. From within spilled a glow of impossible hues—amber, violet, and a deep indigo that carried the weight of eternity. The earth had not cracked. It had opened.

One by one, the six descended into the radiance. Their cloaks caught the light, casting long shadows that trembled like banners across the field. No ropes tethered them; no lanterns pierced their way. They moved with certainty, as though following a path carved long before they came.

The last figure lingered. He stood upon the threshold and turned his gaze outward. Before him stretched the endless expanse of ice, silent and merciless, yet his eyes, crowned in that instant by the flames of the aurora, carried not defiance but sorrow. It was the look of one who knew the burden of centuries, who foresaw both the triumph and the tragedy of ages yet unborn. His lips parted, and though the words were not of human tongue, the wind bore their cadence:

"We must wait for the appointed hour." That was the human translation, though the weight of the words carried deeper than speech—like an oath carved into the marrow of time. Then, in an instant, he too was gone.

The fissure closed upon itself, silent and seamless, as if the ice had never yielded. For a breath, the ground pulsed with a dim glow from below, a light that seeped upward like a heartbeat muffled in stone. It lingered, then faded, leaving only the pale shimmer of the auroras above.

From the depths of polar silence, the vessel stirred. It rose through the veil of drifting snow, an immense silhouette rimmed in quiet radiance, neither flame nor smoke trailing its ascent. Its surface caught the light of the heavens and bent it strangely, as though the stars themselves curved around it. For an instant, the sky bowed—auroras folding inward, veils of green and violet wrapping the hull as though consecrating its departure. Then, as if exhaling a secret, the vessel dissolved into the dark, vanishing without a trace.

The land returned to silence. Snow fell steadily, erasing every scar of intrusion, sealing the plain once more in white stillness. To any who might wander here, nothing had changed. The wilderness endured, endless and untouched.

But the earth remembered. Beneath the frozen crust, corridors newly hollowed exhaled the faint warmth of purpose. In time, a world would be built below, hidden from mortal sight, awaiting the hour foretold.

Above, the wind carried the last echo of voices that did not belong to men, scattering them across the night like embers of a fire long buried.

Above, the aurora continued its eternal dance, indifferent, magnificent. To the world of 1922, nothing had changed. But beneath the Arctic crust, something had taken root—a hidden presence, waiting for the duly appointed hour, when man would be invited to listen.

And then—silence. Not the silence of emptiness, but of something withheld—the earth itself holding its breath. The snow fell thicker, smothering all trace of passage, yet beneath the ice a pulse lingered, faint but insistent, as if the ground had swallowed a secret, it would not release until the appointed time.

It was a silence that did not simply conceal, but promised—return, reckoning, revelation.

ONE

THE FORGOTTEN BOOK

Winston Thornberry was a man in his sixties whose tweed jackets carried the scent of old libraries and whose restless eyes betrayed a mind forever chasing patterns others dismissed as chance. He lived for decades in the damp, rain-drenched heart of the Pacific Northwest, a land where fog blurred the line between earth and sky, and where myths seemed to grow as easily as the towering evergreens. An eccentric, contemplative professor by trade, he had long ago abandoned the notion of coincidence, convinced that every fragment of life—every stray word, every forgotten symbol—was part of a design waiting to be uncovered. A man who lived among stacks of forgotten manuscripts, faded scrolls, and arcane volumes could not afford such a luxury as coincidence. For him, every stray fragment of text, every inexplicable discovery, every tattered margin note was part of a larger pattern. The rational world laughed at such thinking, but Winston had long ago learned that reason alone was a brittle lantern in a vast cavern. He preferred the deeper glow of mystery, however treacherous its light may be.

His study, tucked away in a corner of his house, bore little resemblance to the polished offices of his colleagues. Their spaces were clean and organized, with neat shelves and well-maintained desks, where one could receive visitors and maintain the air of respectable academia. Winston's chambers, by contrast, resembled a vault devoted to knowledge. Dust particles drifted perpetually in the air like the unsettled ghosts of forgotten scribes. Books leaned against one another like drunks after a long night, their spines broken, their titles erased by time. The carpet beneath his desk was worn to the threads by decades of pacing. And the smell—ah, the smell—was of leather, mildew, ink, and that faint iron tang of paper left too long in the damp, dimly lit basement that occupied most of his waking hours. Yet, Winston found comfort in this clutter.

There were no lifeless objects. They were companions from ages past. He often told himself, only half in jest, that he could hear the heartbeat of history in the pages of his books. When he read them late into the night, he fancied that they whispered to him, passing along secrets too fragile to be spoken aloud. It was a lonely way to live, but Winston never considered it lonely. To live without mystery—that, he believed, was true solitude.

That night, Winston had a vision, and the line was blurred between dream or prophetic revelation. He saw himself standing in a wasteland of ice, endless and blinding, the air so cold it burned his lungs. The surroundings dissolved into white silence, a stillness so deep it felt like the end of the world. His clothes offered no warmth. The cold clawed through fabric and flesh, numbing his limbs until he could barely move. He was alone and paralyzed by the weight of the moment.

Then, through the storm, he saw it. A book, unlike anything he had ever seen, floating through the storm. Suddenly and without warning, the Book rested on a pedestal of frost, untouched by snow. Its cover was dark, yet glowing faintly as though lit from within. Around it the air softened. A warmth spread outward, not fire but something purer, deeper—like solace given shape. The icy wind faltered at its presence, and Winston felt strength return to his bones. He stood in awe.

He reached for it, but before his hand touched the cover, the pages stirred as if alive. They curled inward, sealing themselves shut, as the pedestal shook from side to side. A whisper moved through the silence, not heard with ears but pressed directly into his spirit: "*You will seek me... You will vow it. And I will answer.*"

The warmth quickly vanished. The storm surged again, swallowing the Book and the pedestal, causing all things around him to disappear. Winston gasped awake on the tiny cot in his study, drenched in sweat, yet shivering with a chill that seemed not of this world. He often fell asleep in the study following long nights of reading, writing, and researching matters that Margaret, his wife, had no desire to be a part of but this was different. His breathing was shallow, as he struggled to compose himself. He sat upright, staring aimlessly around the room, in a muddled state.

"It's only a dream," he murmured to himself, the words dissolving into the quiet. Slowly, he drew back to the edge of the cot and sat there—motionless, hollow-eyed—staring into the unyielding silence, as though searching for meaning in the emptiness before him. He yawned a few times before returning to the comfort of his makeshift bed.

Morning light slanted pale and gray through the rain-streaked windows. He had awoken before dawn, heart pounding, the final echoes of the dream still clinging to him like mist. The air in his study was cold, his lamp dimly lit, but he could not shake the warmth that had filled him in sleep—the warmth of the Book's presence, luminous and alive. He sat at the edge of the cot, fingers trembling as he tried to recall the sequence of images: his fragile body in the snow, the light beneath the ice, and the whispers that had seemed to speak to him. Logic urged him to dismiss it—a conjuring of the mind, a byproduct of exhaustion—but he knew better. The dream had not come to entertain his curiosity; it had come to summon him.

Winston rubbed the remnants of the dream from his eyes, unsettled by how real the Book had felt. But his breath stalled when he saw a parcel resting squarely on his desk. He had never heard the knock that must have accompanied its delivery late into the night and no members of his household had come to him with knowledge of a delivery or the parcel's existence. But there it simply was—squatting on the pile of unopened correspondence like an intruder that had always belonged.

Winston gazed at the parcel as one might regard a

long-lost friend returned from years of silence—familiar, yet distant. And still, some quiet hesitation within him refused to let his hand reach for it. "Where did you come from?" he whispered as if expecting the parcel to respond. "Could it be?" he asked with uncertainty, without continuing this thought, as he inched closer to the desk to examine the package more closely.

The wrapping was unlike anything he had ever seen. It was not ordinary paper but brittle parchment, yellowed unevenly with age, the edges curling as if scorched by some forgotten fire. A glob of dark wax sealed its flap, but the impression it bore belonged to no heraldry, no university insignia, no private press. It was a circle within a circle, intersected by a line. Simple, stark, and for some reason, profoundly unsettling. There was no note, no sender, no explanation. To most men, it would have been an oddity, a curiosity to puzzle over and then set aside. But Winston was not most men. To him, the parcel was no accident of delivery. It was a summons of sorts, calling him to some unknown challenge that he would hopefully soon discover.

With trembling fingers, he slit the parchment open, his spectacles sliding dangerously down his long, angular nose. Inside was a book unlike any he had ever encountered in decades of rummaging through archives and backwater libraries. Its cover was as dark as obsidian, polished to a sheen that seemed to swallow light. And as he stared at the closed volume resting on the desk before him, he realized with quiet dread that the dream and the Book were one and the same: both alive, both waiting, both calling him forward.

When he tilted it beneath a nearby lamp, the surface glimmered faintly as though alive, pulsing with an inner vitality. No title adorned its spine, no decoration announced its worth. The Book declared its mystery through silence. When he cracked it open, a faint fragrance rose from the pages—a mingling of cedar, ash, and something older still, something that stirred a memory buried so deeply he could not name it. For an instant, his stomach turned with unease. He nearly closed the volume and shoved it back into its wrapping. But curiosity won, as it always did. The first page bore an inscription written in a hand too steady, too deliberate, to belong to any ordinary scribe:

"In the year men counted as 1922, we descended, with high expectations of the earth man's awakening. Yet, we wait still, for the hour when humanity will listen."

The words hit him like a hammer blow. He read them aloud, many times, his voice quivering in the dimly lit light. The syllables seemed to vibrate in the room, echoing from the bookshelves, rippling through the dust-laden air. For one absurd heartbeat, Winston swore the volumes around him leaned closer, listening like old conspirators. His pulse quickened. He closed the Book sharply, then opened it again, unable to resist. Strangest of all, the script itself seemed to shift as he looked at it—not in language, but in tone, as though the meaning resisted permanence; as though the Book demanded faith before revelation.

He pressed both hands into his unruly shock of gray hair and leaned back in his chair. All his life, he had been mocked for chasing after the intangible. At the university, he was the eccentric professor, tolerated but not respected. His lectures on ancient myths and hidden civilizations were met with polite indifference from colleagues who prioritized tenure and grant money. At home, his family regarded his obsessions with weary affection, humoring him the way one might humor a child lost in his fantasies. Yet Winston had clung to a singular creed: that mankind bore an obligation to reach beyond the veil of the visible world, to strain toward the truths that lay just out of reach.

And here, at last, was vindication. The very thought of receiving some form of validation after years of struggling to free himself from taunts and humiliation was simply overwhelming. He felt as if a weight was being lifted from his mind, thus freeing him to delve deeper into mysteries of the unknown. The Book had not come by chance. The dream or vision was a sign aimed at preparing him for this moment. It was no accident. It was a divine invitation confirming that he was chosen.

But, chosen for what?

As he pondered the significance of the moment, he found himself feeling thoughts of unease. The lamplight dimmed inexplicably. A hush fell over the room, as though the entire house paused, holding its breath, waiting for instructions. Cold sweat prickled at Winston's brow. His fingers traced the edge of the dark cover. What was this Book? Who had sent it? But, most importantly, why had it come to him?

Time slipped away unnoticed as he turned its pages. Some leaves bore words in that unnervingly steady script. Others displayed only strange symbols—geometric forms, constellations unfamiliar to any map that seemed to pulse faintly with light when glimpsed from the corner of the eye. He scribbled frantic notes in his journal, connecting half-remembered myths, fragments of scripture, and references to explorers who had vanished into the polar wilderness. His handwriting grew more erratic as the day deepened, his mind racing to keep pace with the torrent of impressions.

Winston knew that the dream was no illusion but a revelation—an unveiling meant to draw him toward the Book's deeper purpose. Yet beneath the wonder stirred something darker: the slow return of that consuming hunger to understand what challenged reason. He felt it coil within him, quiet but relentless, the same restless pull that had once cost him peace, reputation, and love. And still, he could not resist it.

Outside, the world remained oblivious. Students laughed on the campus lawn. Faculty debated safe matters in warm, well-lit halls. His family prepared supper without him, their voices muffled by the study door. Winston knew he had to find a way to somehow blend into what others saw as "normal," without compromising his belief into the higher side of man's evolution. The very thought of accepting the physical plane as the only proof of mankind's existence was a hard sell for him. The ordinary world had already begun to dissolve, many years ago, and the line between real and illusion was more than blurred in the eyes of Winston Thornberry. He knew that the Book's revelations would open unseen doors, leading him down paths only its whisper could reveal.

He had spent the entire day tucked away in his study, buried in the pages of the Book. By nightfall, his spectacles lay discarded, his eyes bloodshot, his posture hunched. He reached for his journal, the one he had long reserved for private observations—pages crowded with fragments of thought, sketches of symbols, and questions that refused to be silenced. He stroked the pages as though they were a living thing and slowly opened to a fresh one. He stared at the page and began to write, almost prayerfully:

"I will find you... Wherever you are hidden, I will come to you..."

The words left the tip of Winston's pen not as idle curiosity, but as a binding vow, written into the pages of his journal like iron sinking into water.

He closed the journal and cautiously focused his attentions on the Book. It did not stir, yet the air around it seemed to shift, as though the room itself had heard and would remember. In writing the promise, Winston had crossed a threshold he could neither see nor retreat from. The moment sealed him. The Book had chosen its reader, and he, in reckless hunger, had chosen it in return.

Something deep within him tightened—a mingling of awe and dread—as though invisible hands had turned his steps onto a road that bent beyond sight. What he mistook for discovery was, in truth, initiation. The hunger that had driven him to this page would no longer belong to him; it would belong to the Book. And the journey it demanded would unmake the life he thought he owned, and remake him into something he had not yet begun to fathom.

Hours continue to slip away unnoticed. Beyond the window, many dawns crept across the sky—pale, indifferent, and remote—while Winston remained anchored in another realm entirely, a stranger to the waking world. The dream lingered like incense in his mind, expanding with each recollection until it became a living architecture—memory and prophecy woven together in secret geometry. With every reflection upon the dream, with every passage traced from the Book, his conviction deepened: the Book had chosen him, and through him its message would be reborn.

When he finally looked up, the room was gray with morning. His journal lay open before him, filled with words he scarcely remembered writing. Asher, his beloved husky, stirred from his place by the hearth, watching with solemn eyes. Winston exhaled a long, weary breath.

"It's begun," he whispered, more to himself than to the dog, while writing in his journal. "And there's no turning back now."

He gave a faint smile, while gently closing his journal. In the stillness that followed, he thought he heard it—a faint exhalation, almost like breath coming from the body of the nearby Book. It appeared that the shadows in the corners of the room deepened, as if listening and waiting for it to whisper words of profound truths. For a moment, Winston froze, telling himself it was only the wind through the eaves. But, deep within, he lingered, knowing that the Book had heard him and was indeed speaking a language that only few could hear.

TWO

THE RIDICULED SCHOLAR

The days that followed blurred into one long pulse of discovery. Sleep came fitfully, interrupted by bursts of writing, cross-referencing, and muttered theories spoken to the empty air. Winston's study, once cluttered, now resembled an excavation site. Pages filled with diagrams, spirals, and symbols spilled across the floor.

Each morning, he entered his lecture hall with renewed purpose. His students noticed the change—the fire behind his eyes, the way his words trembled with conviction.

"We are on the edge of something," he told them one morning, chalk in hand, his voice carrying through the high-ceilinged room. "History is not linear. Knowledge is not cumulative. There are...interruptions—insertions—moments when the veil thins." Winston stood before the lecture hall in his signature tweed jacket with elbow patches, a relic of a bygone academic age. Once, that jacket had been a banner of respect, a garment worn by a man whose lectures brimmed with wit, passion, and daring questions. In those days, students filled the hall early, jostling for the best seats, their notebooks poised to capture every word. Now, the jacket seemed more costume than uniform—threadbare, sagging at the elbows, clinging to a man no longer in step with the time.

The younger students exchanged uncertain glances; one stifled a laugh. Winston pressed on, undeterred. The Book's language had begun to infiltrate his own, phrases echoing like scripture. He quoted fragments without realizing it, tracing circles and intersecting lines on the board as though reconstructing the geometry of revelation.

The lecture hall echoed with a restless dissonance: the rustle of paper, the squeak of shoes on the tile, the metallic ring of a coin flipped carelessly against a desk. These sounds, once mere background to eager silence, now formed a chorus of indifference and ridicule. Whispers spread like smoke across the rows. A cough disguised a laugh. Somewhere in the back, someone stifled a yawn so theatrically that it drew a ripple of amusement. Winston felt each sound weigh against him, like stone set hard against his ribs.

Still, he pressed on. His lecture notes lay untouched at the podium; he no longer trusted their safe, predictable words. Instead, fragments from the dark volume whispered at the edges of his mind, demanding utterance. "Suppose," he began, his voice tense, "that there exists a record—a witness—hidden for a century, or maybe longer. Not written for glory or myth, but for those willing to listen. A book not of history alone, but of warning."

The students shifted uneasily. Some exchanged smirks; others leaned forward despite themselves. Winston's hand brushed the outline of notes hidden in his coat pocket that he wanted to share, but he resisted the impulse to reveal knowledge they were not ready to receive. To place sacred knowledge here, beneath fluorescent lights and skeptical eyes, would feel profane.

"They laughed," he said, his voice deepening. "They laughed at the men who claimed the earth curved beneath their feet. They laughed at those who spoke of hidden worlds and realms beyond the stars. They always laughed. But truth does not ask for laughter, nor does it wait for applause."

He paced now, his shoes tapping the floor like a heartbeat. "What if knowledge—real knowledge—was kept from us until the appointed hour? What if myths are not lies, but memories? What if silence itself has been obedience to something greater than us all?"

A boy in the front row leaned sideways and whispered—loud enough for all to hear—"The old man's lost it again."

Laughter erupted, sharp and merciless. It rolled across the room, breaking his rhythm, stabbing deeper than he would allow them to see. Winston gripped the edge of the podium, steadying himself, though his eyes blazed with a strange light. "Mock if you must," he said, his voice rising above the jeers. "History is written not by the comfortable but by the ridiculed, the forgotten, the ones willing to bear the weight of truth when others refuse. You laugh now—but one day, you will remember these words."

The laughter ebbed into whispers. Some students looked away, ashamed; others smiled with the thrill of their own cruelty. Only a handful remained still, their brows furrowed, caught between disbelief and the uneasy sense that perhaps their eccentric professor was speaking something he should not know.

Winston exhaled slowly, his hands trembling at his sides. The Book was safe, concealed, in the privacy of his study, but its presence still pressed against him, urging him further. He closed his eyes for a moment, listening to the silence beyond the mockery. In that silence, he almost thought he heard it—the faintest whisper of pages turning, speaking through him, guiding his tongue. It was as if the Book itself was present telling him what to say to a gathering of skeptics hungry for fodder.

"We must not scoff at that which we do not understand," he said, his eyes sweeping the room, searching, pleading, for even one ally among them. "Mankind is bound by duty—by destiny—to seek beyond the veil of the known." But duty and destiny were not words these students wanted. A wadded scrap of paper sailed from the back, landing near his shoes. Another snicker, another ripple of laughter. His heart faltered. Once, this hall had been his kingdom. Now it was his tribunal, and the verdict had already been delivered.

The bell rang at last, though Winston hardly noticed. Chairs scraped the floor, notebooks slammed shut, and the room emptied in a rush of laughter and chatter. A few students cast backward glances—half amusement, half pity—but none lingered. Winston remained at the podium, staring at the chalk-dusted surface as though the symbols he had scrawled there might still reveal themselves if only, he looked long enough. His chest ached with the effort of restraint. The mysteries of the Book burned inside, urging him to open their young minds to truth, and silence their laughter with the weight of facts that he had experienced first-hand. But he could not—not yet. Not like this.

He gathered his notes with deliberate care and slipped them into his worn leather satchel. When he finally left the lecture hall, the corridor outside hummed with the chatter of students streaming to their next classes. He walked slowly, head bowed, hoping to pass unnoticed.

"Did you hear him?" a girl's voice rang out just behind him. "A secret record waiting for mankind to listen?" More chatter and faint laughter followed.

Another voice, mocking his cadence: *"Truth does not require applause!"* The imitation drew shrieks of delight.

Winston froze in place. For a moment, the words pressed into him like stones hurled at his back. He almost turned, almost demanded they look him in the eye when they spoke. But what then? More jeers, more disdain. He tightened his grip on the satchel and pressed forward, his footsteps echoing louder than theirs until he reached the quiet stairwell.

There, alone, he paused. Surrounded by the Book's presence, which radiated like a hidden flame, steady and unyielding, he felt again the whisper from his dream: *You will seek me. You will vow it. And I will answer.*

Winston closed his eyes, steadying his breath. *Let them laugh. Let them sneer,* he thought to himself. Their voices were shallow waves against a shore he had already left behind. For he knew, with the certainty of one marked by something greater than ridicule, that truth was never born in applause. It was born in silence—and in silence, it endured.

At home, the walls of his once-cheerful house had grown cold. The rooms where laughter once lingered now echoed with silence. The echoes of mocking from earlier that day in the classroom were still clinging to him like smoke. The house smelled faintly of rosemary and butter, the kind of warmth Margaret always cultivated in anticipation of a pleasant evening.

"Winston?" Her voice carried from the front hall, bright with expectancy. She appeared a moment later, dressed in a dark silk blouse, a string of pearls at her throat. Her lipstick was fresh, her hair carefully arranged. A coat hung neatly over her arm, suggesting that she was ready to go out for the evening.

It took only a glance at his empty hands, his worn satchel, and the distracted fog in his eyes for her expression to change. "You've forgotten..." The words dropped with the weight of certainty.

Winston blinked. "Forgotten? He hesitated. "Did I forget an anniversary...?"

"You're close..." she said lightheartedly. "We're having dinner tonight, with the Harringtons." She paused and continued, now becoming more intense in her tone. "I reminded you twice."

A pang of guilt struck him, but he smothered it

quickly beneath the reflexive shield of excuses. "My last lecture ran long, Margaret. The students—they pressed me with questions. It was impossible to leave when—"

"Pressed you with questions?" she cut in, her voice sharpening. "Or would it be more accurate to say you lost yourself in another one of your...obsessions?" The word stung. He adjusted his spectacles, avoiding her gaze.

"It isn't an obsession," he snapped. "What I am doing is far more important than trivial dinners with people who care only about business gossip and committee seats."

Her eyes narrowed, the pearls at her throat trembling with the rise of her breath. "Trivial? That's all you have to say about the only people who seem to care about me and haven't abandoned us, as have most of our friends?" The volume of her voice grew louder. "You embarrass me, Winston. Do you think I enjoy walking into these rooms alone, making excuses for a husband too distracted with imaginary concepts to remember he has a wife? Now you're forcing me to cut ties with the only friends I have left..."

He set his satchel down heavily by the door and stood facing her. "You knew what I was when you married me."

"Yes," she said bitterly. "A man with passion. A man who believed knowledge could change the world. Not this...half-stranger...who hides in books and forgets his own family exists. I never intended to marry a ghost..." She hesitated. "Winston...I hear that your lectures are becoming strange. Elizabeth says the students are talking. You're speaking of things no one understands."

"Of course they don't," he replied sharply. "Truth rarely announces itself in language that skeptics can recognize."

Margaret crossed her arms. "You used to talk about ideas, not oracles. You're beginning to sound like a man searching for faith in the wrong place."

He looked up then, the lamplight catching the exhaustion in his face. "If knowledge isn't faith, Margaret, then what is it?" Her silence was answer enough. When she finally turned away, he whispered almost to himself, "They'll see, in time."

The silence between them thickened. Winston's throat worked as if to speak, but no words came. Upstairs, a clock ticked steadily, indifferent to them both. Finally, Margaret exhaled, her shoulders stiff.

She set her coat aside with clipped precision, inching closer to Winston. "Well, I guess you've made your choice," she said in an agitated tone. "I hope you enjoy your discoveries." She let out a deep sigh and walked past him, her perfume lingering like a memory of warmth he no longer deserved. She walked over to a nearby chair, and gently sat for a spell, her hands clasped tightly in her lap. Her face was pale, lips pressed into a hard line, eyes weary from years of bearing ridicule not her own.

"Winston," she began before he could respond. "I cannot live like this any longer."

"For Christ's sake...Margaret, give me a break," he cried out, now placing his keys on the side table, as though laying down a sacred relic. "It ain't no picnic for me either; you've heard the laughter," he said softly, now appearing to dial back the anger. "You've seen their ignorance. But we cannot let ridicule silence the truth."

Her composure cracked. Tears welled in her eyes. She stood quickly and began pacing, her hands wringing. "It isn't just the laughter in the lecture hall anymore, Winston," she said, voice rising with every word. "It's everywhere... At church, women glance at me as though I carry your madness on my shoulders. At the grocer's, no one will meet my eye. Even when I walk the dog, neighbors smirk, whispering that my husband has gone insane. Do you understand what that is like?" She paused, now displaying a pained expression. "Better still...do you even care?"

He reached for her hand, but she pulled back as if his touch would burn like fiery coals.

"This is not what I signed up for," she added, now sobbing. "I can't continue to carry this humiliation forever... You need to talk to someone—someone who can help." Her words trembled with desperation. "Look at you...can't you see that you're losing your grip on reality?"

Winston opened his mouth, but no sound came. Margaret's eyes held him with a steady, unflinching gaze—the kind of gaze that had once steadied him in moments of doubt, but now judged him with quiet finality. "If you can't stop this," she said at last, her voice stiff as a wire ready to snap, "then there is nothing more to discuss." She paused, as if deliberately choosing her words carefully, then let out a deep sigh. "You're forcing my hand, Winston, if you can't pull yourself together..."

"Forcing your hand?" His voice broke into a shout, harsher than he intended. "What the devil does that mean? Huh?" He paused, clearing his throat, as if the act could steady the storm inside him. "You want me to leave? Is that what you're saying? You'd throw away everything because I dare to believe in something greater than dinner parties and idle...bull crap?"

The words landed between them like blows, heavier than the laughter of students, heavier than the ridicule of strangers. Margaret—his anchor, his companion through decades of study, the one who had endured his late nights and his eccentricities—was slipping away.

For a moment, neither spoke. The air between them was thick with the unspoken: her longing for a husband she could reach, his terror that the only person who tethered him to the ordinary world was preparing to sever that tie. Finally, Margaret drew a trembling breath, her eyes glistening.

"I don't know if I can stay married to a ghost, Winston." She turned away, her pearls catching the light as she vanished down the hall, her footsteps sharp against the floor. Winston stood frozen, as though his hesitation could shield him from her words. Yet, the silence of the house told him the truth. Ridicule at the university was survivable, but ridicule at home was not.

Several days passed after his argument with Margaret. The sharpness of their words and the exchange between them had dulled into an uneasy quiet. Winston had hoped that time would smooth the edges, and with enough patience and civility life might return to its familiar rhythm. He buried himself in his lectures, determined to recapture the enthusiasm that once animated his students, but the effort felt hollow. His voice, once alive with conviction, now carried a tremor of doubt. The tension between home and work clung to him like a shadow—subtle, persistent, impossible to shake. Even in the lecture hall, he could feel it following him, a silent weight pressing at the edges of every conversation, every glance. He told himself that he needed only to endure—that once Margaret's anger cooled, all would be well again. Yet in quiet moments, when the classroom emptied and the echo of his own words lingered in the air, he felt the unmistakable truth: something had shifted, and it would not easily shift back.

Unbeknownst to Winston, Margaret felt it, too—the slow unraveling of what they once called peace. She told herself that silence was better than anger, but even peace, she discovered, could carry the weight of sorrow. She moved through the house with careful restraint, tending to her tasks as though order might stand in for closeness. But each sound reminded her of the distance between them—the creak of his chair in the study, the faint murmur of his voice rehearsing ideas she no longer understood. Part of her longed to knock on his door, to bridge the space with something tender and ordinary, but pride—or perhaps fear—held her still. She loved him, but his eyes no longer saw her; they searched instead for something beyond reach, something that had already begun to claim him.

Several weeks passed and Winston grew to find peace with the situation. The tension at home and at the university was less than ideal, but he was prepared to deal with it provided that the status quo remained. Unfortunately, weeks later came the final wound. Their daughter, Elizabeth K. Thornberry, stood radiant in her bridal gown, a vision of promise and new beginnings. She stood in front of the mirror admiring the dress, while Margaret hovered nearby, fussing with her veil. In only a brief time, his only daughter was to be married to John, her childhood sweetheart.

Winston stood in the doorway, undetected by Margaret and Elizabeth, smiling softly, with a tiny box cradled in the palm of his hand. Pride swelled in him, eclipsing, for a moment, the pain of recent weeks. His daughter was beautiful—brighter than the morning star. Yet, there was something off about her demeanor. She appeared subdued, lacking the usual enthusiasm of a soon-to-be new bride. Sensing her uneasiness, Winston debated whether he should intervene to see if she was making the right decision. He knew Elizabeth's fiancé and felt that he was by all accounts a standup type of guy. However, something was wrong and now was the time to speak or forever hold one's peace if the goal was to set the record straight. Winston stared at Margaret and could tell from her expression that she, too, sensed something was wrong.

Margaret turned toward Elizabeth, displaying a weak smile. "Are you alright, my dear?"

Elizabeth turned away, lowering her eyes to the floor, showing a clear reluctance to speak. "If you are nervous about marrying John, that's perfectly normal. All brides and brides-to-be get temporary cold feet..."

Winston continued to look on but remained silent, as he waited for Elizabeth to respond. There was a long pause before Elizabeth could bring herself to speak. It was obvious to the most casual observer that the young bride-to-be was in agony. Winston sized up the situation and determined it best to let things play out between Elizabeth and her mother before making an attempt to intervene.

"It's not that, Mother," Elizabeth whispered at last. Her voice carried the tremor of someone standing too close to the truth. Margaret frowned, her hands stilling in the folds of silk.

"Then what is it, my dear? You do love him, don't you?"

"Of course I do," Elizabeth replied quickly, almost defensively. "More than anything."

"Then what troubles you?"

For a moment, Elizabeth said nothing. Her lips parted, closed again, and when she finally spoke, the words emerged like glass breaking softly in her throat. "It's Father..."

Margaret's brow knit in confusion. "Your father?"

Elizabeth turned away, her voice barely above a whisper. "Please, don't let him come to the wedding. I—I can't bear it. Not after everything." The words seemed to echo in the stillness of the room. "I can't endure the embarrassment."

Winston froze in the doorway; breath caught in his chest. He had not meant to listen, yet the truth reached him with cruel precision. Each syllable landed with the sharpness of betrayal, and though his daughter had not seen him, her rejection found its mark.

Margaret's mouth opened as if to protest, but no sound came. In her daughter's reflection, she saw her own failure staring back. And Winston, unseen, stepped backward into the hall, the sound of his retreat swallowed by the hush of that terrible silence.

He stumbled backward into the dim hallway, his breath shallow, his pulse thundering in his ears. The words echoed, relentless, carving themselves into him: *I cannot endure the embarrassment again.*

He pressed his back to the wall, the dark wood cool against his spine, as if it might hold him upright when his legs no longer could. Pride had swelled in him only moments before, rising like sunlight through a storm—but now the light was gone, snuffed out with a single whisper. Elizabeth, his daughter. The one he had cradled in his arms, the one whose laughter had once filled this house with joy. The memory of her as a child, chasing Asher and his predecessors across the yard, her hair tangled by the wind, now collided with the sight of her radiant in her wedding gown—yet rejecting him as though he were a stain upon her life.

His throat tightened, and a sound escaped him—half sob, half strangled laugh. The ridicule of his students had bruised him; the indifference of his colleagues had wearied him. But this—this rejection from his own flesh and blood—was a wound no scholar's pride could endure. He lowered his gaze to the tiny box, clutched against his chest, its weight both anchor and burden. He whispered bitterly into the silence and directed it to Asher, who stood nearby:

"You are all I have left now."

When he returned to his study, he saw the Book that had appeared mysteriously, sitting out in the open on his desk. The cover seemed to glimmer faintly in the half-light, its silence heavier than words. A dangerous thought whispered at the edges of his mind: perhaps Elizabeth was right. Perhaps he had become an embarrassment, a relic, a madman clinging to shadows. And yet...the Book pulsed with quiet certainty, as if to remind him that he had been chosen—not by daughter, nor wife, nor colleague—but by something greater.

Tears blurred his vision, but his jaw set with grim resolve. If he was to be denied as father, denied as husband, denied as scholar, then he would not be denied as servant to the truth. The Book had claimed him. And now, more than ever, he belonged to it. He left the door open, and sat at his desk, hand running over the Book cover without a word. His pride collapsed into dust, yet one look at the Book released a surge of unexplained peace that flooded the entire atmosphere.

That night, alone in his study, Winston sat in his fraying tweed jacket, the forgotten Book open before him. The laughter of students, Margaret's ultimatum, Elizabeth's whispered plea—all of it pressed in, choking the silence. His hands trembled as he opened his journal. Ink blurred as tears fell onto the page, yet none of it appeared to matter.

Journal Entry, December 15, 2021

They all call me mad, he wrote. *They call me lost. Yet, I know I am neither. What is madness, if not the refusal to see the truth that waits beyond the veil? If I must walk alone, then I walk alone. But the truth remains.*" His pen scratched harder, words desperate and defiant.

"Why can't they see...what is so obvious to me?" he whispered to himself. "Is it because I have been chosen?" he hesitated, pen running out of ink. "If I am indeed chosen for a higher call, it is not my desire to lose my family, but neither is it my desire turn away..." Winston was in deep turmoil and continued writing rapidly in his journal. But, deep within there was peace that he could not rationally explain. "Lord, I am a man of many flaws but I cannot abandon you, if you are calling me to do your will on earth." He paused and cleared his throat. "Here I am..."

Out of nowhere, he could hear the lowly whisper of voices speaking to him in what appears to be a harmonious chorus. And all of things that had troubled him no longer mattered.

"*The appointed hour will come, and when it does, they will know.*"

He closed the journal. Around him, the house stood silent, emptied not by death but by absence—the absence of love, of companionship, of trust. Once celebrated for his brilliance, Winston Thornberry had become an outsider, not only to the world beyond his door but within the very walls that had once sheltered him.

And yet, in that void, one companion remained, Asher, a beautiful Siberian Husky, who had been his loyal friend for many years. He had replaced his predecessor, another husky, Buddy, who lived to be twenty years old before leaving this earth. Buddy had been a loyal friend and companion, but as with all things time had a funny way of prevailing in revered matters of life and death.

Asher looked on, curled up next to Winston's chair as a reminder that he was not alone. Winston displayed a brief smile as he gently caressed Asher's head. The dog wagged his tail and Winston reached for the Book that laid open before him.

The Book, its pages faintly alive in the lamplight, whispered a promise that no ridicule, no betrayal, or loneliness would ever be able to extinguish.

Winston knew that he could not continue to live in limbo. He had to make a decision, right or wrong, that would lead him toward the Book's hidden purpose. Yet even as he continued searching for meaning, he felt the slow tightening of obsession begin, that familiar gravity drawing him toward mysteries that refused to be left alone.

THREE

NORTHWARD EXILE

The morning light crept reluctantly through the dining room windows, gray and heavy with drizzle. Winston sat at the far end of the table, untouched tea cooling beside him, his spectacles folded neatly on the cloth as if order might steady him. Margaret moved quietly, pouring coffee with deliberate precision, her pearls absent, her expression guarded. Elizabeth entered last, her bridal gown now replaced by a simple sweater and skirt, her face pale with sleeplessness. For a long while, no one spoke. The only sound was the faint ticking of the clock on the mantle and an occasional move by Asher.

At last Winston cleared his throat, his voice low and uneven. He jumped right into his speech, and did not hold back.

"I heard you yesterday...in the bridal room," he said, not lifting his eyes from the table. Elizabeth froze, her hands tightening around the chair. Margaret looked sharply at him, her lips parting, but no words came. "I heard every word," he continued, his voice sharpening.

"That you cannot endure the embarrassment of your own father. That my presence is something to be hidden." He finally raised his gaze, his eyes wet but blazing. "Did you for one minute give thought to what you said and how your words would pierce through my heart like a sword?" There was a brief pause.

"Do know what that day means to a man...? To hear his own child banish him from her joyful moment, as though he were a criminal?"

Elizabeth swallowed hard, her voice trembling.

"Father, I didn't mean—"

"You meant it," he cut in, harsher than he intended. He leaned back, his chest heaving. "I have been ridiculed by students, dismissed by colleagues, laughed at in every hall I have walked... But I never thought the crushing blow would come from my own flesh and blood."

The silence pressed down heavy. Margaret reached across the table, her voice careful.

"Winston, this is a very important day for Elizabeth. She was afraid that you may lose it in front of everyone... It wasn't meant to wound."

His hands curled into fists on the table. "Afraid?" he muttered bitterly. Afraid of what? The truth? There was a long and awkward silence.

"It's always fear... And because of it, I am not a father, not a husband, not even a man to be trusted at my own daughter's wedding." His eyes softened then, remorse flickering through the anger. "Perhaps I am not the man you remember. Perhaps I have failed you both. But if truth is to cost me even this—then so be it." He rose slowly, taking his spectacles and satchel. "I will be away for a time," he said quietly. "A few weeks, perhaps more. Don't ask me where, or when I will return. You wouldn't understand, and I cannot explain." His gaze lingered on Elizabeth, then Margaret, the weight of both love and betrayal heavy in his voice. "But when I go, remember—this was *not* my choice." He reached into his pocket and pulled at a small box, placing it on the table next to Margaret. "You know what to do with it..." he said in a voice filled with mystery and angst. He turned, his footsteps echoing in the hall until the front door closed behind him.

His sudden absence left Margaret and Elizabeth in silence, staring at the place he had sat, the small box, the shadow of his absence heavier than his presence had ever been.

The days that followed were best described as a time of quiet unraveling. Winston could not help feeling as though the world itself had shifted half a step away from him. Colleagues still greeted him in the corridors, but their eyes slid past his face, their smiles too measured, too careful. Even his lectures—once filled with the sound of his own conviction—fell into uneasy silence. Students took notes dutifully but without curiosity, afraid to laugh now, yet more afraid to listen.

At home, conversation dwindled to necessity. Margaret spoke less, her kindness replaced by a practiced restraint, the kind born of weariness rather than anger. Elizabeth's visits grew infrequent. When she did appear, she kept to safe topics—the weather, her work, trivial things that avoided the raw edge of what none of them dared to name.

But Winston felt no bitterness. The ache that had once flared into anger had cooled into something stranger—acceptance. He understood now that revelation demands solitude. The Book had not come to be proven in lecture halls or debated over wine and dinner. It had come to be lived and would serve as a beacon of hope for those searching for answers.

Each night, when the house was still, he returned to his study. He no longer wrote feverishly but with deliberate calm, recording not thoughts but instructions—as though taking dictation from the unseen. He charted dreams, fragments of symbols, faint impressions that seemed to press upon him from somewhere beyond sight. And as he worked, the same message repeated itself with increasing clarity: *You will not find what you seek here.*

By the time the first frost of winter spread across the windows, he had stopped attending faculty meetings altogether. A formal notice came from the university—concern worded as compassion, a request for rest, perhaps a leave of absence. Winston folded the letter neatly, placed it inside his journal, and stared for a long while at the flame in the hearth.

"Rest," he murmured. "Yes. That's what they think I need."

He rose, crossed to the window, and looked out over the snow-dusted campus. Beyond the familiar roofs and chimneys stretched the gray horizon of the north, wide and unknowable. Something stirred within him—a quiet certainty that his path lay beyond that line, where no map would guide him and no laughter could reach.

The wind pressed against the glass as if to answer. He did not smile, but his eyes softened. For the first time in months, Winston felt neither sorrow nor fear. Only purpose.

The morning, he decided to leave, the world was unnervingly still. A thin mist hung over the campus lawns, softening the edges of things, turning familiar shapes into uncertain silhouettes. It was neither dawn nor full morning—the kind of hour that feels suspended between choices.

Winston moved quietly through the house, careful not to wake Margaret. Asher followed at his heels, paws soundless on the worn floorboards. The old dog watched every movement—the gathering of journals, the careful wrapping of the Book, the methodical placing of each item into the leather satchel that had accompanied Winston through decades of travel and lecture.

He paused by the doorway of his study. The lamp was still on from the night before. Winston hesitated making his final entry into the journal.

To seek the truth is not madness, he had written, *but obedience.* He read the words once more, then drew a line beneath them.

On the small table near the window lay two sealed envelopes. One bore Margaret's name, the other Elizabeth's. He had written them the night before, though he wasn't certain why—not apology, not explanation. There were no words that could soften what he was about to do. Still, the act of writing had steadied his hands.

He placed the letters on the mantel, weighed them

down with the small brass compass Margaret had given him years ago—a token of direction, though it had long ceased to point anywhere meaningful.

"You'll take care of them, won't you?" he said softly to Asher. The dog tilted his head, ears pricking, as though he understood. Winston smiled faintly. "No, I suppose not. You're coming with me."

Outside, the air bit at his face as he stepped into the gray morning. The street was empty, save for the slow drift of leaves across the pavement. Behind him, the house stood silent, its curtains drawn. He waited for the expected rush of doubt, but none came. Only calm.

By midday, he was on a train heading north, the landscape unfurling like a fading memory—cities dissolving into fields, fields into forests, forests into the white silence of distance. He wrote in his journal as the train rocked gently beneath him, noting the way the light changed, the way the world seemed to grow quieter the further he traveled.

At dusk, the sky over the horizon deepened into blue-gray steel. Somewhere ahead lay the edge of the known world and beyond that, the place of his dreams, the place that had been calling him since the first night the Book appeared.

Winston closed his journal and looked out through the frost-kissed glass.

"I'm coming," he whispered, not to himself, but to something unseen. "Wherever you are hidden—I will find you." The words lingered in the cold air like a vow. The world had dismissed him. The Book had not.

Days later, back home, the lecture hall was

unusually full. The atmosphere thick with a restless energy, and students eager to departure for the Christmas holidays. Whispers curled through the rows like smoke, carrying rumor and speculation. Word had spread that Professor Winston Thornberry, once a celebrated name in these very halls, was to be replaced. Some claimed he had gone mad; others whispered that the university had quietly pushed him aside. For the students, the spectacle was almost entertainment, and many filled the seats not out of respect but out of old-fashioned curiosity.

When the visiting Professor Jordan West Morgan entered—a tall man with a measured stride, gray at the temples, and eyes that carried both authority and kindness—the noise faltered. He moved with a presence that commanded attention, his very silence chastening. He placed his notes on the podium, adjusted his spectacles, and scanned the restless faces with a gaze sharp as glass.

"Before we begin," he said firmly, his British accent crisp as frost, "there is something to be addressed." He let the words hang in the air, cutting through the whispers.

"Professor Thornberry has been granted a sabbatical. I will be filling his lectures for the foreseeable future." The announcement drew murmurs, then bursts of laughter from the back rows. Someone clapped mockingly. The sound was cruel, echoing in the vaulted room like a jeer from the gallows.

Professor Morgan slammed his hand down upon the podium, his voice rising like a sudden storm.

"That's enough!" His words cracked like thunder. The room fell to a hush, though defiance still glimmered in a few eyes.

"I have heard how you treated Professor Thornberry," Morgan continued, his voice steeled with anger. "We've all heard... And you should be bloody ashamed! Many of the greatest minds in history were mocked, ridiculed, even persecuted. Galileo was threatened and silenced for daring to claim the Earth revolved around the sun. Charles Darwin endured endless scorn for his theories of natural selection. Nikola Tesla was dismissed as mad." He paused. Unease spread across the students like frost climbing glass panes. The professor's voice softened, yet carried more weight in its calm.

"You may not understand Professor Thornberry's work. Perhaps even he cannot fully articulate it. But the courage to pursue truth in the face of scorn—that is something all of us should aspire to."

For a long moment, no one spoke. The lecture hall—so often filled with derision—now seemed a cathedral of silence. Yet the words came too late. Winston was gone.

Weeks later, the church bells rang in jubilant peals. It was Christmas Eve. The streets were filled with carolers and the jubilant sound of nearby holiday shoppers. The day was supposed to be a happy time of jubilation; but, for Elizabeth Thornberry, the joyous day carried a hollow ache. Dressed in her bridal gown, radiant as spring, she searched every corner for the one face she longed to see. But her father was nowhere. She had expected distraction, perhaps an awkward remark or eccentric gesture, but absence—utter, unbroken absence—was something she never anticipated.

In the bridal chamber, she turned on her mother, her voice breaking with grief.

"Did he call?" Elizabeth asked. Margaret lowered her eyes to the floor and shook her head. "Where is he? Why did you let him leave?" she said, now appearing to blame her mother for his absence. Before Margaret could respond, Elizabeth continued in an angry tone. "Why didn't you try to stop him?"

Margaret tried to explain, words stumbling like stones in her mouth. Elizabeth shook her head violently, tears splashing onto her gown. The bridesmaids looked on, before trying to console, but their efforts failed.

"I never wanted him gone! I just wanted him to stop—to stop the madness, not to vanish. You drove him away!" Elizabeth continued sobbing, as if totally forgetting that she made it clear that she did not want him to attend the service.

Margaret hesitated, as if debating whether to speak and remind Elizabeth of the role she had played in making sure that her father would not attend the service. After a moment of reflection, she concluded that silence was answer enough. For in that silence lay guilt, regret, and the weight of choices too late to undo. It was clear that Elizabeth was already feeling the weight of her ill-guided decision and her wedding day would forever carry the scar of absence—a father lost not to death, but to exile.

The church bells tolled softly in the crisp afternoon air, their peal announcing what should have been one of the happiest moments of Elizabeth's life. The aisle gleamed with a runner of ivory satin, flanked by rows of delicate white roses and candlelit lanterns that cast a golden shimmer across the pews. Guests turned expectantly, their faces bright with smiles, their voices hushed into reverent silence.

But in the bride's chamber, just moments before the music began, Elizabeth sat trembling. Her veil had been arranged, her gown smoothed, her bouquet pressed gently into her hands, yet her heart carried a weight no lace or flowers could disguise. Her mother walked closer, her own eyes red-rimmed, though her expression tried to remain composed. In her hand was a small, worn velvet box. She pressed it into Elizabeth's palm without a word. "This is from your father," Margaret whispered.

Elizabeth hesitated, and stared at the box. She instantly recognized it as being from her father. Fingers unsteady, she opened the box to reveal a delicate bracelet of filigreed silver and tiny gemstones, its design unmistakably old—fragile, timeless, and radiant. She recognized it as her great-grandmother's bracelet; a piece Winston had often spoken of with reverence.

Tears welled uncontrollably as she lifted it from its velvet nest, the cool weight of it pressing against her skin. Winston was not there but the gift was a whisper of his presence, a bittersweet tether between them.

"I can't..." Elizabeth choked, lowering her head as tears slipped freely down her cheeks. "I don't deserve..." Before Elizabeth could finish her sentence, Margaret knelt before her daughter, clasping her trembling hands.

"Of course, you do," Margaret murmured. "You must. He would want you to walk down that aisle with strength, not sorrow."

Elizabeth wept silently for several minutes, her shoulders shaking beneath the veil. Then, drawing in a long, shaky breath, she fastened the bracelet around her wrist, letting its cold shimmer anchor her. She rose, steadied, though emptiness still hollowed her chest.

When the music swelled, she walked the aisle with grace, with her uncle Jonah. The congregation marveled at her beauty and poise. To the outside world, it was a flawless ceremony: vows spoken with clarity, rings exchanged with trembling joy, applause breaking into jubilant celebration as the couple sealed their union with a kiss.

Yet through it all, an invisible absence lingered. The place where her father should have been—beside her, behind her, smiling with pride—remained vacant, although filled by Winston's younger brother. Even as the crowd erupted in cheer, even as the petals fell and the sun streamed golden through the windows, Elizabeth's heart bore the quiet wound of loss.

The bracelet glimmered faintly against her wrist as she clasped her husband's hand. It was beautiful, treasured, but it did not fill the empty chair, nor silence the question that would haunt her for years: why had he not been there?

The reception hall was alive with laughter and

music, the clink of crystal glasses mingling with the rhythmic hum of a string quartet tucked neatly in the corner. Tables shimmered beneath soft candlelight, their centerpieces of white lilies and roses standing tall in slender glass vases. Everywhere Elizabeth looked, there was motion—friends dancing, children darting between chairs, cousins raising toasts with flushed cheeks and shining eyes.

She smiled, of course—her new husband's arm draped proudly around her, their first dance a graceful sweep across the polished floor, the room erupting in applause at every twirl. To the guests, she was radiant, a bride basking in the glow of her wedding day. But beneath the practiced smile, Elizabeth's chest still ached with hollowness.

During the speeches, that ache deepened. One by one, voices rose in joy—her bridesmaids teasing about childhood mischief, her uncles joking about family quirks, her mother offering tender words that drew a sheen of tears from every corner of the room. Yet when the time came for the 'father of the bride' toast, a silence rippled. Margaret stood again, lifting her glass, her words carefully chosen, warm enough to fill the gap yet not enough to erase it.

Elizabeth lowered her gaze to the bracelet gleaming on her wrist, its silver catching the candlelight. It was beautiful—timeless—but it reminded her more of absence than presence. She turned it slightly, running her thumb across the delicate links, wishing the hand that had given it could have been there to hold hers.

Later, when the cake was cut and laughter swelled

again, Elizabeth slipped away for a moment. She stood near the window, the night sky stretching endlessly above, her reflection faint in the glass. The merriment carried on behind her—joyful, unbroken—but in her own heart, the night carried a shadow.

Her husband, John, joined her quietly, sliding an arm around her waist. She leaned into him, grateful, yet still aching. He kissed her temple, whispering,

"You look beautiful, but there is an eerie sadness about you." He paused. "I'm sorry Winston could not be here, but I hope you are happy, with me?"

She nodded, her throat tight. "Yes," she said softly. And it was true—she was happy. But her happiness was laced with grief, a contradiction she could neither speak aloud nor banish.

As the music swelled once more and they were called back to the dance floor, Elizabeth allowed herself one final glance at the stars. Somewhere, she hoped, her father thought of her too.

The church bells had long since fallen silent, and the last of the guests had drifted away into the evening. Candles sputtered in their holders, their light bending over flowers that now seemed tired from the weight of the day. Elizabeth sat alone in the bridal suite, her gown spread about her like fallen snow, her veil cast aside.

Margaret entered quietly, her hands folded before her, pearls glinting faintly against the dim light. She closed the door softly, as though gentleness might lessen the sting of what had passed. Elizabeth did not look up. Her eyes fixed on the mirror before her, but she did not see her reflection—only the empty space where her father should have stood hours ago. Her voice, when it came, was raw.

“Why didn’t you ignore my silliness and insist that he should come?” she whispered to her mother.

Margaret stopped short. “Elizabeth—”

“You could have said something, Mother, so I would realize my foolishness. You could have told me that he had to be there.” Her voice cracked, the words tumbling out with the force of all she had held back. “Every girl dreams of her father walking her down the aisle. Every girl but me...”

Margaret’s lips parted, but no words followed. Her silence filled the room like smoke, suffocating, undeniable. In that silence lay guilt, regret, and the weight of choices too late to undo.

Elizabeth turned from the mirror at last, her eyes glistening. “I know you tried to protect me from embarrassment, but at what cost? Now I’ll never forget that empty space... Never.”

Margaret’s shoulders sagged, her composure breaking. She reached for her daughter’s hand, but Elizabeth pulled it back. The two women sat in silence, divided by a decision neither could undo. For Elizabeth, her wedding day would forever carry the scar of absence—not a father lost to death, but to exile, to silence, to the weight of choices made in fear. Margaret stood, trying to be strong walked toward the door.

“I’m sorry,” she said in a broken tone. “I’m really sorry.”

Later, the bridal suite was quiet at last. The bustle, the music, the endless congratulations—all had ebbed into memory as the door clicked softly shut behind them. Candles still flickered along the dresser; their flames faint compared to the brilliance of the day just past. Elizabeth slipped out of her wedding garb and sat at the vanity, staring at her gown and veil folded away like a relic of a moment that already seemed impossibly distant.

Her husband, exhausted but glowing, soon drifted to sleep, his even breathing filling the silence. Elizabeth sat at the vanity, hair unpinned, her reflection pale and luminous in the dim light. Her eyes were red at the corners, not from laughter, but from the tears she had swallowed down throughout the day.

Slowly, she lifted her wrist. The bracelet gleamed, delicate and steadfast, its silver catching the candle's glow. She unfastened it and cradled it in her palm, running her fingertip over the filigree. The cool metal was a link to a past she both cherished and mourned—a hand-me-down not just of family, but of memory, of presence lost. She pressed it to her cheek, eyes closing, as if the gesture might bridge the emptiness left by her father's absence.

"You should have been there," she whispered, her voice breaking in the stillness. For the first time that day, she allowed herself to weep without restraint, her body shaking with sobs she had hidden from everyone else. After a long while, the tears softened. She placed the bracelet carefully back upon her wrist, fastening it as if sealing a promise to carry him with her, even in absence. Rising to her feet, she moved to the bed, slipping beneath the covers, one hand resting protectively over the silver band.

Her husband stirred and turned toward her, pulling her close without waking fully. Elizabeth rested her head against his shoulder, eyes drifting shut. And though the joy of her wedding day was marred by emptiness, she clung to the quiet hope that the bond between father and daughter—though fractured—was not beyond redemption. The last candle flickered out, leaving her in darkness, yet the faint weight of the bracelet against her skin felt like a single, enduring light.

FOUR

THE SILENT DEPARTURE

Days later, the world as Winston had known it was gone. The clatter of railways, the echo of station halls, the murmur of human life—all faded behind him like a dream dissolving with dawn. The final leg of the journey was by air, a chartered flight bound for the northern frontier. The chill of the tarmac cut through Winston's coat as he stood at the base of the narrow boarding stairs, Asher pressed close against his leg. The husky's breath plumed in the frigid morning air, visible in rhythmic bursts, steady and loyal. Winston adjusted the strap of the heavy canvas bag slung across his shoulder, its weight a reminder of the supplies he had gathered: thermal gear, journals, food rations, lanterns, and—most carefully packed of all—the Book.

The twin-prop plane waited, its fuselage streaked with frost, engines groaning against the cold. A few men in heavy parkas loaded crates into the cargo bay, their voices muffled by scarves and the steady whine of the wind. Winston clutched his ticket tighter; the paper already crumpled from his restless grip.

Asher bounded up the stairs first, tail wagging, nails clicking on the metal steps. Winston followed more slowly, his boots heavy, each step echoing like a tolling bell. At the threshold he paused, turning briefly to look back. The horizon was pale, the sun hidden behind a wall of cloud, and the city behind him seemed all ready to recede—his home, his family, his failures shrinking into distance.

Inside the cabin, he slid into a seat by the small round window. Asher curled at his feet, head resting against Winston's boots with a soft sigh. The flight attendant offered a quick smile before moving down the aisle, but Winston hardly saw her. His thoughts were elsewhere.

He pressed his hand to the satchel at his side, feeling the shape of the Book beneath the layers of wool and leather that always seem to bring comfort. For weeks it had consumed him, pulled him away from everything he once thought unshakable. Elizabeth's rejection. Margaret's silence. His colleagues' mockery. All of it had led him here, to this narrow seat on a plane bound for the northern edge of the world.

Winston leaned his forehead against the cold glass. Outside, snow flurries chased across the runway like restless spirits. The engines roared, the ground trembled, and the plane began to move.

He closed his eyes, whispering to himself more than to Asher:

"There's no turning back now."

In the dim hum of the cabin, Winston felt both dread and resolve. His life as he had known it was finished. Ahead lay only ice, silence, and whatever destiny awaited him beneath the northern sky or whether it would be discovered that he is indeed mad.

Winston knew the North Pole was no place for men to linger. Maps called it nothing more than drifting ice, a crown of white floating upon a restless sea. There was no soil, no permanence, only the endless groan of shifting floes. But the Book whispered differently. In its strange symbols and shifting passages, it spoke of a hidden place beneath the endless white—a ridge of rock swallowed by glaciers, that hid a secret world.

The pilot, a weathered man with ice in his beard, said little. "No one goes this far in winter," he muttered during a brief moment of turbulence. Winston merely nodded. There was no need to explain. He was not traveling *to* a place; he was traveling *toward* something.

Others saw only ice and desolation. But Winston saw an invitation. If the ice drifted, then his cabin would drift with it. If the cold threatened to devour him, he would endure as the Book endured—fragile in form yet eternal in meaning. And if no human could survive there unaided, perhaps that was the very point. It was meant for him alone.

Thus, impossibility no longer mattered. Whether on shifting icecaps or hidden stone, Winston would stake his claim where no man lived. For there, the book promised, truth waited in silence.

Far from the bells of his daughter's wedding, Winston Thornberry would trudge northward. His only companion would be Asher, a loyal white husky with eyes like pale fire and a gait steady as the tide. Together they would brave the Arctic winds, their figures dwarfed by the immensity of ice and sky. Days would bleed into nights without boundary, the world reduced to snow, wind, and the rhythmic crunch of boots and paws.

As the hours passed, the rhythmic drone of the engines lulled him into a state between waking and dream. He thought of Margaret's face in the lamplight, Elizabeth's laughter when she was small, Asher's steady presence beside him. They drifted through his mind like constellations half-remembered—bright, distant, unreachable.

The plane shuddered as it descended through the last veil of gray clouds, the world below stretching out in an endless sheet of white. Winston pressed his forehead to the cold window, his breath fogging the glass as he studied the barren landscape that would soon cradle him. The North Pole, albeit it the fringe of the high Artic, was not welcoming—it was fierce, sharp, and alive with a silence that could swallow a man whole. Yet, had chosen this exile, and if he had chosen wisely, he knew the forces that beckoned him to come would not betray him.

The plane dipped low through a ceiling of gray cloud, and the world below opened into a wilderness of ice and barren rock. This was no city, no settlement—just the ragged fringe of the Arctic, where the tree line ended and the tundra began its endless march northward. Here, the forests were not forests at all but stands of stunted spruce and birch, twisted and bent beneath decades of wind. Beyond them stretched nothing but white—ice fields and the frozen ocean, an unbroken expanse pointing toward the Pole.

When the plane finally descended, the world was silent but for the shriek of the wind. They landed on a narrow stretch of ice, where a lone outpost stood like a forgotten sentinel at the edge of creation. The pilot cut the engine as they skidded onto a rough airstrip carved into permafrost, little more than gravel and snow tamped down hard. "Last stop north," he muttered as Winston disembarked.

He stepped out into the cold. The air struck him like glass, sharp and clean. Each breath burned, yet felt purer than anything he had drawn in years.

The pilot unloaded Winston's supplies—food, instruments, fuel, books, and the single trunk that contained his notes. "Cabin's that way," the man said, pointing toward a line of dark pines barely visible through the snow. "No radio past this point. You'll be on your own."

"That's precisely the point," Winston replied.

He pulled his coat close, squinting against the wind. Somewhere in this desolation, tucked against a ridge that still bore the bones of trees, his cabin waited. A fragile foothold on the edge of eternity. The air bit him instantly—needles of frost clawing at his skin, burning his lungs. He pulled his wool scarf tighter, the great canvas bag heavy across his shoulder, his other hand clutching the handle of a battered trunk. The tarmac gave way to a rugged path carved into the snow, a single snowmobile waiting, its engine coughing to life at his command.

The ride was long, the landscape a shifting monotony of white ridges and skeletal trees that clawed against a horizon forever pale. By the time the cabin came into view—a dark smudge of timber against the snowbound earth—his hands were raw, his body stiff. Yet his heart quickened, for in this desolation lay a kind of grim sanctuary. Winston repeatedly covered Asher with heavy wool blankets but the vibrations of the snowmobile made it difficult to keep him covered.

The vehicle growled across the tundra, its treads grinding over wind-carved drifts and stretches of frozen gravel. Behind Winston, the airstrip had already vanished, swallowed by distance and swirling white. Ahead, the land rose unevenly, ridges blackened with stone and the occasional clutch of trees—spruce twisted by the ceaseless wind, their branches gnarled but stubbornly alive. This was the tree line's last stand, the world's edge, where earth yielded to the Arctic's endless desolation.

By the time the cabin came into view, Winston's face was raw with cold, his hands stiff inside his gloves. The structure huddled against the base of a ridge, its roof heavy with snow, its logs darkened by years of weather. A curl of frost clung to the eaves like lace, and the narrow windows looked out with the blank stare of a hermit keeping secrets.

He cut the engine, and the sudden silence was deafening. Only the wind spoke now, threading through the trees with a low, mournful hum. Winston stood still, canvas bag slung across his shoulder, the great trunk thudding into the snow at his feet. He felt, absurdly, that the land itself was watching.

After a while, the cabin greeted him with more silence, its roof appearing to sag under the weight of snow, its door stiff but yielding when pushed open.

The cabin was smaller than he imagined—stone and timber, half-buried beneath the drifts. As he approached the entry way, the cabin door resisted when he pushed, stiff from ice, then gave with a groan. The door creaked as he entered. The air inside was strangely warm, carrying the faint scent of cedar and smoke, lingering from seasons past, though the hearth was cold. Dust coated the shelves, yet the table had been cleared, as if waiting for a guest. On it lay a single object—a weathered lantern, its glass faintly glowing from within, though no flame burned.

The stone fireplace loomed at the center of the room, black with soot, its cold hearth like a mouth hungry for flame. Winston dropped his bag, stacked kindling, and struck a match. Soon fire sprang to life, the crackling heat spilling outward in waves, wrapping the cabin in a fragile sense of welcome.

Asher padded in behind him, shaking snow from his coat, before curling near the hearth with a sigh of contentment. Winston stood for a moment in silence, studying the modest space. The timbers creaked in the wind, the shelves bowed with wisdom, the fire's light flickered like a benediction. At the edge of the world, far from everything he had known, Winston Thornberry had arrived. To the world he had vanished, but to himself he had at last come home.

He drew a slow breath, as if feeling the Book's presence hum faintly against his arm. He closed his eyes now, sensing a message of sorts, though no words were exchanged.

You have reached the edge of the world—and the beginning of something far older.

Outside, the wind rose again, sweeping across the frozen plain like a voice speaking in a language he had always known but never understood. Inside, the fire crackled, shadows dancing across the rough-hewn walls. He unpacked supplies methodically—cans stacked, gear arranged, blankets thrown across the cot that sagged in one corner.

Smoke curled up the chimney as warmth bled slowly into the room. Winston removed his gloves, rubbing life back into his fingers, and let his gaze sweep across the cabin. Books lined the sagging shelves, their spines faded with age, titles barely legible. In the dim light, they seemed more than objects—silent witnesses, waiting to be read, or perhaps to read him.

He busied himself with the small tasks of settling in—stacking the supplies he had brought, spreading blankets across the cot, arranging lanterns and tools where he might need them. When at last the room felt less like a tomb and more like a refuge, Winston turned to the shortwave radio resting on a side shelf. He fiddled with the knobs, coaxing life into it. Static filled the air first, sharp and restless. Then, from the static, fragments of sound began to bleed through—distant voices, clipped and foreign, snatches of languages carried across the polar sky.

He leaned closer. Through the hiss came a faint melody, wavering and sweet, as though it had traveled centuries to reach him. A guitar strummed softly, a voice half-swallowed by the noise, but familiar in tone—like the folk songs of his youth. For an instant, Winston felt transported back to the Pacific Northwest of his student days, evenings filled with Dylan, Mitchell, and Simon. The song lingered only a moment before collapsing once more into static.

Winston exhaled, a dry laugh slipping out. "Even here," he murmured, "ghosts find a way to sing."

Asher's ears pricked, his head lifting toward the door. A low growl rippled from his throat. Winston followed his gaze, every muscle tensing. The fire crackled. The wind moaned. But at the door, the heavy silence seemed to thicken, waiting.

He forced himself to step forward, hand brushing against the journal in his coat pocket. He would write tonight—record the details, test his sanity on the page. But as he reached the door and laid his palm flat against the wood, a chill deeper than the cold outside threaded through him.

For a moment, he was certain: he was not alone. He looked around carefully and focused his attention on the fire, before returning and lowering himself into the old armchair beside the hearth. The weight of the day pressed against him, heavier than the journey itself. He removed his glasses, rubbing the bridge of his nose, then reached into the pocket of his coat. There, wrapped in a scrap of cloth, was the twin to the gift he had sent Elizabeth: a faded photograph of his grandmother wearing the same bracelet that now adorned his daughter's wrist.

He held the photo close, his throat tightening. He could picture Elizabeth's face even now—radiant in her gown, the hall filled with music, joy blooming around her like spring. Yet threaded through that vision was the hollow ache of his absence, a decision that gnawed at him. He imagined her hand brushing the bracelet, her tears held back before the world but flowing freely in secret.

"I should have been there," he murmured, the words bitter against his lips. The fire cracked, spitting sparks, but offered no answer. He leaned back, staring into the flames, his heart torn between regret and a stubborn conviction that his path, lonely as it was, carried necessity.

Outside, the wind howled across the barren expanse, but inside the cabin, Winston's world shrank to the faint warmth of the fire and the cold weight of memory. Somewhere far away, his daughter had danced beneath candlelight, her laughter trailing into night. Here, in exile, he sat alone—watching shadows flicker, clutching a photograph, and wondering if she could feel his love through the emptiness he had left behind.

The fire had settled into a steady rhythm, the wood sighing as it gave up its warmth. Winston reached for his leather-bound journal, the one he had carried faithfully for years. Its edges were worn, its pages filled with the scrawl of a restless mind. Tonight, in the silence of his new solitude, he opened it again. The pen felt heavy in his hand, as though it carried not just ink, but the weight of every choice that had brought him here.

He paused, staring at the blank page. His breath fogged faintly in the cold air, the fire's glow casting a flickering light across the desk. Finally, with a hand that trembled more from sorrow than from chill, he began to write.

Journal Entry, January 1, 2022

"This day I have arrived at the cabin. The journey was long, the air brutal, but I am here, settled by the fire with provisions enough to endure. And yet, no distance, no frost, no silence of the Pole can numb the ache within me. Only days ago, my only daughter prepared to wed her childhood sweetheart, John Farrington. Today, Elizabeth became a bride. Today, I usher in a New Year, filled with wonder and opportunities for new beginnings."

The ink smudged where his hand lingered too long. He set the pen down for a moment, pressing his fingers against his brow, fighting the images that rose unbidden—her face lit by joy, her veil trailing like morning mist, her arm linked with another man's as she walked down an aisle where he should have stood. He forced his hand to continue.

"I was not there. I chose not to be. I gave her what I could—a fragment of the past, a bracelet that belonged to my grandmother, that she might wear a piece of me in my absence. A poor substitute for a father's hand, for his voice, for his pride. I imagine she wept when she opened it. Perhaps she felt betrayed. Perhaps she cursed me. And she would be right to do so."

The fire cracked sharply, startling him. He glanced up, eyes burning, then lowered them back to the page.

"Yet I could not bring myself to stand in that hall, beneath the stares of those who know me as less than I once was. My path calls me northward, to solitude, to discovery, to the silence that might one day redeem me. But tonight... tonight I feel only absence. Hers and mine."

His script faltered into a shaky line. He closed the journal softly, as though shutting the words away might quiet the ache. Leaning back in the chair, he stared into the fire, the shadows dancing like ghosts across the walls.

At last, he whispered into the stillness, as though Elizabeth might somehow hear: "Forgive me."

The wind pressed against the cabin and the world beyond was endless white. But inside, Winston sat alone with his fire, Asher, his journal, and the unshakable knowledge that even in exile, he could not escape the love—and the loss—of his daughter.

As he sat in solitude within the weathered cabin, he felt as though, to the world, Winston Thornberry had vanished. Yet to himself, in this desolate silence, he had finally arrived.

The cabin was modest, but resolute—its walls groaning beneath the assault of the wind, like a sentinel holding vigil against eternity. There was a calming presence in the place, as though it had been waiting for him, embracing him despite the sorrow pressing heavily on his heart.

The great stone fireplace dominated the room, its flames dancing and spilling warmth that reached beyond mere heat. It stretched into the corners like a benediction, softening the edges of exile. Along the walls, shelves sagged beneath the weight of books—tomes worn and whispering with wisdom—reassuring Winston that perhaps the answers that had eluded him in the world he left behind might yet be found here.

Asher lay content by the hearth, his dark eyes lifting often to Winston, tail thumping lightly against the floor. In the dog's quiet companionship, there was no judgment, no absence, only loyalty and the comfort of presence.

Winston sat for a long while in the chair by the fire, his hand resting on the armrest polished by years of use, until again he reached for the leather-bound journal and began to write.

Journal Entry 2, (Continuation) January 1, 2022

"This night I mark my arrival. The cabin stands firm, though worn, its walls braced against the endless wind. I find in it a strange solace, as though I were meant to sit within its silence. To the world, I have disappeared. But here—here I exist."

He paused, listening to the wind clawing at the shutters, the fire sighing in response, before writing on.

"Yet even as I settle here, I cannot escape the ache of this day. My daughter was recently wed, and I was not there. I picture her smile, her dress, her hand trembling as vows were spoken. I gave her only a token of the past—a bracelet that once belonged to my grandmother. Beautiful, yes, but a poor

substitute for a father's hand, for a father's blessing. I wonder if she wept when she opened it. I fear she did. And if her tears were not of joy, then the blame rests upon me."

The words wavered, ink pooling where the pen lingered too long. He set it down, pressing his thumb against the smudge as though trying to hold back what could not be undone.

"But I could not stand among them, not now, not as the man I have become. My path leads here, to solitude, to questions that demand silence to be heard. I tell myself that one day she will understand—that my absence was not abandonment, but necessity. And yet, the truth gnaws at me: I should have been there. Forgive me, Elizabeth."

He closed the journal gently, as though tucking away a confession too raw to linger in the open air. Leaning back, Winston let his gaze fall into the fire, its light flickering against the walls like restless spirits. Asher stirred beside him, nudging his hand with a cold nose, grounding him once more in the present.

Winston sat in the glow, feeling the sharp ache of absence, yet clinging to the fragile hope that in this solitude he might uncover the answers—and perhaps, in time, a path back to the love he had left behind. But, for now, he would have to settle for a good night's sleep and the hope that a new day would bring.

The first night passed without much sleep. The wind raged outside, battering the cabin walls as if testing his resolve. Inside, the silence between gusts was immense—a silence that seemed not empty but *inhabited*. Winston sat by the lantern's faint, pulsing light, his journal open, the Book resting beside it.

Eventually, he wrote without aim, as if recording for an unseen reader: *The air hums as though alive. I feel watched, but not in fear. It is like being read.*

He let out a deep yawn, rekindled the fire and finally slipped into sleep.

The first light of morning crept through the frost-laced window, thin and pale, filtering across the cabin floor in muted streaks. Winston stirred beneath the weight of heavy wool blankets, the cold nipping even through their layers. For a moment he lay still, listening—the groan of timbers, the faint pop of dying embers, the wind prowling across the ridge. Then came the steady sound of Asher's breath beside him, loyal and reassuring, anchoring him to the present.

He rose slowly, his joints stiff, the air sharp enough to sting his lungs. The fire had nearly gone out during the night, leaving the room icy and brittle. He knelt at the hearth, feeding it with kindling, coaxing flame back to life. Soon the fire cracked and climbed again, painting the walls with amber light. Asher padded forward, stretching, before curling once more into the warmth.

Winston pressed his hand to the door, steadying his breath, listening. The wood was cold beneath his palm, vibrating faintly with the rhythm of the wind. Nothing stirred outside. No footsteps. No sound but the storm's sigh.

He almost turned away, but then his eye caught it—something pale caught between the frame and the door. A sliver of paper, edges damp, quivering with each draft that pushed through the seams.

Winston's hand tightened. Slowly, he pulled it free.

The paper was rough, yellowed as if it had weathered many years, the ink scrawled in a hurried, uneven hand. He held it to the firelight but he could not read it. He rushed to retrieve his glasses, but the words were too faint to be seen with the naked eye.

Faded letters swam before his eyes, but no visible message. His first thought was absurd—perhaps some scrap carried by the wind. But no, he dismissed that immediately, as it was clearly a deliberate attempt to convey a message, pressed carefully into the door while he slept or while he turned his back.

Asher rose from the hearth, growling low, ears pitched forward toward the shutters. Winston's gaze darted to the window.

There was nothing but the white blur of storm.

He set the note on the desk, smoothing its edges with trembling fingers, still attempting to read the faded message. The firelight made the ink shimmer, dark and certain. He forced himself to whisper words aloud: "What does this mean?"

The sound of his voice broke the silence, but did nothing to dispel the anxiety that had taken root. If anything, the cabin felt smaller now, the walls closer, the shadows deeper. The shortwave radio hissed on the shelf, spitting static like a restless whisper. Then, cutting through it, a brief burst of song—just a line, half a verse. A familiar one, though warped by distance. *Don't think twice, it's all right.* The guitar strummed once, twice, then vanished again into the void. Winston stared at the radio, heart thudding. Coincidence. It had to be coincidence, he thought to himself. But as he looked back to the paper lying on his desk, its message unclear, he could not decide what unsettled him more—that someone had found him here, at the edge of the world...or that his mind might be beginning to betray him.

As the day grew into evening, Winston set about the tasks of survival. Outside, snow crunched beneath his boots as he stepped into the cutting wind, axe in hand. The ridge loomed overhead, crowned in frost, its shadow stretching long across the clearing. He split logs in measured rhythm, each strike echoing like a drumbeat in the frozen stillness. His breath rose in clouds, the sweat beneath his coat quickly stiffening into ice. When the woodpile grew high enough to reassure him, he gathered a pail of snow and brought it inside, setting it to melt and boil over the fire. He moved with methodical precision, arranging supplies on the rough-hewn shelves, checking his maps, sharpening tools. The cabin became less a shell and more a dwelling, shaped by his hands, claimed by his presence.

And yet, through each task, the absence followed him. As the axe rang against wood, he thought of Elizabeth's laughter echoing in a hall of music. As the snow melted into water, he imagined the clink of champagne glasses raised in her honor. Even the fire—steady, loyal—called to mind the candles that must have lit her reception.

When at last he sat again at the table, steam rising from a tin cup of boiled water, Winston reached once more for his journal. He did not open it right away; instead, he traced the leather cover with his fingers, staring into the fire's glow. His reflection in the darkened window looked older, wearier, and yet resolved.

The North demanded everything: labor, endurance, silence. It would strip him bare until only truth remained. He had come here to face that trial, to find answers the world had drowned in noise. But as the morning settled over the ridge and the wind clawed anew at the shutters, one truth remained unshakable—his heart, no matter how far he fled, still beat in rhythm with his daughter's.

Life in exile, soon hardened into ritual. Winston chopped wood at dawn, his breath pluming in the air like smoke from some ancient altar. He melted snow for water, simmered beans and dried meat in battered pots, and filled journal after journal with notes, questions, and fragments of half-mad revelation. Asher trailed faithfully at his heels during long walks across the tundra, their silhouettes two small figures swallowed by constant drifts of snow. Yet strangeness clung to the cabin.

One night, as he dozed by the fire, the telephone on the wall—a relic not even connected—rang shrill and insistent. He lifted the receiver, but only silence answered. When he replaced it, faint crackles lingered, as though distant voices pressed against the line. Another evening, a knock rattled the door. He rushed to open it, but nothing stood there—only snow shifting in the howling wind. He returned to the table, used as a desk, and found a piece of paper with faded letters. However, upon closer viewing and right before his eyes the faded letters now appeared. A folded sheet of paper lay waiting on his desk with visible lettering. The handwriting was elegant, unfamiliar, with a message brief yet heavy with promise:

"Welcome."

Winston sat heavily at the desk, the note beside him like a living thing. The fire popped close by, but its warmth did nothing to steady his hands as he opened his journal. His pen scratched hard against the page, the letters jagged, urgent.

Journal Entry, January 5, 2022

"Tonight, I found a message that only days ago was hidden by faded ink. Now, tonight, the message is clear and I am welcomed into my new environment. But, by whom? The message was not there when I arrived. I checked the door myself. I am certain of it. Someone must have placed it while I slept—or while my back was turned. The thought chills me more than the wind outside. Yet, I do not embrace fear. I feel validated and somehow assured that I am on the right track and will soon know why I am here."

He paused, listening. The radio hissed in the background, a faint thread of static weaving through the silence. He glanced over his shoulder, then pressed the pen harder, ink pooling dark.

"I cannot dismiss this as an accident. The paper was too deliberate, the script too certain. Yet the alternative—intrusion—is worse. How could anyone have followed me here? How would they know where I would stay? And if they are here...why play at games? Why not reveal themselves?"

Asher's claws clicked softly on the floorboards as he circled near the hearth. Winston glanced at the dog, grateful for the steady presence, then returned to the page.

"Perhaps solitude is already gnawing at me. Perhaps the note is my own creation, though I have no memory of writing it. Madness has many doorways; am I at the threshold of one? Still—the note is here, real, tangible. I can touch it. I can see it. This much is undeniable. And, all I can do at this point is wait..."

He underlined the word twice, the ink digging into the paper. Then he set the pen down, breathing hard, staring at the page as though it might betray him.

The radio spat again, a burst of foreign chatter, then silence. Winston closed the journal slowly, his hand resting on the cover as if to hold his words captive.

For the first time since arriving, the cabin did not feel like a refuge. It felt like a stage.

Winston again stared at the letters as the firelight danced across his tired face. He stroked Asher's fur absently, eyes fixed on the door as though expecting another knock. He whispered half in jest, half in fear:

"I don't think that we're alone..." He paused, eyes curiously surveying his surroundings, as Asher looked and let out a faint bark. "Have you been expecting me?" he then murmured light heartedly, as if expecting a reply.

The wilderness had claimed him, but solitude was not his lot. He could not let go of the feeling that something or someone was watching and waiting for the right moment to make a revelation. In his heart,

Winston felt the stirrings of destiny, rising like heat from beneath the endless snow.

The cabin had settled into its familiar silence. Winston sat in a nearby armchair reading the Book that had mysteriously appeared at his home and sent a subtle message that could only be described as an invitation. The fire crackling behind him, and with Asher lifting his head and offering a low whine, Winston began to slowly touch the pages of the Book.

Tucked between the front pages of the Book was a weather slip of parchment. The edges were damp from snow, the handwriting jagged and hurried. As he gathered the paper in trembling hands, it was as if he could hear a voice whispering through the crackle of the fire, faint but undeniable:

"Wait..."

His pulse quickened as he hurriedly rose from the table and rushed to the front door. He stepped outside, the cold immediately swallowing him. The ridge loomed in moonlight, shadows stretched long and empty across the drifts. No footprints marred the snow other than his own from earlier on that day. Still, the sensation of eyes lingered, burrowing into his back as he shut the door and dropped the latch.

Winston returned to his desk, where he observed the Book snap shut beneath his palm. He looked on but was filled with uncertainty. He had no idea what was happening but rose abruptly, the chair scraping harshly across the floorboards, to look around. He seized the lantern, its light flaring, and swept it across the room.

"Asher," he whispered, voice tight. The dog padded

close, ears sharp, tail stiff. Together they moved through the cabin, the glow of the lantern pushing shadows from one corner only to deepen them in another.

He pulled open cupboards, one after another, their hinges groaning. Nothing but empty shelves, dust, and the faint musk of disuse. He crouched and tugged open the narrow drawers beneath the workbench—spare nails, a rusted hammer, coils of twine. No sign of intrusion. The radio hissed and sputtered, filling the silence with its restless whisper. Every few moments it spat a syllable, a note, as though mocking his search.

He moved to the bookshelves, running his hand along the spines, eyes darting between titles he half-remembered. One by one, he tugged at volumes, pulling them forward, even stacking them on the floor to check the space behind. Dust motes rose in the lamplight, swirling like ghosts. Nothing.

His breath quickened. He turned to the floor, prying at the boards near the hearth where the wood looked darker. The crowbar screeched against the grain as he forced it up. Beneath held nothing but cold dirt and the faint smell of earth long shut away.

Asher whined, backing toward the door. Winston's lantern shook in his hand as he scanned the room, heart hammering.

"There's no one," he whispered to himself. "No one here." Yet the words felt hollow, fragile against the press of silence.

He set the board back into place, knelt beside it, and let the lantern's light fall on the note still lying on the desk.

"Welcome."

Winston swallowed hard, lowering himself into the chair once more. And yet the sense of being watched clung to him like a second skin.

Asher returned to the hearth, curling reluctantly into the fire's glow. Winston leaned back, closing his eyes, but his thoughts churned. He wondered if he had not found an intruder because there was none to find—because the trespasser was inside him, scratching notes from his own unmoored mind.

The lantern sputtered low, shadows lengthening. Somewhere deep in the static, the radio sighed out a faint line of song, half a verse, broken by silence. Winston shivered. The cabin felt emptier than ever—emptier, and yet unbearably full.

By morning, another note appeared, resting atop his books:

"We see you."

Winston sat hunched over the desk, the fire casting long, restless shadows across the walls. His pen hovered above the page, trembling faintly in his hand. At last, he pressed down, forcing himself to capture the thoughts that had clawed at him all night.

Journal Entry, January 6, 2022

"There are notes that continue to appear at times and places that escape my notice. At first, I thought them tricks of the wind—scraps blown from nowhere—but I cannot deny their words. This morning: "We see you." How did they find their

way inside? The door was barred, the windows latched. I searched every corner, every crevice, and found nothing. Yet the notes remain and continue to appear."

He paused, listening to the faint moan of wind pressing against the timbers, the hollow whistle seeping through the chimney. Asher stirred restlessly by the hearth, ears pricked, tail twitching.

Journal Entry 2, January 6, 2022

I tell myself solitude plays tricks. That the mind, left in silence, begins to shape ghosts from shadows. And yet...if it is not madness, then it is something worse. Someone has marked me. Watches me. Knows I am here.

His script grew hurried, ink smudging beneath his hand.

I cannot be sure what is real. The notes are tangible—I hold them, I read their words—but the silence beyond the walls offers no clue, no sound of footsteps, no proof of presence. Perhaps I am unraveling already. Perhaps the North has teeth sharper than frost.

He stopped, staring at what he had written, his breath quick and shallow. With deliberate care, he closed the journal, as though sealing away not just his words but the unease creeping through him.

The fire popped sharply, a coal breaking apart, and Winston flinched. His eyes darted to the door, the window, the shelves sagging with books. Every shadow seemed alive, every creak in the wood a footstep.

And though he told himself it was imagination, he

could not shake the feeling as he doused the lamp and lay down—that even in the depths of the North, he was no longer alone. Even checking the chimney. Nothing. Asher circled him nervously, ears twitching, as though sensing what Winston dared not speak aloud. Was someone truly watching him in this desolation? Or had solitude already begun to unravel his mind?

The days and nights were beginning to blur and he tried to use his time to record his experiences on a daily basis in order to maintain accurate records in his journal.

As night fell again, he sat rigid by the fire, the journal open but his pen unmoving. Every creak of the timbers, every groan of the wind seemed now a signal, a whisper, a warning. And though the room was warm, a chill spread through him deeper than the frost outside—an unshakable certainty that he was no longer master of this solitude.

The wind had battered the cabin all night, clawing at the shutters like a restless hand. When dawn finally came, its light was pale and weak, filtering through the frost on the windowpanes. Winston rose groggily, his body heavy from a night of shallow, broken sleep.

He moved automatically—stoking the fire, boiling snow for water, laying out his tools. For a few blessed minutes, the rhythm of survival quieted his mind. But when he reached for his journal, intending to steady himself with writing, his breath caught.

The journal lay closed on the desk, exactly where he had left it—but its strap had been undone. He was sure he had fastened it the night before. A tremor of dread ran through him as he lifted the cover. Inside, between two pages of his own scrawl, a slip of paper waited. Not left at the door, not dropped by chance—hidden within his journal, where no one should have been. His hand shook as he unfolded it.

"You cannot hide."

The words were neat this time, deliberate, written in an ink that bled faintly into the paper. Winston's pulse thundered in his ears. He glanced at the door, still barred from the inside; the windows, still latched; Asher, still curled at the hearth, head lifting as though sensing his master's fear.

A wave of cold broke over him deeper than the chill of the cabin. Whoever—or whatever—had left the note had been inside while he slept. Had touched his journal. Had known precisely where he would look. His mind splintered between two explanations. One: he was unraveling, planting the notes himself, lost to some creeping madness. Two: someone else was here, unseen, slipping through his sanctuary like smoke.

Winston shut the journal with a snap, his breath coming fast. For the first time since arriving, the cabin no longer felt like a refuge but a trap—a stage where someone else wrote the script and he merely acted his part. Behind him, the fire popped sharply. Asher growled, low and uncertain, staring at the door. Winston whispered, more to himself than to the dog:

"This is real. It has to be real." Yet even as he said it, he couldn't tell which possibility frightened him more—that someone was hunting him, or that he was losing his mind. Neither choice was appealing.

The wind had quieted by nightfall, leaving the cabin wrapped in a silence so dense Winston could hear the creak of its timbers as if they were breathing. The fire burned low, a dull orange glow licking at the stones, while Asher lay with his nose on his paws, ears twitching at every faint groan.

Winston could not sit still. His eyes kept returning to the journal on the desk, the strap buckled tight now, as though the leather could guard against intrusion. But fear gnawed at him—fear of what he might find come morning.

He lit a single lantern, the flame small, trembling, and moved about the cabin with measured intent. At the door, he spread a thin layer of ash across the threshold—any step would mark itself clearly. At the window, he tied a slender thread from the latch to the shelf nearby, so fine it was almost invisible in the dim light. One tug, one shift, and he would know.

In the corner, he pulled a book from the shelf and set it precariously upon another, balanced just so. A careless hand, even the faintest vibration, would send it sliding to the floor with a sound he could not ignore.

When his preparations were complete, Winston stood in the center of the room, lantern raised, scanning the space that had seemed so welcoming only a night before. Now the shelves sagged like watching eyes, the shadows pooled like figures crouched and waiting.

He returned to his chair by the fire, journal clasped to his chest, and sat with Asher pressed close to his feet. His pen scratched once more across the page, his words uneven:

Journal Entry, January 7, 2022

If the traps are undisturbed by dawn, then madness is the culprit. If they are sprung, then I am not alone. I pray, God, that the lesser evil is true.

He shut the book, leaned back, and forced his eyes to remain open. The cabin seemed to hold its breath with him, every groan of timber louder than the last. And though the night deepened, Winston knew sleep would not come—not while he waited to learn whether his enemy was indeed within the cabin or within himself.

FIVE

THE RUNAWAY

The first gray light of dawn pressed through the frosted windowpanes, a faint shimmer against the cabin walls. Winston stirred awake in his chair by the fire, his head heavy, his journal still resting open on his lap. The room was cold, the fire burned low, but it wasn't the chill that woke him—it was the crackle of the shortwave radio, left on the shelf where he'd tuned it the night before.

The air was filled with static, broken by bursts of distant voices—half-English, half-lost in the ether. A broadcaster droned faintly in German, fading into silence. Then, without warning, a fragment of music drifted through: the hollow strum of an old guitar, a voice weathered and plaintive, singing of roads and time.

It was the sort of music Winston had always gravitated toward—folk and early rock, the kind he'd grown up with in the Pacific Northwest. Songs by Bob Dylan, Joni Mitchell, Simon & Garfunkel—music steeped in reflection, rebellion, and melancholy. The kind of music that felt less like entertainment and more like conversation with the past.

The melody rose above the static for a few brief, haunting measures, then collapsed into white noise again, leaving only the hiss of emptiness. Winston leaned forward, his elbows on his knees, staring at the radio as though it had conjured the sound from his own memory rather than from the air.

Asher stirred at his feet, ears pricked, eyes fixed on the door. The traps—ashes across the threshold, thread strung taut at the window, the precariously balanced book on the shelf—waited for his inspection. But Winston sat still, listening to the radio's restless whispers, the song that came and went like a ghost.

Finally, he rose, lantern in hand, and turned toward the door. His breath hung in the air, each step measured, deliberate. It was time to see if the night had left him proof—of intrusion, or of madness. The lantern's glow trembled as Winston moved to the door. The thin layer of ash he had scattered across the threshold lay undisturbed, smooth and unbroken. No prints, no smudges, not even the faintest trace of a brush or shift. He knelt closer, heart hammering, but the truth was plain: no one had passed through in the night.

Straightening slowly, he crossed to the window, eyes narrowing at the thin thread stretched taut across the latch. It remained exactly as he had left it—unbroken, unmoved, fragile as a spider's line. He touched it gently; it hummed back at him, intact. A faint strum of guitar floated from the shortwave radio, half a verse of some nameless folk tune, before dissolving back into static. Winston's jaw tightened.

Turning to the corner, he lifted his lantern toward

the stack of books. The one he had balanced precariously on the edge remained balanced still, its position as steady as if unseen hands had preserved it. No one had touched the books. No one had been here.

His throat worked dryly as he set the lantern down and raked his fingers through his hair. "Nothing," he muttered, the word harsh against the silence. "Absolutely...nothing."

Asher wagged his tail once, uncertain, then laid his head back down. The dog seemed to trust the stillness; Winston could not.

He paced the cabin, each turn sharper, more agitated than the last. The notes were real. He had held them, read them, tucked them away in his journal. He had *not* imagined them. And yet the traps mocked him with their emptiness, as though the night itself conspired to gaslight his senses. The radio crackled again, voices overlapping in a blur—snatches of weather reports, foreign chatter, a burst of laughter quickly drowned in static. Winston froze, staring at the device, a surge of anger rising in his chest.

"Are you laughing at me now?" he snapped, the sound of his own voice startling in the still room. The cabin offered no answer, only the restless hiss of the airwaves and the slow drip of melted frost from the eaves. He turned away, jaw tight, his frustration coiling into something darker. If the traps revealed nothing, then either he was losing his grip—or his unseen visitor was cleverer than he imagined.

Winston sat heavily at the desk, the leather journal waiting like an accuser. He flipped it open, pen scratching hard against the page, the words tumbling in jagged strokes.

Journal Entry, January 9, 2022

The traps show nothing. No step in the ash, no thread disturbed, no book fallen. Yet the notes are real. I have them in my hand, tucked between these very pages. How is it possible? Either I am losing my mind, or my visitor slips through this place like smoke, unseen, untouched. I will not be made a fool by shadows. I will not. Am I dealing with an invisible force that takes liberties with my mind? Or, am I dealing with a supernatural being with superior intelligence who is trying to send me a message?

The nib dug too deep, tearing a groove into the paper. He threw the pen down, pushing back from the desk, his breath ragged. The cabin seemed to lean in on him, the groan of its timbers mocking, the hiss of the radio a constant whisper in his ear. He stood abruptly, gripping the lantern, scanning the room.

"If you're here," he called out to the silence, "show yourself." His voice echoed off the beams, hollow, unanswered. Asher gave a low whine, unsettled by his master's agitation. Winston drew in a long breath, forcing his hand to steady.

"Fine," he muttered. "Then we'll see how clever you truly are."

The morning quickly faded into evening. He began his preparations anew. He laid fresh ash across both doorways and windows, thicker this time, impossible to cross without leaving a trace. He tied not one but three threads at different heights across the latches, invisible snares for any hand that dared intrude. He wedged a mug at the top of the doorframe, balanced so precariously it would shatter at the faintest push. And when he was done, he stacked his books deliberately into towers along the shelves, fragile cairns of knowledge ready to tumble at the lightest disturbance.

By the time dusk fell, the cabin looked less like a scholar's retreat and more like a fortress of fragile alarms. Winston stood in the center, chest heaving, lantern light flickering across his face.

"If someone comes tonight," he whispered, "they will not slip through unseen."

The radio crackled from its shelf, spilling a thin, warbling verse of Dylan's "*A Hard Rain's A-Gonna Fall*" before collapsing again into static. Winston's head snapped toward it, his stomach twisting at the words.

For the first time, he wondered whether the voices carried by the airwaves were warning him—or mocking him. Either way, the silence was no longer a refuge. It was a cage. The storm rattled the cabin with the fury of a living thing, snow hurling itself against the windows in sheets of white. Winston hunched over the rotary telephone, his brow furrowed, voice raw with frustration.

"Come on," he muttered, twisting the cord and pressing the receiver hard against his ear. The line sputtered with faint crackles, whispers of a signal—yet never a voice, never an answer. Each time he thought he heard something, it was swallowed by static.

Behind him, the forgotten book lay open on the desk, its symbols faintly shimmering in the lamplight. At the edges of his perception, Winston thought he heard something else—a low, humming vibration beneath the wind. He rubbed his temple, telling himself it was the storm.

Asher, curled on the rug, lifted his head suddenly. His ears twitched, his gaze fixed on the door. Winston caught the movement but ignored it, too consumed by his futile call. Then came the sound. A low creak—the door easing open. Winston turned, startled, just in time to see Asher nosing the door ajar, his thick coat bristling against the gale.

"No—Asher!" Winston slammed the receiver down and lunged for the door, but too late.

Asher bounded into the night, vanishing into the whirling white. For a moment Winston simply froze, disbelief etched into every line of his face. Then terror gripped him. Out there, in this cold, even a strong beast like Asher could freeze to death. The thought of his companion—the only friend who had not abandoned him—perishing in the snow broke something within him.

"Why did I come here?" he whispered, his voice trembling. Then he pounded the doorframe with his fist, rage and despair mingling. "What the hell am I doing?"

Was it madness, after all, to think he could escape ridicule only to be abandoned even by his dog? He tore on his heavy coat and stumbled into the storm, the wind biting like knives.

"Asher! Asher!" he shouted, his voice whipped away into the vast emptiness. He tripped through the snow, calling until his throat burned. Only silence answered.

Asher, meanwhile, padded through the drifts with a strange determination. The storm no longer seemed to buffet him; his ears twitched as though guided by something beyond sound. He pressed forward into a hollow between ridges where the snow swirled in spirals, not random, but patterned. And there, beneath a drift of ice, a light pulsed faintly.

The Seam. It glowed with hues not of the natural world—violet and indigo, threads of gold weaving like script across the surface. Asher lowered his muzzle, sniffing curiously, then pawed at the frozen crust. The light responded, flaring briefly, humming with a resonance that made the air tremble. For a long moment, Asher stood enraptured, head tilted as if listening to a voice beyond hearing. When at last he turned back, the glow seemed to follow him, a faint luminescence clinging to his fur.

Hours later, back at the cabin, Winston had collapsed against the doorframe, exhausted, and fearing the worst. Tears froze on his face as he wept bitterly. All of a sudden, there was a strange noise. At first, he thought it was only the wind—a low cry threading through the pines. Then came the sound again, nearer this time, fragile but unmistakable: a bark, hoarse and broken, carried on the frozen air. His heart lurched. He stumbled to the door and flung it open.

Through the drifting snow, a shape emerged—

small, limping, resolute. Asher. His fur was rimed with ice, his gait unsteady, but his eyes—those familiar, faithful eyes—still burned with life. Winston fell to his knees in the snow and the dog pressed against him, trembling, burying his head into the man's chest as though to prove he was real.

"My boy…oh, my brave boy," Winston whispered, his voice breaking into something between laughter and a sob. He clutched Asher's body, feeling the warmth radiate through the frozen fabric of his coat. The smell of fur, of earth, of home was almost too much to bear.

When he finally looked into Asher's eyes, Winston saw something new there—something ancient and knowing. The same faint glow he had seen in the fissure's light flickered now within them, gentle and steady. Asher's return was not mere survival. It was a message.

Winston held him tighter, the truth settling like fire beneath the ribs. He was not alone in this place. The world beneath the ice had chosen to give something back. Asher entered the cabin—shaking off snow, tail wagging, eyes bright with a fervor Winston had never seen before. He looked well, considering he had disappeared for hours.

"Asher," Winston breathed. He dropped to his knees, clutching the dog, burying his face in the warm fur. Relief surged through him in a sob. "Don't you ever do that to me again. Do you hear me? I can't—"

His voice cracked, and he buried the rest in silence. But he sensed that something was different about Asher.

He was not the same. A faint, metallic scent clung to his coat—ozone and cedar mingled. His eyes seemed lit with urgency, as if he had seen something wondrous, terrible, or both. He paced, pawing at Winston's sleeve, then at the door, then back again, whining insistently.

"What is it, boy?" Winston whispered, unease prickling at the back of his neck. Asher gave a sharp bark, tail rigid, gaze fixed on the storm beyond. Winston followed his eyes, his own pulse quickening. The dog pressed close, insistent, nudging him toward the door as if trying to guide him, to tell him of the glowing secret beneath the ice. Winston was rightfully concerned but soon realized that night was once again upon him and there was very little that could be done in the dead of night.

That night, long after Asher had settled back on the rug, Winston sat at his desk, pen scratching against paper. His journal entry was brief, almost cryptic:

Journal Entry 2, January 9, 2022

The wilderness is no longer empty. I know in my heart of hearts that Asher has made contact with someone or something out there and has safely been returned, as a sign of what is out there. I know that I am on the verge of a breakthrough...

Winston laid the pen aside, its final scratch still echoing faintly in his ears, and let his gaze sink into the fire. The flames rose and fell like living memories, their dance mirrored in the hollow of his eyes. Outside, the storm had hushed, but the silence that replaced it was no gentler. The snow whispered against the glass with the soft insistence of a voice that would not be ignored.

Deep within, Winston knew he was not alone. The air itself seemed to lean in, attentive, charged with the breath of a presence unseen. Something—no, some*one*—was near, watching, waiting. The question was not whether he would encounter it, but whether, when it revealed itself, it would bear the face of kinship or the mask of something altogether alien, a creature to which the word 'life' could scarcely be applied.

He closed his eyes, feeling the weight of his choices press upon him. The bridges to his old life had been burned with his own hand—family estranged, reputation shattered, laughter trailing behind him like shadows wherever his name was spoken. To turn back now would not restore what was lost; it would only crown him with ridicule, confirming him as the fool everyone believed him to be.

No, retreat was impossible. The only path left was forward, into the uncertainty that called from beneath the ice, into the presence that watched from the shadows of the unseen. Whatever awaited him—wonder or horror, revelation or annihilation—he would meet it with the last fragments of courage he possessed.

And so, with the fire crackling low and the snow whispering like prophecy beyond the windows, Winston Thornberry steadied his heart. Destiny no longer lingered on the horizon. It sat in the room with him, patient, inexorable, demanding to be faced. The cabin glowed with a fragile peace, shadows flickering against the timber walls like memories coming home. Asher lay curled beside the hearth, his breathing deep and even, the soft rise and fall of his chest more reassuring than any human word. Winston watched him for a long time, unable to look away. The dog's return had broken something open inside him—a dam of disbelief that had held back hope for too long.

He rose and approached the small window, looking out into the vast, frozen expanse. The wind had calmed, and the snow glittered faintly under the cold shimmer of the moon. There, in the quiet heartbeat of the Arctic night, he felt it—the subtle hum that lived beneath the stillness, like the pulse of something vast and unseen. It was no longer menacing. It was music.

"You found them, didn't you?" he whispered to Asher without turning. "You went where I couldn't... and they sent you back." The words trembled out of him, half prayer, half revelation. For the first time since arriving, Winston felt certainty bloom within him—quiet, unshakable. The path he had chosen, the ridicule he had endured, the pain of leaving his family—it had all led here, to this place of luminous silence. He turned back to the fire, eyes damp but bright.

"I was right," he said softly, almost in awe. "They're here, Asher. All of it—all the signs, the geometry, the whispers—it's real."

Asher's ears flicked at the sound of his name. He lifted his head briefly, then rested it again with a deep sigh, as if in agreement. Winston smiled, a rare, genuine smile that seemed to ease the lines etched by years of doubt and sorrow.

"We're close now," he said, kneeling beside the dog. "Closer than ever. We must keep going and embrace whatever lies ahead."

Outside, a soft wind moved through the pines, carrying with it a faint shimmer of light that danced across the snow—like the echo of distant watchers, approving. Winston closed his eyes and breathed deeply, grateful at last. He no longer felt alone in the cold. He felt chosen.

SIX

THE DESCENT

It was over two weeks since Asher had run away and returned. Something was wrong, and it was clear that the husky was not himself. The change had been subtle at first—missed meals, a strange disinterest in the scraps Winston laid out, restless pacing before the door. But in recent days, Asher's behavior had deepened into something troubling. He moped at Winston's feet, head pressed against the floorboards, eyes haunted with a distant gleam. At night, he whined softly, as though hearing a sound Winston could not.

Winston sat at his desk, spectacles low on his nose, the forgotten Book open but unread. His hand hovered over his journal; pen poised above the page. At last, he began to write.

Journal Entry, January 28, 2022

Asher is failing. He turns from food. His coat dulls. He whines at shadows, or perhaps at silence itself. I fear I have dragged him into exile for no purpose but my vanity. Have I doomed him to freeze and starve beside me in this forsaken place? God forgive me if so. Margaret would say I am mad. Elizabeth would not look at me at all. And perhaps they are both right. Yet here, in this wilderness, Asher is all I have. If I lose him, I lose myself. Please grant me the wisdom and clarity to know the role you would have me play, so I don't lose the blessings I have in search of something that I was never meant to know.

He set the pen down, staring into the fire with hollow eyes. The words looked back at him from the page, damning in their honesty. He thought of Elizabeth's wedding day—the way she had pleaded for him to stay away, the way her voice broke when she spoke of the "embarrassment." His own daughter was ashamed of him. And Margaret, her face cold with finality, demanding, in her own way, that he leave rather than ruin what remained of her life. They were gone. And now, even Asher seemed to be slipping away.

Winston could still hear his only daughter's fractured voice uttering the word "*embarrassment*"—a word that pierced him deeper than any accusation. His own daughter, ashamed to call him father and shamefully demanding that he not attend her wedding.

"What have I done?" he whispered softly, now reflecting back on the marble expression displayed on Margaret's face, during their last quarrel. Her once gentle eyes were emptied of all tenderness. They were lost to him, consigned to the silence of absence. And now, as he watched Asher falter, it seemed even his last companion was slipping beyond his reach.

The next morning, Winston trudged into the snow with his dog at his heels, determined to find answers. The air was brittle, the kind that burned the lungs, each breath a punishment. He wandered across ridges and hollows, scanning the horizon, searching for something—anything—that would explain the strange malaise gripping his companion. But there was nothing. Only endless white, a silence so complete it rang in his ears like a bell. By noon, he returned to the cabin, shoulders slumped, more defeated than ever.

Out of desperation, he turned to the Book and stared at the pages, as if waiting for them to give him an answer.

"How could I have been such a fool!" Winston's voice erupted with such anguish it seemed to claw at the rafters. The sound was part cry, part confession—an echo of all the ridicule, the laughter, the whispers that had hounded him. In a violent surge, he swept his arm across the desk, sending volumes and papers cascading to the floor. The crash resounded like thunder, as if the accumulated knowledge of his life had turned traitor, abandoning him in his hour of need.

Asher flinched at the sudden fury. The loyal dog rose slowly, ears pressed back, eyes filled with a sorrow so deep it was almost human. He whimpered—soft, uncertain—yet that sound carried more weight than the scorn of colleagues or the silence of family. In that fragile cry, Winston heard the terrible truth: even here, even now, his violence had the power to drive away the only companion left who still bore witness to his existence. His rage shattered, giving way to a hollow despair. He dropped to his knees among the fallen books, their scattered pages whispering accusations in the firelight.

"My only friend," he choked, reaching trembling hands toward Asher. "Forgive me."

His voice dissolved into bitter sobs, the kind that seemed to rise from some place beneath words. And in that moment, with his arms wrapped around the trembling dog, Winston understood the cruel symmetry of his life. To his students, to Margaret, to Elizabeth—he had already become invisible, a ghost they dismissed, an absence more palatable than his presence. If he lost Asher, too, what remained of him? What meaning would there be in continuing, unseen and unheard, in a world that had already erased him? The thought carved itself into his heart like prophecy. Long before he would descend into the luminous halls of the hidden city, Winston Thornberry knew what it was to be a ghost.

"What have I done?" he cried out.

That night, Asher grew restless again. He pawed at the floor, then the door, whining with insistence. Winston, weary, tried to soothe him.

"Enough, boy! Not tonight." But Asher barked, sharp and sudden, then stood rigid, staring at the door with unblinking eyes. Winston frowned.

"What is it you see? For Christ's sake, show me!" Winston's voice cracked in the silence, half-command, half-plea, trembling with the desperation of a man who had nothing left to lose.

Asher whined again, louder this time, his body stiff

with urgency. He circled once, then planted himself before Winston, pawing insistently at his coat, eyes burning with a strange insistence—as if he bore a message from some realm Winston could not enter alone.

The professor's hands fumbled at the hooks of his heavy overcoat. He snatched his hat from the peg, shoved his scarf beneath the thick collar, and with a resigned tremor slid his arms into the sleeves. His movements were clumsy, hurried, yet deliberate, as though his body already knew the journey could not be refused. The boots came last—heavy, stiff with cold. He stamped them against the floorboards, each thud resounding like a drumbeat of inevitability. His chest rose and fell in ragged breaths as he reached for the latch.

The door groaned as it opened. A gust of frigid wind tore into the cabin, scattering loose papers and dimming the lamplight to a fragile flicker. For an instant, Winston thought he heard something in that wind—not merely air, but a voice, low and mournful, like words stretched beyond comprehension. He hesitated, heart hammering. Asher did not waver. The dog leapt into the storm, snow rising around him in a spray of white. At the threshold he turned, his shape caught in the moonlit blur, eyes reflecting with a brightness that seemed unearthly. He barked once, sharp and commanding, and then bounded forward, swallowed by the swirling dark.

Winston gripped the doorframe, staring into the howling whiteness. A shiver traced his spine, not from the cold but from the certainty that beyond the veil of storm something waited—something that had summoned his dog, and now summoned him. He drew a ragged breath, pulled the door tight behind him, and stepped into the storm. The snow bit at his face, the wind howled like a warning, but the trail of paw prints already marked the path before him. Somewhere in that swirling void, Asher led on, and Winston—whether toward revelation or ruin—had no choice but to follow.

They crossed the frozen expanse in silence, Winston's breath harsh in the night air, Asher's paws moving with a certainty that defied the storm. The dog led him down into a hollow where the wind swirled in strange, deliberate patterns.

And there, beneath a sheet of ice, light pulsed faintly, like veins beneath translucent skin.

The time had come. The fissure before him shimmered. The ice beneath his boots hummed, a low vibration that seemed to rise not from the earth but from the marrow of his own bones. Winston stood motionless, feeling the wind sweep around him in long, spiraling gusts that carried neither threat nor chill, only a strange solemnity—as though the elements themselves paused to bear witness.

He tightened the strap of his satchel, feeling the weight of the Book pressed against his chest, its presence both anchor and compass. Asher stood beside him, tail low, eyes fixed on the luminous opening ahead. Together, they faced the impossible.

Winston's mind was a storm of names and memories—those who had dared to believe that the boundaries of the world were not fixed but living, waiting to be crossed. Admiral Richard Byrd, whose journals spoke of warm lands hidden beyond the poles. Jules Verne, whose imagination cracked the crust of the Earth itself. Madeleine L'Engle's vision of light folding upon itself like time undone. Even the Urantia Book, that strange, luminous gospel of unseen worlds and celestial origins.

And above them all, one name rose like a flame in the cold: Jesus of Nazareth—who walked upon the waters, spoke to the storm, and opened passages not through ice or stone, but through the unseen corridors of the spirit. They had all, in their way, pierced veils the world called impenetrable.

Now it was his turn. He smiled faintly, the lines of age softening under the light.

"They all followed the call," he murmured, voice trembling. "Not one of them turned back."

The fissure widened with a sound like a sigh, the light within deepening into hues of gold and violet. Asher whined softly and took a step forward, glancing back only once before moving into the glow. Winston hesitated only a moment longer.

"Forgive me, Margaret. Forgive me, Elizabeth," he whispered. "But the world has kept its secrets too long."

He drew one final breath of the frozen air, lifted his face toward the pale sun, and stepped after the dog—into the light, into the silence, into the hollow heart of the Earth. The fissure closed behind them with no sound, no mark, no trace—only a faint shimmer on the snow, like the lingering afterimage of a miracle.

The Seam. Winston stopped short, heart pounding. The glow bled through the snow in threads of violet and gold, weaving into symbols that shimmered and shifted when he looked directly at them. The air vibrated with a hum that resonated in his bones. Asher approached fearlessly, sniffing at the Seam, tail low, ears pricked. He turned to Winston, eyes alive with insistence, as though commanding him to see what lay hidden.

"Dear God," Winston whispered, his voice trembling with awe and terror. His breath fogged in the bitter air, vanishing almost as soon as it left his lips. He fell to his knees, the weight of the moment pressing him into the snow as though the earth itself demanded reverence.

His hands, unsteady with both cold and revelation, brushed the icy crust. Beneath his fingertips the snow gave way to light—living light, veins of gold and violet pulsing as though the ground itself carried a heartbeat. As he cleared more of the surface, the glow brightened, spilling across the hollow, casting shadows long and spectral. For an instant, Winston thought the shadows themselves moved with a will, bending toward him like witnesses.

Tears stung his eyes. *This...this is what Asher had seen. This is what he had tried to tell me.* A lump rose in his throat, thick with gratitude and shame. The dog had led him here, faithful where all others had forsaken him. Margaret's scorn, Elizabeth's rejection, the jeers of his students—all of it was momentarily silenced by the loyalty of one creature who had not turned away.

Then the impossible happened. The light shifted, pulsing faster, as if it had recognized his presence. A deep tremor rolled through the ice, not violent, but measured, like a chord struck upon some hidden instrument of the earth. Slowly, gracefully, the Seam began to widen. The ice did not fracture; it did not shatter. It *parted,* fluid and elegant, as though invisible hands were drawing back curtains to unveil a stage that had waited centuries for its audience.

A current of warm air rose from the opening, brushing against Winston's frozen skin with the caress of a memory long forgotten. It carried a fragrance that made him shudder—a mingling of cedar and stone, of incense and earth, impossibly ancient and yet so familiar. It was the scent of something enduring, something that had waited with infinite patience for him, for this moment.

Winston's tears spilled freely now, cutting hot paths down his wind-burned cheeks. He pressed a trembling hand to his chest, overcome.

"I was not mad," he whispered hoarsely. "I was not mad!"

Asher pressed close to his side, eyes gleaming in the otherworldly light, his breath steaming in the night. The dog gave a low whine, not of fear, but of recognition, as though he too understood that they stood upon the threshold of a mystery greater than either had ever dreamed.

For the first time in his long exile, Winston Thornberry did not feel abandoned. He felt *summoned.*

Asher slipped through without hesitation. Winston hesitated only a moment, torn between awe and terror, before following. The descent was slow, each step echoing against walls that shimmered with crystalline veins of light-script. The symbols ran like rivers along the stone, rearranging themselves when he blinked.

The acoustics were uncanny: his breath, his heartbeat, even the creak of his boots returned to him amplified, transformed, as if the cavern itself were alive and listening. The space opened suddenly, and Winston staggered forward into a cathedral of ice and stone. Pillars rose like frozen trees, branching into vaults that glittered with their own auroras. Water dripped somewhere far above, each drop ringing like a bell. He turned in a slow circle, mouth open, eyes wide, struggling to comprehend the enormity of what he beheld.

Asher stood calmly at the center of the cavern, tail swaying, eyes fixed on the glowing script as though he understood it. For a moment, Winston thought his companion looked regal, transformed by the light into something more than mortal canine. His knees buckled, and he sank to the floor again, tears burning his eyes.

"Could it be?'

All the ridicule, all the pain of rejection, all the exile—it had led to this moment. From the surface, he could see what appeared to be an underground city. The joy of the moment filled him with great peace, a type of peace that he had never before experienced. Yet, he knew this was his first encounter and he would not be able to absorb the fullness of the moment. The entire experience was overwhelming.

That night, he returned to his modest cabin, feeling as if the weight of the world had been lifted.

Journal Entry, February 1, 2022

Tonight, I followed Asher into the earth. I swear that I have gone to that very spot many times before, in my dreams but tonight it was different. The ice opened, which was their way of welcoming us. The walls themselves breathed with light, and the silence sang with songs of blessings and praise. I do not yet understand what it means, but I know this: the world above is not the only world. The wilderness is no longer empty—it is alive, and it waits for humanity to rise and take its rightful place in the universe.

Winston carefully shelved his journal to the side and stared at Asher with a renewed look of love and appreciation. Asher, unlike before, appeared to be refreshed and returning to his own self.

"We're going to be okay, boy," he called out to Asher. Then he burst into laughter. "I am not mad, after all. Everything in life that's happened...has led to this moment. They were all wrong, because we are finally home!"

SEVEN

GHOST AMONG TITANS

The following day, Winston and Asher returned to the place he referred to as the Seam. The cavern opened into vastness, a place so immense that Winston felt himself reduced to less than a shadow. The vaulted ceiling stretched upward like a cathedral without end, its walls veined with shimmering light-script that pulsed in slow, deliberate rhythms. The acoustics were uncanny—every shuffle of his boots, every breath he took came back to him multiplied, transformed, as though the air itself was alive and listening. And then he saw them. Figures—tall, regal, and impossibly luminous—moved with measured grace across the chamber. Their garments shimmered like woven starlight, and their faces wore a serenity beyond human comprehension. They spoke in tones layered with harmonics, voices like chords of an organ, rising and falling in waves of impossible beauty.

Winston's heart nearly stopped. For an instant, he thought the weight of the sight itself would crush him. These were no phantoms, no illusions conjured by hunger or loneliness. They were real. Flesh of light, bone of radiance. This was his vindication, the proof that all his suffering had not been in vain.

The beings were magnificent, their every gesture imbued with an otherworldly purpose. They moved in perfect harmony, slow and deliberate, their luminous hands tracing symbols across the walls that flared brighter at their touch. Their voices rose in polyphonic tones, a celestial music that seemed less heard than felt, resonating in Winston's chest until his very bones vibrated.

Tears blurred his vision. His throat tightened with reverence and terror. Stumbling forward, he spread his arms wide, his voice bursting out of him as though it had been waiting there for decades.

"I am here!"

The cry tore through the vaulted chamber, splintering into a thousand echoes that rebounded like an army of voices, each one pleading, desperate. For a heartbeat, Winston expected them to stop, to turn, to greet him as one who had at last answered some ancient summons. But they did not turn. The beings continued their solemn procession, heads bent toward one another in silent conference, their music weaving around him as though he did not exist.

"I am here!" he shouted again, louder this time, the sound cracking against the immensity of the space. His heart racing; his hands shook. Still, no response. Panic flared. He waved his arms, his voice raw.

"Look at me! For God's sake, look at me!" His words echoed, but only the silence of disregard answered him.

He ran forward, close enough to reach one of them. Trembling, he extended a hand, his fingertips grazing the edge of a luminous garment. But the contact was an illusion—his hand passed through as though through mist. The figure did not falter, did not pause, did not so much as acknowledge a ripple of disturbance.

Winston fell back, his heart hammering. "No..." he whispered, a moan rising from the pit of his being. He tried again, pushing through the space where the being stood, only to find himself swallowed by light and emptiness. It was like pulling on a dream that dissolved in his hand. His knees struck the stone floor. He clutched his head, sobs ripping through him.

"I gave up everything!" he wept bitterly, voice shattering into hoarse fragments. "My wife, my daughter, my name...all of it, for this moment. And you cannot even see me."

The beings glided on, radiant and remote, their music swelling to a grandeur so beautiful it seemed to mock his insignificance.

Asher whimpered at his side, pressing close, his eyes fixed on the beings. The dog saw them—of that Winston was certain. And yet the cruel truth tightened its grip: his only companion bore, perhaps, more recognition from these luminous titans than he, Winston Thornberry, the man who had sacrificed all to find them. He pounded his fist against the icy floor, his voice breaking into a final cry:

"I am not nothing! I am here!" But only the echoes answered him—hollow, pitiless, returning his desperation like a mirror of despair. Winston's heart nearly stopped. For an instant, he thought the weight of the sight itself would crush him. These were no phantoms. They were real. They were his vindication.

After trying unsuccessfully to make some type of contact with the beings, Winston grew weary and decided to retreat. He motioned for Asher to follow him as he headed back to the cabin. However, before he could return, something happened.

At first, there was no sensation—no falling, no motion, only the feeling of being carried, as though suspended in the breath of something vast and living. Then, slowly, light began to return. It unfolded in ribbons—blue, gold, and silver—coiling around him in silent harmony. The air was warm, almost weightless. The cold and the roar of the surface world were gone.

Winston opened his eyes. He stood on a narrow ledge overlooking an expanse so magnificent that his mind refused at first to name it real. Miles below stretched a valley bathed in perpetual dawn—its light soft and internal, radiating not from a sun above but from the very air itself. Crystalline spires rose like cathedrals of glass and stone, reflecting hues of living color. Rivers of light wound between them, flowing as though thought itself had taken form.

He gasped. "It exists..."

Asher barked once, the sound startling and pure. The dog stood poised at the edge of the ledge, his fur aglow with the faint luminescence of the place. There was no echo—only resonance, as if the space itself absorbed sound and returned meaning.

Far below, figures began to emerge—as the others

had been, they too were tall, radiant, clothed in garments that shimmered. Their movements were slow, deliberate, filled with a grace that transcended human measure. Each one bore an inner light, soft but unceasing, and though Winston could not yet see their faces, he felt the unmistakable impression of *welcome.* His breath trembled. He descended the stone path spiraling down into the valley, the air vibrating faintly with unseen harmonies. The closer he came, the stronger the warmth grew, until the very tension in his heart seemed to dissolve.

The first of the beings approached him. Its eyes were vast, luminous, reflecting not light but memory. The being spoke, and though no sound crossed its lips, the words bloomed within Winston's mind as gently as breath:

"You have come where others turned back."

Winston swallowed hard, tears blurring his vision. "I believed," he whispered. "Even when no one else would."

"Belief was the door," came the reply. *"But humility opened it."*

These sentiments were etched in his mind, although no words were spoken or exchanged between Winston and the regal beings.

Behind the being, the others gathered—six in all, just as the Book had foretold. They stood in a semicircle, their presence neither male nor female, neither old nor young, but timeless, like living ideas clothed in light. Asher sat at Winston's feet, tail motionless, eyes locked on the beings with serene understanding.

One extended a hand—long, luminous, almost translucent—and from its palm blossomed a shape: the same circle-within-circle symbol that had sealed the Book.

"This world," the voice continued, *"was never hidden from you. Humanity turned its eyes away."*

Winston fell to his knees, overwhelmed by the immensity of it all—the beauty, the peace, the unbearable clarity. Everything he had lost, every ridicule and exile, every unanswered question, had led him here.

"Why me?" he asked, voice cracking. "Why choose me?" They did not speak his language but their mind was able to translate his thoughts and transmit their message.

"Because you listened when others mocked. Because you sought truth not to conquer, but to understand. The earth remembers such souls. Few remain."

The air shimmered. The valley brightened, and for a moment, Winston thought he saw faces in the light—familiar, fleeting—those of dreamers, explorers, prophets, poets. All the ones who had ever looked beyond the veil of certainty.

"You are not the first to find us," said the being, *"but perhaps the last who will still believe."*

Winston bowed his head. "Then let me learn. Let me serve whatever purpose brought me here."

The being stepped closer, touching a hand to his brow. *"Then you shall see as we see, and remember what the surface has forgotten."*

In that instant, light enveloped him completely—not blinding, but revealing. His thoughts became sound, his fears dissolved, and in their place came music—vast, harmonic, infinite. He saw the Earth as it truly was: alive, conscious, yearning for restoration.

And through it all, one truth rose above the rest, clear as the crystalline air: The hollow was never emptiness. It was remembrance—the memory of what humanity had once known and lost.

Winston wept. He was no longer the ridiculed scholar, no longer the exile. He was a witness to the unseen world, and at last he understood that revelation was not given to the worthy, but to the willing. Those who were willing to believe were the chosen.

He stood suspended in a brilliance unlike any light he had ever known. It was neither blinding nor soft, but alive—like a consciousness that could see through him. The air shimmered with colorless fire, and from within it emerged the regal beings, whose forms wavered between substance and spirit. Their eyes, if they could be called that, seemed to draw him inward, reflecting his own thoughts back to him purified of fear and pretense. He looked on in awe before them, their presence radiant yet weightless, as though composed of thought itself.

He felt both infinitesimal and exalted, as though standing before the architects of creation. No mouths moved, yet a voice filled the chamber, resonant and eternal. One among them spoke—not with sound, but with vibration that pulsed through his chest and mind alike.

"Humanity's forgotten covenant reveals the deeper purpose of your existence beneath the Earth."

It was a truth he had always sought but never dared to name, now revealed in a single, impossible instant. A thousand questions surged within him, but before he could speak, another pulse of light enveloped the space. The beings began to dissolve into waves of luminous mist, and Winston reached out in vain, desperate to hold on to their presence.

However, before he could respond or even draw breath, the light surrounding them flared to brilliance, and without passage of time or motion, Winston found himself back in the cabin—alone, trembling, and uncertain whether he had been granted revelation or merely returned from a dream too vast for the human tongue to hold.

The next moment was silence. The warmth of the cavern was gone, replaced by the cold stillness of his cabin. His lamp flickered as though mocking the radiance he had just witnessed. He stood trembling, the echo of their words still humming in his bones.

Was it a dream, or had he truly stood in the presence of the Regal Ones? He could still smell the faint mineral scent of the earth and feel the hum of something vast receding beneath his feet. Alone once more, Winston realized that his encounter had changed him in ways he could not yet understand. For though he had been returned to the world above, part of him remained beneath the ice—among those who remembered what mankind had long forgotten.

Hours seemed to pass, or perhaps only moments—time itself felt unreliable. Winston sat at his desk, pen trembling in hand, the journal open before him like a waiting witness. The page stared back in silence, expectant, almost alive. He tried to write, but language felt crude, a tool too blunt for what he had seen.

Asher sat peacefully on the floor next to the fire place, eyes fixed on Winston, as if waiting for him to make the next move.

He managed only fragments: *light without source... beings beyond matter...covenant forgotten...* Each phrase collapsed under the weight of its own inadequacy. He stopped, pressing the pen to his lips, eyes unfocused. The memory of the beings lingered not as vision but as vibration—a deep, spiritual resonance that hummed faintly in his chest.

He wondered if anyone would believe him. Perhaps no one was meant to. For the first time, he understood why prophets are called madmen and why revelation so often drives one to solitude. Looking around the cabin—the worn desk, the frost-rimmed window, the half-burnt logs—everything seemed smaller now, like remnants of a discarded dream.

He whispered into the stillness, half-in prayer, half-in awe, "Why me?" But there was no reply, only the faint echo of wind across the tundra, as if the Earth itself had closed its lips around a secret too sacred to speak aloud.

Winston paused for a brief moment before pulling his journal from the desk. Pen in hand, he started writing.

Journal Entry, February 8, 2022

Today was glorious, albeit a bittersweet moment. I will never forget this day. I saw them for the very first time with my own eyes. The beings, which I will for now refer to as the Regal Ones or the Titans, were magnificent, tall and regal in appearance. Their garments shimmered, as if stitched from constellations, their every gesture imbued with an otherworldly purpose. They moved in perfect harmony, slow and deliberate. There was a celestial aura in their tone that vibrated throughout the chamber. The entire experience was moving and brought me to a place of great emotion. I foolishly expected them to stop what they were doing, turn around and greet me. Instead, they acted as if I was invisible. They did not turn. The beings continued their solemn procession, heads bent toward one another in silent conference, their music weaving around me as though I did not exist. However, when I reach a place of absolute surrender, I was lifted to a place of absolute peace, love and beauty as never before seen or experienced in my Earthly realm. And, it all happened in the mind without speaking one word.

I have seen them. Not in dream, nor in the delirium of frost and solitude, but in that thin realm where truth wears no disguise. The Regal Ones—beings of impossible radiance—stood before me as if time itself bowed in their presence. They spoke not in language but in knowing, and the knowing pierced me like light through water.

"Humanity's forgotten covenant reveals the deeper purpose of your existence beneath the Earth."

The words still echo, not in my ears but in the marrow of my soul. I do not understand them fully—perhaps I am not yet meant to. But I feel as though something ancient within me has been reawakened, as if the Earth itself called me by name.

When I returned, I found no trace of their light—only the quiet breath of wind against the windowpane. And yet, everything hums differently now. Even the shadows seem to listen. I sense that what I have witnessed was not the end of my search, but its beginning.

If I am to carry this message, I must first become worthy of it. The light reveals, but it also exposes—and I fear it has shown me how little of myself is yet prepared for truth.

Still, I will write. I will remember. For perhaps one day, when I am ready, the Earth will open again, and they will return.

For all the years of searching, for all the sacrifices—the family lost, the career destroyed—he had found the proof he longed for. Yet proof meant nothing if it could not be acknowledged. He was a ghost among Titans, invisible, unheard, irrelevant.

Winston wrote furiously by lamplight, page after page spilling from his pen until the fire sank to embers and the clock crept past one in the morning. His hand trembled, his ink-stained fingers aching, but still he pressed on, determined to capture every detail before memory betrayed him. Only when exhaustion weighed on his eyelids did he pause, setting the pen aside.

On impulse, he rose, and walked over to the nearby window. He stared aimlessly through the window and quickly walked away. He put on his heavy coat, and stepped out into the frozen night. The air was brutal, sharp as glass against his skin, but above the horizon the Moon circled low, casting its silver light across the endless snow. It did not rise or set—it drifted sideways, eternal, patient, like a sentinel pacing the world's edge.

The snowfields shimmered, each drift gleaming like crystal, the landscape transformed into a dreamscape of silver and shadow. Winston stood transfixed, his heart aching with a mixture of wonder and sorrow. *Was it madness? A dream? Or had he truly walked among Titans?*

"How strange," he whispered. "To be unseen by those I sought, yet watched over by this pale guardian of the night."

Asher pressed close to his leg, and Winston rested a trembling hand on the dog's head. Together they gazed at the circling Moon, two solitary witnesses at the edge of the world, their silence deeper than any vow. For the first time since entering the hidden city, Winston's despair softened. The Moon had not turned away. And in its quiet light, he found the courage to face whatever mystery awaited beyond the veil of ice. He looked into the heavens for one last time and returned inside. He closed the door, rubbed Asher's head and returned to his desk.

Shaking, he tore open his journal and began to write again by the trembling moonlight that danced along the walls.

Journal Entry, February 9, 1922

"They are real. I have seen them with my own eyes. To be here is vindication. The beings are magnificent—tall and regal. Their voices rose in celestial music." He paused.

"I am here!" he proclaimed loudly.

"They are real! He whispered, as Asher whined

softly, pressing his muzzle against Winston's trembling hand.

Winston slowly pushed away his journal and retired for the night.

When dawn came, it arrived without color. A pale, ghostly light spilled through the narrow window, resting on the clutter of maps, notebooks, and instruments scattered across the cabin floor. Winston stirred from a shallow, dream-ridden sleep, his body heavy as if gravity itself had deepened overnight. For a moment he lay still, uncertain whether he had truly awakened—or whether he still lingered in that realm of vision and light.

The hearth had gone cold. He rose, wrapping his coat around him, the floorboards creaking like old bones beneath his steps. Everything appeared the same, yet nothing felt familiar. The air was dense, humming faintly, as though some invisible current still passed through the room.

Then he saw it—the faintest shimmer upon his desk, like dew catching light that was not there. At the center of the page upon which he had written the night before, a single symbol had appeared: a spiral of fine, silvery dust, forming what looked like an unbroken path descending inward. He touched it with trembling fingers; it dissolved instantly, leaving behind a subtle warmth on his skin.

His breath caught. The logical part of his mind raced to explain it—condensation, static, fatigue—but his heart knew better. Something had crossed the veil between worlds, leaving this gentle mark as both reminder and summons.

He turned toward the window. The Arctic horizon stretched endlessly, silent and white, yet he no longer saw desolation. Beneath that frozen crust, he now believed, lay the pulse of another world—the covenant spoken of, still waiting to be fulfilled.

He whispered into the quiet, "I am listening." And for the briefest instant, he thought the Earth whispered back.

The following days unfolded in a strange, lucid stillness. Winston went about his routines almost automatically—tending the fire, mending his boots, melting snow for water—yet every movement carried a sense of consecration, as if he were performing sacred rites rather than mundane tasks. He could not shake the memory of the spiral that had vanished beneath his touch. It haunted him with its simplicity: a single line turning ever inward, as though urging him to follow where reason could not go.

He spent hours poring over his maps, tracing the coordinates that had once seemed theoretical curiosities. Now they glowed with new meaning. Beneath the polar crust, beneath the magnetic void where compasses faltered, he felt certain the pathway to the Seam awaited him. The Regal beings had not merely revealed themselves—they had called him.

One evening, as the sun dipped below the horizon and the aurora began its spectral dance, Winston stood outside the cabin. The ice fields shimmered with green and violet fire. He thought of Admiral Byrd, of Verne's explorers, of prophets and poets who had dared to follow whispers the world dismissed as madness. He realized he had joined their company—not by intention, but by inevitability.

Inside, he began preparing for descent. Journals sealed in wax, provisions measured, instruments recalibrated. He recorded one final note before closing the last of his equipment cases:

"Truth lies not upon the surface, but in the hollow that waits beneath. I have been shown the door; it would be cowardice not to enter."

The wind rose outside, rattling the shutters like a restless spirit. Winston paused, feeling that familiar vibration return—the silent pulse beneath the Earth. He knew then that the time of waiting had ended.

Tomorrow, he would go beneath the ice.

EIGHT

THE COUNCIL-DEBATE

For a moment, the memory of the towering figures came rushing back—faces radiant, voices woven like chords of a celestial hymn. He froze, staring at the cabin ceiling, heart thudding. Had it truly happened? Or had his weary mind conjured it as a fevered vision? The question electrified him. He laughed aloud, startling Asher, who lifted his head from the rug with a quizzical yawn.

"Dream or miracle, we shall know today, eh boy?" Winston declared, swinging his legs over the cot. His voice brimmed with a vitality he had not known in years, as though the years of ridicule and despair had been momentarily erased.

On this particular day, he bustled about the cabin with unusual energy. The kettle rattled as he set it on the iron stove, the sharp scent of boiling water soon rising. He fumbled with his journal, scribbling notes even as his spectacles slid down his nose.

"Tall, luminous, harmonious—real or imagined?" he muttered, tapping his pen against the margin. His words spilled across the page with the urgency of a man desperate to capture the fleeting wings of wonder.

"We did it old boy?" he said, while looking over his open journal. "They invited us and we came..."

Asher padded over, tail wagging, head tilted as if amused by his master's frenzy. Winston crouched down and took the dog's face in his hands.

"If only you could speak, old friend," he said softly. "What tales we would tell the world together. You saw something—I know you did. And if I am not mad, if it was real, then..." His voice trailed off, but his eyes shone with eagerness, like a boy on Christmas morning, as he prepared for the day.

Hours later, Winston donned his tweed jacket, patched at the elbows, and tied his scarf with a flourish as though preparing for an audience. He put on his heavy coat, now inching closer to the door. He glanced back once more at the fire, its embers glowing warmly.

"Oh, Margaret, if you could see me now," he murmured, not with bitterness, but with something dangerously close to joy. "I am not mad..."

He slowly opened the door. The morning air rushed in, biting yet invigorating, and before him lay the endless expanse of snow. Somewhere beyond that white horizon lay the truth—whether dream or revelation—and Winston Thornberry was determined to find it.

Far below the frozen surface, light pooled in a chamber vast and solemn. The council of luminous beings gathered once more, their voices weaving chords of deliberation into the air. They spoke in tones that were not readily apparent to the human ear. Yet their gestures appeared to display a mixture of tranquility and concern.

"They are coming..." was the translation of Speaker One's words.

"We must decide this matter before they arrive," interrupted Speaker Two.

"Yet he is operating under the mistaken belief that we are his vindication," intoned Arioth, Keeper of Restraint.

"He would carry us back as a banner to silence his doubters. That is not readiness—it is vanity cloaked in discovery." A ripple of assent moved through the circle, though not unanimous. Lumen, voice of compassion, looked on.

"But did you not see his tears? You heard the way he begged to be seen. Even the animal felt his anguish. There is sincerity there." Lumen's bright tenor rose in protest.

"Sincerity is not stewardship, my dear Lumen." Arioth countered with an aura of firmness.

"Sincerity can turn to pride in an instant. If we show him too soon, the true mission, he will seize the light as possession, not as the true gift it was meant to be."

"Has he not shown the proper degree of reverence to the Book?" Seraphiel, a being of light and radiance, lifted her hand and the chamber hushed. Her radiance deepened, the harmonics soft yet firm. "We must remember the appointed hour. It is been 100 Earth years." She paused. "He has come further than most, but the soil of his heart is still restless. If we sow now, the harvest will be weeds."

"Earth is a dark jungle filled with weeds of questionable origin." Arioth added in summation.

The Archivist stepped forward, dipping a finger into the basin of still light. Winston's image flickered across its surface: pacing, scribbling furiously, his eyes alight with desperation. The basin revealed not only his movements but his motives—anger at those who mocked him, hunger for validation, a gnawing loneliness.

"There is much work to be done with the subject…" the Archivist observed.

"He burns, but without clarity. He seeks us to silence his ghosts, not to serve the truth."

"Then let us hide what he seeks," Arioth interrupted.

"Let the Seam vanish from his eyes. If he is ready, he will learn to wait. If he is not, he will wander until he is emptied of himself."

Lumen's voice rose again, urgent. "And if hiding breaks him? If despair drives him into ruin, then we shall have our answer…"

"Better despair than corruption," Seraphiel replied gently, though the weight in her tone silenced the chamber. "Better he be broken than the knowledge be profaned," she continued.

"Least we not forget that Earth is a distant planet, quarantined from the rest of the heavenly host as part of the rebellion," Arioth said firmly and with power in his voice.

"Though it is our desire to restore Earth to its rightful place in our planetary system, our observations of more than one hundred years reeks of immaturity, greed, lust for power and failure. We cannot force the hand of time." He paused, as if reading the thoughts of the council members. "No matter how much we want to save this planet, the inhabitants must desire to save themselves." He paused again, longer this time. "This planet is doomed to destroy itself, unless we intervene. But our intervention cannot be at the expense of other more evolved civilization who have made right choices and decisions throughout the ages of time to move into higher planes."

The expression on Arioth's face was one of profound sadness and dismay.

The council bowed their light in assent. With a gesture, Seraphiel extended her hands, and the chamber trembled with resonance.

"Let him learn that discovery is not conquest," Seraphiel said displaying a pained expression.

"When he comes seeking as servant, not claimant, then the veil will lift. Until then, we must wait, as must he..."

"He has all of the answers that he needs to find himself, hidden deep in the belly of the Book," Arioth said firmly.

"It is not the appointed time," Seraphiel said, her voice like a current of wind passing through crystal. "And yet," she added softly, "let him descend once more—only once—to behold the city in its fullness, that he might remember what lies beyond the reach of mortal eyes."

Arioth bowed his head in long contemplation, the

light of his form flickering as though touched by unseen tides. When he finally spoke, his tone carried the quiet authority of the Council itself:

"So shall it be. He shall glimpse the city again, but never as before. The veil must remain between our realms, for the purity of this world cannot yet abide the shadows of pride that cling to humankind. Henceforth, his communion with us shall be through the language of dreams—symbol and whisper, vision and silence. The Seam will fade from sight, hidden not in punishment, but in mercy, until the appointed hour when wisdom and humility meet as one."

The chamber darkened to a dim, golden hush as the decree settled over all. Even the light itself seemed to bow in reverence.

"It is not the appointed time..." Seraphiel whispered with profound sadness. "It is not the appointed time."

The words 'the appointed time' moved like a refrain across their harmonics, sealing the decision. High above, on the surface, the glowing Seam faded like ink in snow. Where once veins of light pulsed, only blank ice remained—smooth, perfect, impenetrable.

Back in his cabin, Winston could not sit still. His hands shook with anticipation as he gathered his satchel, notebook, and a half-loaf of bread.

"Come, Asher," he said briskly.

"We'll go back. We'll find it. We'll prove I was not mad."

"I will try to take pictures..."

The dog wagged his tail, but there was something guarded in his eyes, as though he already knew the truth.

Winston strode into the white silence, his heart thundering like a distant drum, unaware that the Seam he sought had already been veiled by a council whose wisdom ran deeper than the oldest ice. Though Winston believed his motives to be pure, the council discerned truths invisible to human eyes. They had watched him with patient vigilance and knew that his heart was not yet tempered enough to bear the weight of revelation. The messages entrusted to them were not fragile curiosities, but truths of a super-universe—designed to restore Earth to harmony and precision—and such truths demanded readiness beyond mere longing.

And Winston did long, with every fiber of his being. He hungered for something greater than himself, though he could not fathom the role destiny had cast for him in the fragile survival of mankind. The raging storms, fires, floods, wars, greed, corruptions, intolerance on Earth for difference: these evils were no accident. It was all part of Earth's journey to a higher celestial plane.

Unbeknownst to Winston, his life had been under quiet observation for decades. That inner ache for truth, that restless fire, had marked him as one chosen to walk the narrow path on behalf of humanity. Every decision, every stumble, every small act of defiance or devotion had been woven into a longer design—a preparation for this very threshold. Yet no special path was carved for him, no shield from error, for such protection would have emptied his journey of meaning.

And so, the council waited, hearts heavy with restraint, as they watched him falter, knowing that even his missteps were part of the crucible. For Winston, as for all who seek, the path to truth was not gifted but forged—choice by choice, breath by breath—an evolution shaped not by intervention but by the hard, luminous work of self-discovery.

NINE

THE CITY

Time could not be measured in that place. There was no sun to rise or set, only the steady glow of an inner dawn that seemed eternal. Winston had walked among the luminous towers with the Regal Ones, their presence both humbling and uplifting, like walking in the company of living conscience. They led him to a great chamber at the heart of the valley. The air there shimmered as though filled with invisible wings. At the chamber's center rose a structure of glass-like crystal shaped like an inverted spire. He was filled with many questions, and was especially curious upon seeing the same sigil on the ice—the circle within the circle, intersected by a line—as on the Book.

"*You have seen its shadow,*" a being etched in Winston's memory. "*It is the mark of balance—the meeting of the seen and the unseen. We came to preserve what humanity abandoned: the harmony between spirit and intellect, between creation and compassion. Above, your world divides these as if they were enemies. Here, they are one.*"

Winston's throat tightened. "You mean…we broke something?"

The beings regarded him with eyes that held both sorrow and love.

"Not broke," one said gently. *"Forgot."*

The chamber brightened. Along its walls appeared shifting visions—images of early civilizations guided by light, of prophets visited by dreams, of explorers glimpsing impossible things before retreating in fear. Among them, Winston saw faces he recognized: Byrd, Verne, Galileo, Christ—and, to his astonishment, his own reflection shimmering faintly among them.

"Why me?" he whispered.

"Because we listen closely to those who doubt themselves," came the reply. *"And you, Winston Thornberry, have doubted enough to become teachable."*

Asher stirred beside him, ears pricking as a low resonance filled the chamber—a sound that was not sound at all, but understanding made audible. The beings raised their hands, and from their palms unfurled patterns of living light. He saw the Earth, vast and radiant, veins of light running through its core like arteries of thought.

"Your world is alive," they said together, their voices harmonizing like music. *"Every act of kindness, every cruelty, every prayer, every silence—it all shapes the pulse of the planet. We are its memory, waiting for humanity to awaken."*

Winston trembled, overcome by the magnitude of it.

"Then there is hope," he said with growing excitement. "You're telling me it can be restored?"

"Hope," one replied with a faint smile, *"is not given. It is remembered."*

Winston fell silent, his gaze fixed on the radiant heart of the chamber. A strange peace began to settle over him—not the stillness of resignation, but of understanding. He saw now that his exile had never been punishment. It had been invitation.

"Then teach me," he said finally. "If there's still time, teach me how to help restore what we've forgotten."

The beings exchanged a long, luminous glance, their light deepening to a golden hue.

"You must first remember that no truth belongs to one individual alone," they said. *"Even revelation must return to the surface, or it withers in the dark."*

Winston lingered long in that valley of light. Days—or what passed for days—slipped through his grasp like water. He walked among the radiant gardens where every leaf shimmered with awareness, where the very air carried the scent of creation still unspoiled. Here there was no hunger, no decay, no argument between heart and mind. It was a place of impossible balance, and for the first time in years, he felt whole.

Yet even in that perfection, a restlessness stirred. It began as a whisper, almost inaudible, threading through his thoughts like wind through reeds. The Regal Ones sensed it before he spoke.

"You long for the surface," one said, not accusingly, but with gentle understanding.

Winston bowed his head. "I fear it. And yet, I do."

The being's light dimmed to a softer hue. *"Fear is*

not the enemy of purpose, Winston Thornberry. It is the shadow that reveals it."

He lifted his gaze. "You said I must remember what was forgotten. That revelation must return to the surface. But you also said not all are ready to hear. How, then, can I speak?"

"Not all will listen. But some will feel."

The beings led him to the valley's heart once more, where the inverted tip of crystal glowed brighter than ever. The air vibrated with a low resonance that seemed to echo from the very bones of the world.

"This is the Source," one said. *"From here, all things are joined—the seen and the unseen, the living and the departed. Every thought, every breath is recorded in its light. From here, the memory of the Earth flows upward like rivers into the sea."*

Winston stepped closer. "And I…I must carry it?"

"No," the being replied. *"You must become it."*

The words pierced him. Light streamed outward, wrapping him in warmth that defied description. He saw flashes of the surface world: Margaret and Elizabeth, faces drawn in sorrow; the lecture hall filled with laughter; the night he first opened the Book. And beneath it all, he saw the web that bound every soul to every other—an invisible network of thought and compassion pulsing through the planet's heart.

"What you teach must not come from pride," the voices said together, *"for pride builds monuments, not bridges. Speak softly, write truth in humility, and the few who are ready will awaken. This is your mandate."*

Winston trembled. "And if I fail?"

"Then you will have joined the company of all who tried. And the world will still remember that you tried."

He sank to his knees. "I cannot go back to them unchanged."

"That is the purpose," came the answer. *"To be changed, and yet return."*

The beings raised their hands. From the Source poured a stream of golden light that touched his brow. It did not burn; it sang. Every particle of his being seemed to remember its origin. When the brilliance faded, Winston found himself once more at the fissure, Asher standing faithfully beside him. The light behind them pulsed once more—then began to recede.

"Go, *Witness,"* the final voice called. *"The surface sleeps. It is time to wake them."*

Winston understood. They were not asking him to stay. They were preparing him to return to the surface. Wiping his eyes, Winston let out a big yawn, realizing for the first time that he was dreaming. He yawned once again and stood to stretch. Everything seemed so real.

"Was any of it real?" he asked himself. As he closed his eyes, he saw the fissure sealed behind him, silent as breath, and realize that closure to his north pole experience was rapidly approaching. He pressed a hand to his chest, as if proving to himself that he was alive and the moment was real. He looked down at Asher and smiled.

"That was one hell of a dream, old friend," he whispered. "We've got a lot of work to do..."

TEN

THE WILDERNESS WITHIN

Winston set out at first light, his satchel slung across his shoulder, his breath unfurling in pale ribbons against the frozen air. The cold bore down with quiet insistence, yet it no longer governed him. Something else moved beneath his awareness—measured, attentive—as though the land itself had taken note of his passage.

The Seam was real. Not as discovery, but as acknowledgment. It had allowed itself to be seen. That knowledge settled over him with a gravity he did not resist, carrying with it the unsettling sense that he was no longer merely an observer, but a participant in something patiently unfolding.

He knew he would soon return to the Pacific Northwest, to lecture halls and familiar routines, yet the life awaiting him already felt provisional. What he had encountered would not follow him openly; it would remain where it was, vast and unmoved. Still, it would *know* where to find him.

His fingers closed around the satchel. Inside were his

sketches of luminous veins etched through stone, his careful notes on warmth without source, and the lingering scent of cedar—faint, persistent, and wholly out of place. It clung to him now like a quiet mark, a sign not of possession, but of notice. He had crossed a threshold, and something ancient had taken his measure.

Asher trotted faithfully behind him, but Winston noticed his steps were slow, his gait uneven. Every so often, the dog stopped, nose to the ground, eyes fixed on something unseen.

"Come along, boy," Winston urged, voice tight with impatience. "We'll be there soon."

Hours passed. He crested the ridge, heart racing, but the hollow before him was blank—nothing but ice and snow, smooth as though no hand, no paw, no miracle had ever disturbed it. He staggered forward, dropping to his knees. His gloves scraped the surface, desperate to find even the faintest trace.

"I don't understand..." he muttered.

"It was here. I saw it, I touched it, we touched it..." His voice cracked into the barren silence. He clawed at the ice until his nails tore through his gloves and his fingers stung with blood. Still nothing—no glow, no fissure, only the indifferent face of frozen earth.

The wind rose, carrying his anguish across the expanse. Winston threw back his head and roared.

"Do not hide from me!" his voice echoed back, a cruel imitation of the plea that had gone unanswered in the city of light.

Behind him, Asher whined. The dog lay down in the snow, chest heaving, eyes glazed with fatigue.

Alarm pierced Winston's frenzy. He stumbled to Asher's side, cradling the animal's head in his arms.

"No...not you, too," Winston whispered, tears freezing on his cheeks. "You're all I have left."

For a long moment he stayed there, his fury dissolving into grief. The ice beneath him was merciless, the horizon endless, and the knowledge he had sought now receded like a phantom dream. He pressed his face into Asher's fur, the warmth fading beneath his touch.

"Have I come this far only to be mocked by silence?" he asked the void. "Have I given up everything for a mirage?" he wept bitterly.

By the third day of searching, Winston was a ghost of himself. He was physically and emotionally spent. For he had combed the hollow and surrounding ridges until his boots were shredded and his skin raw with frost. Each time he returned to the cabin empty-handed, he convinced himself he had simply missed the landmark, that tomorrow would yield the seam.

Each morning, he set out again, driven less by hope than by a feverish refusal to surrender. Deep within, he knew his hope was fading and sooner or later he was left to face his demons. The land offered him nothing but echoes—memories so otherworldly they seemed less like recollections and more like visions, testing his spirit until he could no longer tell where truth ended and mystery began. The line between truth and illusion was blurred, leaving him adrift between wonder and doubt. Snowstorms rolled in like endless curtains, blotting out distance, mocking his persistence. His maps blurred, his compass wavered, and still he trudged, a lone figure against a wilderness vast enough to swallow nations.

One evening, as dusk deepened into polar night, he pressed farther than ever before, ignoring Asher's whines. The dog circled him anxiously, but Winston waved him off.

"Not tonight, old friend. Tonight, we find it." His voice cracked with desperation, a brittle thread against the howling wind.

The storm grew merciless. Snow stung his face like needles; ice crusted on his beard. His legs numbed, his arms trembled. He stumbled, fell, rose again, until at last his strength failed. He collapsed face-first into the drift, his breath shallow, heart pounding like a hammer muffled by distance.

"So, this is how it ends..." he thought dimly. "Not vindication, not revelation—just another fool frozen in pursuit of ghosts."

Images rushed him: Margaret's cold eyes, his daughter's rejection, the council chamber where he had cried out in vain. But it was Asher's face that lingered, loyal, wounded, refusing to leave him even as the world turned away.

Through the blur of snow and failing vision, he felt movement at his side. Asher's warm body pressed against him, whining, pawing at his chest. Then the dog's teeth tugged at his sleeve, pulling, urging, dragging.

Winston groaned, forcing his eyes open. The storm spun around him like a wheel of knives. He let Asher pull him, crawling inch by inch, until his hands touched the cabin doorframe, rough wood biting into his numb palms. With the last of his strength, he staggered inside and collapsed by the hearth.

Hours later, warmth returned to his limbs in sharp waves of pain. He lay wrapped in furs, Asher curled against him, chest rising and falling in sync with his own. He stroked the dog's head weakly, tears burning his frozen cheeks.

"You saved me," he whispered hoarsely. "Twice over. First from loneliness, and now from death."

The fire crackled, the storm outside raged, but within, Winston realized a truth more terrible and more beautiful than any seam of light: he was not in control. The mystery could not be seized, only awaited. He had given up his family, his reputation, and nearly his life—and still the hidden city remained closed.

For the first time, Winston did not resist. Weakness came upon him gently, like the first unmistakable signs of sickness. He coughed, cleared his throat, and shut his eyes, heat rising beneath his skin. Asher pressed against him, and Winston held the dog close, surrendering to the warmth and the moment.

"I failed..." he whispered in a broken voice. "Maybe, it's time we headed back."

The cabin walls groaned against the wind as Winston slumped back onto the cot, his chest rattling with every cough. The fever had hollowed him, leaving his limbs heavy, his head fogged with a dull, persistent ache. Even Asher lay close but watchful, ears pricked as though measuring each ragged breath.

The fire sputtered, embers threatening collapse. Winston forced himself to rise, every joint protesting.

He stumbled to the woodpile, fingers clumsy as he placed the logs onto the coals. The flames caught reluctantly, casting long shadows across the cabin.

Supplies were running low—half a sack of flour, a few stale biscuits, and a dwindling measure of dried meat. The thought of hunger gnawed at him as sharply as the cold. He lowered himself onto the floorboards, back against the chair, and pulled his journal into his lap. His hand trembled as he lifted the pen, but his resolve hardened.

Journal Entry, February 23, 2022

The snow tried to claim me today. For hours, I wandered searching for the hollow space that once pulsed with light. I returned half-dead, lungs afire, limbs like stone. Was it vision or madness? Did I descend once into a city of harmony, or was it fever and imagination conjured by a desperate man?

I long for certainty. Instead, I have coughs that tear my chest, dwindling food, and silence that mocks me. Yet still I write. I cannot help it. There is a compulsion beyond reason to record, as if my words matter to someone beyond these walls. Perhaps they do. Perhaps they do not.

If I perish here, let it be known: I sought truth, even if truth eluded me. I hungered not for wealth or acclaim, but for meaning. Whether that meaning was found or invented, I cannot say. And yet...

Here he stopped, the pen slipping as a shiver coursed through him. The cabin's single window drew his gaze. Beyond the glass, snow swirled in silver ribbons. For a heartbeat, he thought he saw her—one of the towering beings, luminous, serene. A smile lingered on her face, a smile that radiated warmth in defiance of the storm.

Winston gasped, blinking hard. When he looked again, there was nothing but the storm and the pale moonlight. But the air within the cabin shifted—less heavy, almost kind. He pressed his hand to the journal, the words trembling into being.

I am not alone. Even if only a phantom, the vision bore hope where despair had settled. Hope is as necessary as bread, as fire. If she is real, then perhaps I am closer than I dare believe. If she is not, then even my imagination is merciful. Either way, I endure. I wait. I will not yield.

He closed the journal, breath hitching with exhaustion, and leaned his head against the wall. Asher inched closer, laying his head on Winston's knee, as the fire brightened, as if it too had caught a measure of borrowed strength. He gave way to the silence, as if he resolved to let the silence be what it was.

The cabin groaned in the wind as night fell, its walls quivering under the storm's weight. Winston sat hunched at the desk, firelight flickering against the spine of books and the half-frozen panes of glass. His journal lay open before him, pages crowded with frantic sketches of ridges, fissures, half-maps that led nowhere. The ink blurred where his hands had pressed too hard, smudges testifying to his growing unrest.

He dipped his pen, the tip scratching like a blade across paper.

"I have searched every hollow, every seam in the ridge, but the way is gone. I know what I saw—streets lit from within, a city unlike any built by human hand. Faces that bore the weight of wisdom untold. The Regal Ones live, hidden beneath the ice. Yet the earth itself has swallowed the gate, and I am left to wander in circles like a blind man chasing shadows."

He paused, staring at the words, then pressed on, the pen cutting deeper into the page.

"Have they hidden themselves from me? Or have I only imagined it? No—my mind is clear. I touched it with my eyes. Still, why do they not reveal themselves again? Do they test me? Have I failed some measure I cannot name? I confess the thought tears at me: perhaps they saw in me not faith, but pride. Perhaps they have judged me unworthy."

The fire popped, scattering sparks. Winston looked up sharply, heart pounding, but the room was empty. Only Asher stirred, lifting his head briefly before sinking back into sleep.

Winston set the pen down, his hand trembling. He leaned back, eyes burning, and whispered to the empty room: "Am I being prepared—or punished?"

He glanced at the window then, and for the briefest instant, he thought he saw a reflection not his own: another tall figure, still and radiant, watching him with eyes both sorrowful and stern. He blinked hard, and the glass showed only his own weary face, lit by firelight.

Slowly, he bent again to the journal, scrawling the last words of the night.

"Tonight, I glimpsed one of them—though whether with my eyes or with my madness, I cannot say. If it was real,

then hope remains. If not, then I am lost to my own vanity. God help me discern which is true."

He again closed the book with a shuddering breath, the sound of the leather snapping shut echoing in the small room. The fire sank lower, shadows pressed closer, and Winston sat motionless in the silence—caught between revelation and delusion, waiting for an answer that did not come.

The fire dwindled to a faint glow, its last embers pulsing red like the heartbeat of the room. Winston slumped in the chair, journal closed upon the desk, his hand still resting on the leather cover as though to guard it even in sleep. His breathing slowed, uneven at first, then settling into the rhythm of exhaustion. The lantern had guttered out hours before, leaving only the fire's dying breath and the pale wash of moonlight seeping through frost-veined glass.

Asher lay curled by the hearth, ears twitching though his body remained still, his dark eyes open longer than his master's. Then, at last, even he succumbed to the pull of slumber, head lowering onto his paws with a reluctant sigh.

The cabin grew still.

And in that stillness, the air shifted. The timbers creaked with a sound not wholly their own. From the corners, soft and almost inaudible, a murmur rose—like the brushing of many voices woven together, low and fluid. Words too faint to distinguish slid against the silence, syllables dissolving before they could be grasped. The whispers coiled along the walls, threading between the shelves, circling Winston where he slept.

His brow furrowed, lips parting as though to answer some question in his dream, but he did not wake. The whispers bent closer, a tide of sound he could not hear, yet one his spirit seemed to feel. Their tones were neither threat nor comfort, but something stranger—measuring, weighing, deciding.

The last ember broke in the hearth, scattering into ash. The whispers lingered a moment more, then receded, sinking back into the dark wood, the frozen stone, the silence of the ridge.

And then—from the corners, from the walls, from the very stones of the hearth—came a whisper. Not one voice, but many, braided together, soft as breath on glass.

The sound wound itself around Winston, circling him, testing, measuring. "*Not ready…not yet…the shadow of self-clings still…the eye turned inward more than outward.*"

Another voice overlapped, deeper, resonant, like wind through hollow stone.

He has seen, but he does not understand. He desires the crown before the burden. Vanity clouds the vessel."

The murmurs rose and fell, a tide of judgment washing over the cabin. Winston stirred faintly, his lips parting in unconscious protest, but he did not wake.

The whispers bent closer, as though the council of Regal Ones leaned unseen above him, cloaked in light his eyes could not bear. "*We will hide the path. The city will close to him until his heart is made new. Let him hunger, let him wander, until he learns to seek without self.*"

The air grew heavy again, still, empty, as though nothing had ever moved there but the wind.

Winston stirred once, muttering, then fell deeper

into sleep, unaware that he had not been alone; unaware that judgment had been passed in his very presence.

Time was not marked at the North Pole by sun or moon, but by deepening comprehension. The air was heavy with wisdom, too vast to grasp all at once.

The Regal Ones watched him with patience beyond time itself, their light neither diminishing nor demanding. They had shown him the Source, the luminous heart that bound all things together—but they had not yet granted him the fullness of its truth.

One evening, if 'evening' could be said to exist in that unbroken dawn, Winston stood at the precipice overlooking the valley. The hum of the living light pulsed beneath him, in rhythm with his heartbeat. And yet, his thoughts had begun to drift—to Margaret, to Elizabeth, to the laughter that had haunted his lectures. He imagined himself returning, the misunderstood scholar finally vindicated.

The idea came unbidden, but once it entered, it grew. The notion that he, Winston Thornberry—the man who had been mocked, dismissed, pitied—would at last be proven right. That they would have to listen. That they would have to see.

The thought burned bright as pride always does: self-righteous, disguised as purpose.

"You still hear the echoes of men," came the voice behind him.

He turned. One of the Regals, tall and luminous beyond description, stepped forward. The light around its form dimmed, revealing eyes like molten silver—beautiful, unyielding.

"You seek not only to reveal truth," the being said, *"but to be praised for finding it."*

Winston's lips parted, but no defense came. His mind filled with fragments of past humiliation, each one rising to justify his desire. He wanted to say that he had earned the right—that he had suffered enough to deserve recognition. But even as the thought formed, shame crushed it.

"I—" he began, his voice catching. "I only want them to know...that I wasn't mad."

The being's expression softened, but its tone did not. *"And that, Winston Thornberry, is why you cannot yet carry the full Mandate."*

The air trembled. A subtle shift passed through the valley—something unseen, but felt, like the closing of a great unseen door.

"You mean," he stammered, "I am not worthy?"

"Not yet," came the answer. *"To reveal truth, one must love truth more than the self who bears it."*

Light gathered between the being's hands—a crystalline sphere, pulsing faintly. Within it, Winston glimpsed vast shapes of thought, music, and memory. The vision drew him forward, but when he reached out, the sphere dissolved.

"This is the Seam," the being said. *"The meeting place of the worlds—the covenant between what is above and what lies beneath. To pass through it is to see all as one. But pride clouds the eye. Vanity fractures the lens."*

Winston fell to his knees, trembling. "Then what must I do?"

"Continue the journey," the voices answered in

unison. *"You have seen the outline of truth, but not its depth. It cannot yet dwell in you without distortion. Go, live among men again. Fail. Forgive. Remember. When humility outweighs your hunger for recognition, the Seam will open, and you will see as we see."*

The light around them dimmed to a soft glow, the valley sighing as though in sorrow. Winston wept—not from despair, but from understanding. He knew now that revelation was not an achievement. It was surrender.

"Then I will go," he whispered. "Even blind, I will go."

The being stepped forward and placed a hand upon his brow. *"Then even in blindness, you will begin to see."*

The valley brightened once more, and Winston felt himself lifted—not by power, but by mercy. The fissure appeared again, the path homeward glimmering faintly in the cold blue light.

Asher waited beside him, calm, patient, knowing.

"Go, seeker," came the final whisper. *"The journey is not finished. The hollow has only mirrored what lies within you. Now, return—and become whole."*

The light faded. The fissure sealed. And Winston Thornberry, humbled and trembling, knew that he would begin his ascent toward the surface world—not a prophet, but a man still learning how to listen. He let out a deep sigh and returned to the cabin, where he slept peacefully throughout the night.

ELEVEN

SEEN

He woke to the gentle click of the stove settling as it cooled and the mouse-scratch whisper of wind sifting snow across the eaves. For a long minute he lay still, the ache in his limbs a dull tide receding. Heat pulsed back into his fingers, painful and human, and he counted that pain as blessing. Asher breathed against his ribs, warm and steady. Winston's hand found the dog's ruff and rested there, grateful as prayer.

When he finally rose, it was with the care of a man learning again how to be in a body. He fed the fire. He made tea. He forced a mouthful of bread past a bruised throat. He did not speak. The journal lay open on the table like a wound. He stared at it, at yesterday's last uneven line—"*I cannot force a door that is not mine to open*"—and bowed his head.

"Thank you," he whispered, not to the journal, not to the fire, and not only to the dog but to the heavens. While letting out a loud yawn, he added, "For a second chance."

He did not set out at dawn. He waited until

midmorning, when the pale light flattened the world and the cold was merely apocalyptic, not cruel. He wrapped Asher in an extra layer of cloth beneath the dog's harness, checked his straps twice, and only then shouldered his satchel. There was no fever in his step now, only a quiet, deliberate resolve.

They walked without hurry, pausing often, letting the world be the world. Where the snow had drifted into ribbed dunes, Winston traced the wind's work with his eyes as if reading a script in a language he had only begun to learn. Where the ice revealed old fractures—healed, sealed—he touched them with his glove like a physician feeling for pulse.

The hollow, when at last it received them, was bare as bone.

He did not fall to his knees. He did not scratch at the indifferent ice until his blood woke it. He simply stood, Asher at his side, and breathed.

"If this is to be a closed door," he said softly, "then let me dwell on its threshold like a friend... No petition. No proof to carry back like a trophy. Only presence. If there is anything to teach me, teach me how to wait."

The wind moved, seams of snow lifting like sighs. Asher's ears pricked. Winston closed his eyes.

At first, he heard only the familiar: the shallow sibilance of cold, the slow rasp of wool on wool as he breathed, the faint chuff of Asher's nose sorting scents from nothing. Then—barely there, as if hidden behind the ordinary—a tone. Not the choral grandeur of the city's harmonics, not the layered music of the beings' speech, but a single note, true as a plumb line. It seemed to come from under the soles of his boots.

He opened his eyes. The ice had not changed. Yet the world had altered a fraction, and his own posture had altered with it. He realized his shoulders had lowered without his telling them to, that something inside him had set down a heavy bundle it had carried for so long it had forgotten it was a burden. He exhaled, and in that exhale the note deepened—precisely by the distance between grasping and letting go. He laughed—a small, astonished sound that fogged and vanished.

"Is that it?" he asked the air. The single note answered by becoming two. Not louder, not brighter; simply fuller, as if space itself had remembered a forgotten dimension. Asher made a low sound, not a growl and not fear, merely recognition—the sound a creature makes when it finds an old trail under fresh snow. Winston pressed his palm to the ice. It was cold, iron-cold, and yet beneath it he felt the faintest thread of warmth, like a pulse through a glove.

"Thank you," he said, and meant the words with a depth that surprised him. "For the note...for the waiting."

He stayed a long time without demanding more. He breathed and listened and did not measure the worth of the silence by what it yielded. When at last he turned to go, he did so with reluctance and without resentment, the way one leaves a friend who must remain where they are. It was then that the air changed. He felt it before he saw it: a hush gathering upon the hush, a clarity joining the cold.

Snow that had been mere weather began to fall

in a pattern—no two flakes alike, and yet in their descent a coherence, as if the invisible were sketching a geometry around him. He turned back toward the hollow. A small brightness had kindled within the ice. It was nothing like the golden veins of his first discovery. It did not blaze or beckon. It breathed. A seed-light, steady as a sleeping child's chest. He took a step and then stopped, unwilling to turn reverence into pursuit. Asher sat, tail thumping once, twice, then stilled.

The brightness did not swell. It merely stayed. And from it—no, not from it exactly, but through it—came a voice.

It was not a sound that struck the ear. It was a shaping of the space within his chest. A chord formed where despair had lately lived, and words took their form from that chord like frost taking lace upon a window.

"Winston Thornberry."

He gasped. The name rung true the way iron rings when struck well. He lifted his eyes to the blank sky and then lowered them, unable to decide where to bow.

"I am here," he replied, but the old insistence was gone. The words were simple, like setting a cup upon a table.

"We have seen you," the voice said. And, though it was plural, it was also singular, like a river speaking with the mouths of its tributaries.

"We have heard the sound you make when you are emptied of demand." It would have been easy—so easy—to weep in triumph, to seize upon being seen as

vindication. He felt that old lightning leap toward his tongue—and felt it fall away of its own accord, as if the body had decided to refuse the taste of pride. He lowered his head.

"Then forgive me," he pleaded in earnest. "For the days I arrived as a conqueror at the door of a house not mine."

"There is nothing to forgive..." the voice said, and he believed it, because the tone held neither indulgence nor judgment. *"There is only the task of becoming able to carry what you ask to carry."*

He swallowed. His hands had begun to tremble. Asher leaned against his thigh.

"What is that task?" Winston asked. "Tell me what to do and I will do it... Tell me what to bring and I will bring it. Tell me what to leave and I—d"

He stopped. The voice waited, and in the space of that waiting he heard himself: the barter, the bargain, the human urge to purchase mystery with vows. He exhaled a shaky laugh.

"I am doing it again."

"Yes," the voice replied. *"But you are learning not to..."* the voice added.

Something like kindness—older than comfort, harder than reassurance—moved through him.

"Listen, then. You ask of knowledge. But knowledge is not provision; it is precipitation. It falls where the air has become capable of rain."

"I don't understand."

"You will... In your world, men take light and hammer it into proof. They build engines from wonder and sell the

engines to kings. We cannot give you what you would spend that way, even by accident."

He thought of headlines, of lectures prepared to slay the snickering of his former students, of Margaret's face when confronted with a glory she could not deny—and of the quiet venom such triumph would contain. He winced as if at a taste on the tongue.

"I don't want to wound them," he said. It surprised him that it was true. "I wanted to be right so loudly…I forgot how to be right quietly."

"Then a door has turned upon its hinge," the voice said. "There will be other hinges…"

The light within the ice brightened by less than a breath. In that fraction of brightness he sensed others, the council beyond the Seam—their harmonics held in check, their deliberations gathered now not as barriers but as blessings. A name came to him, not learned but remembered: Seraphiel.

"Are you—" He could not finish. The dog's head lifted, as if he, too, felt a presence approach a threshold.

"I am one of many and not like the many…" the voice said, and he understood that titles were only bridges for his mind to cross into something vaster. *"You have asked for a task. We give you a practice"*

"A practice?" He raised his brow, as if muddled by the statement.

"Come and keep company with the Seam each day you are able—and on the days you are not, in your heart. Bring no demands and no witnesses. Do not measure what is given. Leave when you are called away by compassion, and return when you are called back by silence. What you

cannot open, attend. What you cannot carry, do not grasp. When you have learned to receive as one who will not squander, we will speak again."

He stood very still, trying to take in everything that was being said. Although the voice tried to appear familiar, there were still certain things that he could not understand. The words were not rules, yet he felt them settle around him in ways that appeared to make a different kind of growth possible.

"And if I fail?" he whispered in a solemn voice.

"Then you begin again. As the Moon circles. As the tide corrects itself against the shore."

He almost smiled. "And if I succeed?"

"Then what sleeps will wake..." the voice said, and the echo of the council's earlier promise moved through him like a remembered blessing. *"Do you understand the cost?"*

The word stuck.

"Cost?"

"To be given sight is to be given debt. Knowledge will require you to choose between your hunger and another's safety. Between the glory of being known as right and the goodness of keeping what is right from being devoured. We ask now: will you pay that cost, if asked?"

He thought of Asher—of the warm weight at his leg, of the rough pull at his sleeve in the storm. He thought of Margaret and Elizabeth, not as judges but as fragile people moving through a loud world. He thought of the uncounted men who would break the ice with machines and sell the river beneath if he put the map into their hands.

"Yes," he said, though the word shook. "If asked."

Silence followed—not empty, not approving. A silence like a hand resting on a shoulder without pushing or pulling.

"Then practice..." the voice said, and the small light dimmed—not gone, only returned to seed. We will see you when the hour has ripened.

The area around him shimmered with light that seemed to come from nowhere and everywhere at once. The Regal being stood before him—tall, radiant, eyes that seemed to carry the memory of stars. Her voice was a river of sound, fluid and musical, yet her words broke against Winston's understanding like waves on stone.

Fragments reached him: "*...within you...light...power to sustain...*" But the meanings eluded him, scattered like snow carried by the wind. He pressed his hand to his chest, coughing, feeling the frailty of his body, the gnaw of hunger in his belly.

"I do not understand," he whispered, his voice ragged with desperation.

The being's gaze softened, as though she looked not upon his weakness but into a depth he could not see. She raised her hand, and the air itself seemed to answer. The icy currents shifted, and suddenly the area around him grew warm. A loaf of bread, fragrant and steaming, materialized upon the ice before him. Winston staggered backward, trembling.

"Miracle..." he gasped. "You—you would feed me?"

But the being shook her head, her smile touched with sorrow. The bread crumbled into light and dissolved, as though reminding him that the power was never hers to give. She touched her palm to her chest, then extended it toward him, a gesture of transference. Her voice wove into his mind—not words, but a truth that pierced like fire:

"What you seek outside has already been kindled within."

His heart leapt, but his mind recoiled. He shook his head.

"No...I am only a man. A scholar. I can observe, record—but such powers..."

His voice broke into silence. The being's eyes gleamed with both patience and grief. She stepped back, her form dissolving into radiance. For a fleeting moment, Winston felt as though something within him stirred—a spark, ancient and unyielding, pressing against the walls of his doubt. But like a dream upon waking, it slipped away before he could grasp it.

He fell to his knees, clutching Asher, the weight of revelation heavy but incomplete. He reached into his satchel and pulled out his journal. He scrawled desperately across the page, though his hand shook with fever and longing:

Journal Entry, March 1, 2022

They say the spark is within. They say it is mine. But I cannot see it...cannot wield it. Lord, grant me a heart to remember and eyes to see what is given to me before it is lost.

Beyond the sacred area of discovery, the being's voice lingered in the ether, projecting a radiant hue that saturated the surroundings. The being's voice was carried on unseen currents, a message not just for Winston but for a fractured planet:

"*When Earth's children awaken to the divine spark within, then greed will wither, hate will vanish, the wounded earth will heal. But until that hour, the light remains unseen.*" The area of discovery dimmed. Winston, exhausted, curled against ice, which appeared to have turned to stone, whispering softly into the air.

"I will try... I will try..."

The air lightened. The geometry of snow fell back into randomness. Asher sighed, as if a long watch had ended, and pressed his head into Winston's palm.

Winston did not shout, did not run, did not demand the light return. He stood a while in the wide Arctic quiet and then bowed—not sure to whom, not needing to be. When he turned toward the cabin, the world seemed no less white, no less cold. But the whiteness had become a page, and the cold a clean blade that had cut away the fever that had almost killed him.

On the way back he spoke softly to Asher, as one speaks to a companion more than to a pet.

"We will come each day," he said. "We will keep company with the door. We will not rattle it."

The dog's tail thumped once, twice.

At the ridge Winston paused and looked back. The hollow lay unmarked, the surface as smooth as untroubled thought. He felt, not saw, a listening beneath it, as if the earth itself had leaned closer. He raised his hand in thanks, silly gesture that it was.

Back in the cabin, he opened his journal and wrote

without hurry. He did not attempt to capture everything. He did not ornament. He set down what he had been given like bread on a table:

Journal Second Entry, March 1, 2022

I was seen. I was not proved right; I was invited to become right. I was given a practice, not a secret. If the cost comes, I pray to love it more than I fear it.

He closed the book and sat very still. The stove clicked again, settling. Outside, the light thinned toward a long afternoon that would not end soon. He and Asher shared the last of the bread. When the dog looked up at him, Winston felt no ache to be acknowledged by a council or a world. The look was enough.

"Tomorrow..." he said to the quiet, "...we go and wait."

And from deep under the ice—half echo, half divine summons—he heard the call to patience. The path was his to choose, the burden his to bear, and in that freedom lay both his trial and his destiny. For though the vision had faded, the intent remained: it was the desire of the luminous ones to guide humanity into a new era of consciousness, *when the spark within each soul would blaze forth to heal the wounds of a broken world.*

TWELVE

MANDATE

The days that followed arranged themselves around a new axis as Winston kept company with the Seam.

He rose without haste, brewed his tea, fed Asher in small portions he would accept, and walked the familiar path. Sometimes he spoke, sometimes he didn't. Often, he read aloud from his journal—not proclamations, but fragments: a remembered line of poetry, a note about the way snow squeaks when the cold passes a certain threshold, a confession written the previous night. If the ice listened, it did so without comment. If the hidden city waited, it was with the patience of mountains.

There were no spectacles. No rending of ice or pillars of light. Only a sense, some days faint as breath on old glass, that the world beneath the world was nearer than his own pulse. On those days, a tone returned to him—a single true note that steadied his hands.

On the seventh morning, snow fell straight down, a mercy after weeks of side-blown knives. Winston arrived at the hollow and sat. Asher lay beside him, chin on paws. They watched the white curtain stitch the sky to the earth, the Seam erased, the map made honest: *Here there is nothing you can claim.*

"Then I will not claim," Winston whispered. "I will attend."

The brightness came as a seed again, no larger than a thumbprint, a warm hush inside the cold. Winston inclined his head but did not rise. Words moved through the winter like a low tide filling channels in sand.

"*Winston Thornberry*"

"I am here."

"*The appointed hour approaches*," the voice replied.

"*Not triumph, not alarm, just the gravity of a bell struck once at dusk. You have asked what must be carried. Today we speak of the weight and how not to mistake it for a crown.*"

Winston swallowed. "I am listening."

"*Knowledge among your kind is first treated as proof, then as leverage, then as fire.*" The air around him seemed to widen as the voice continued. "*Our task is not to keep you from the fire. Fire cooks and warms. Our task is to keep you from burning what must not be consumed.*"

"What must not be consumed?" His breath plumed in the stillness.

"*Wonder. And the living.*" A cadence like winter sunlight touched his chest. "*We will show you small things that bear large consequence. We will give you a pattern, not a weapon. And you will become, if you consent, the sort of man through whom patterns can pass without becoming knives.*"

Winston's throat tightened. "I consent," he said. The words surprised him with how ordinary they sounded, as if agreeing to carry wood. "But tell me how to keep wonder from becoming proof, leverage, fire."

"*You will be asked to choose.*" The voice was gentle and unrelenting. "*Choose obscurity over applause; stewardship over spectacle; the safety of the unready over the speed of the curious. When you err—and you will—you will begin again without theatrics. You will keep your vow not to rattle the door.*"

A second resonance entered, lower, rich with frost. Winston recognized it, somehow, as Arioth—the restraint he had once bristled against.

"*Hear the cost plainly,*" the deeper voice said. "*You will be given a sign and a sentence. The sign: a geometry in the sky that no man can counterfeit. The sentence: you will not publish a syllable of what you learn until the sign appears.*"

Winston's breath snagged. "Not publish...anything?"

"*Not as proof.*" The first voice returned, Seraphiel's chord folding around his fear. "*You may write what shapes you for goodness. You may speak what humbles you into service. You may teach your students—one day—how to listen. But the city beneath the ice, the acoustics of light, the instruments—these remain sealed until the sky writes what we will show.*"

"What geometry?" His voice quivered with awe and dread. "When?"

"*You will know it when it draws near.*" A finer tone added itself, bright and young—Lumen's hopeful thread. "*It will be like the Moon correcting its path across the horizon, and the aurora bending to name a word not yet spoken on the surface."*

Winston's mind leapt, the old lecturer inside him assembling diagrams, producing a chalkboard only he could see. He caught himself, smiled ruefully.

"Forgive me," he said. "I almost turned your sentence into a lecture before it had cooled."

"*You are learning,*" Seraphiel said, and the brightness warmed.

"What of my family?" The question escaped before he could polish it. "Margaret. Elizabeth. If I am to be obscure, if I am not to publish—what of making amends? What of being seen by them not as a madman but as—" He stopped, a little ashamed of the word that had set fire to much of his life. "As right."

"*Love them without needing them as witnesses. You don't need to prove anything to them.*" The answer came without hesitation. "*Write them no proofs, offer them no maps. Offer them bread. Return what was broken where it was broken, not where you have become strong.*"

He closed his eyes, saw a kitchen he had not set foot in for months: Margaret's back at the sink, Elizabeth's careful mouth holding stillness like a plate that might shatter. "I have no idea how to do that," he admitted.

"*Then you will practice.*" The phrase had become a climate around him. "*Practice is a mercy. It allows the impossible to arrive in increments.*"

A hush, full of listening. Snow dusted his hat brim. Asher sneezed softly,

then resettled, shoulder pressing against Winston's boot.

"Tell me the warning," Winston said, voice low. "You said there is a warning."

For a heartbeat the air went very clear, the way a window clears of fog when a hand wipes it. When Seraphiel spoke again, the tone threaded grief into resolve.

"There are those above who will sense the shape of what you carry long before you speak it. Some will come as patrons. Some as skeptics. Some as thieves. We ask you to discern between hunger for truth and hunger for use."

"How?"

"By what they do with small things." Arioth again, austere as ice. *"Give them something that cannot be leveraged: silence, a delay, a task of compassion. If they bristle, if they bargain, if they demand spectacle, you will know their true appetite."*

Winston nodded slowly, feeling the weight of a new kind of measurement settle in his hands. Not the calipers of proof—the scales of motive.

"And if I fail?" he asked, barely above a whisper.

"Then the harm will be real," Arioth said, never one to soften consequence. *"But not final. We will close what must be closed. You will weep. You will begin again. The world will survive your error. You are not its savior; that is part of why we trust you."*

He laughed once, unexpectedly, allowed the humility to sting and sweeten.

"I accept that."

The brightness gathered, then braided itself with a vibration he felt in bone rather than ear. The ice beneath the surface seemed to become instrument—strings struck, not by hands but by the passing of meaning.

Lines of faint light lifted across the hollow, no more than hairs, barely visible even if one knew to look. They formed a lattice, hovered, and resolved into three simple figures, as if someone had drawn in air with a thread of mercury: A circle. A doorway. A palm, open.

"*Your first pattern...*" Seraphiel said. "A *circle: return. A doorway: threshold, not conquest. A palm: empty, so that it might receive.*"

Winston reached up without reaching, the way a man reaches for a note in a song and finds his voice enlarging to meet it.

"Circle, doorway, palm," he repeated, committing the shapes to memory rather than to proof.

"*Return. Threshold. Empty,*" Seraphiel intoned, each word echoing like a bell struck in the deep. "*Carry this until it remakes you. Only then will the next figure be revealed.*"

The meaning eluded Winston, slipping through thought like water through open hands. Yet something in the cadence—ancient, patient—rooted itself within him. He bowed his head, accepting the charge he could not yet comprehend. In the quiet that followed, he felt the vast intelligence of the Regal Ones watching—not judging, but waiting—for the day when his heart would remember what his mind could not.

The lattice faded like breath dispersed. The seed-light dimmed. Wind resumed its small errands among the drifts. He did not feel abandoned. He felt entrusted.

He remained until his knees ached and his toes warned caution. Rising, he brushed snow from Asher's fur, scratched the ruff that had been a handle on the night of his near-death, and began the walk home.

Halfway to the cabin, the sky brightened not with sun but with a pallid widening—the kind of light ice makes when it tells the eye that day is happening, even if the sun is elsewhere attending other latitudes.

He stopped on the ridge and took out his journal. He did not write the lattice. He drew the words it had left in him: Return; Threshold; Empty.

Back at the cabin, he cooked broth and coaxed Asher to sip. He swept the floor, not because it mattered to the ice but because it mattered to becoming the kind of man through whom patterns could pass without becoming knives. He wrote a letter he did not send to Margaret, and in it he said nothing about light-script or cities. He apologized for leaving the window latch broken last winter. He apologized for being louder than his love. He asked nothing in return.

That night he dreamed—not of chambers or councils, but of his classroom. The rows were empty. He stood at the lectern with no notes. Chalk dust floated like slow snow. A young man entered—one from years ago, the kind who raised his hand only to show he had a sharper question than the one asked. Winston waited. The young man lifted his chin.

"What makes this true?" the student asked.

Winston, in the dream, did not reach for a proof. He reached for a broom and began sweeping the chalk dust from the floor. "Return," he said quietly. "Threshold. Empty."

The young man frowned, as if tricked. Winston kept sweeping until the boards shone. He woke smiling, the kind of smile that has tears waiting politely behind it.

Days braided themselves to this practice. Some opened like hands; some closed like fists. On the closed days he did not accuse the door. On the open days he did not congratulate himself. He simply returned.

Toward the end of the fortnight, the sky offered him an answer that was not an answer. The aurora rose—pale at first, then like poured silk, green and violet, sheets upon sheets. He stood outside the cabin with his hat in his hand and watched it write its long unwinding on the night. For a suspended heartbeat, the veils bent into a shape almost word like—almost circle, almost doorway—and then dissolved back to river. He laughed aloud into the bitter cold.

"Not yet," he said, and felt the joy of understanding a refusal.

Inside, he wrote a last line before sleep: *"I will not hurry the hour that would save me from the worst version of myself."*

Winston pushed the journal aside. He drew the blanket over Asher and lay listening to the stove tick its soft applause. Above the ice, the dawn lifted and lowered its shimmering veil; beneath it, the council kept their patient vigil, holding the silence of ages as one might cradle a bowl of light. And within that patient bowl lay a man, a dog, and a practice—small, ordinary things that pulsed with quiet meaning. Yet in those humble rhythms—the tending of fire, the sharing of warmth, the endurance of faith—the first true scaffolding of a mandate was being formed. It would cost him much, and save more than he would ever know.

The fire burned low that evening, its amber glow

caught in the tired gleam of Winston's eyes. The wind pressed gently against the cabin walls, whispering over the frozen vastness beyond. He had returned from the depths weeks ago, yet the silence of that hidden realm still lingered in his bones, humming beneath each heartbeat like a secret vow.

On the desk before him lay his open journal—pages crowded with sketches, equations, and trembling lines of half-remembered words. None of it came close to the splendor he had seen. The language of the surface was too narrow for what lived below. And so, at last, he set aside the urge to explain and began, instead, to remember.

He sat for a long time, the pen idle between his fingers, the cabin wrapped in the soft murmur of wind and flame. The world above and the world below seemed, for that moment, to breathe in unison. He felt no need for proof, no hunger for revelation—only a still gratitude that all things, seen and unseen, continued in their appointed rhythm. When he finally closed his eyes, it was not with weariness but with wonder. For in the hush between heartbeats, he sensed it again—the pulse of the Earth, steady and forgiving—reminding him that the Seam had never truly vanished. It had simply moved within. The Seam was never beneath the ice—it was within the soul that dared to seek it.

THIRTEEN

SURFACE

The world had gone thin. Days came like paper—translucent, easily torn—through which the old ache of hunger and the new ache of knowledge showed at once. Winston moved quietly in that frailty: boiling water, feeding Asher in careful portions, laying another stick on the fire as if tithing to warmth. He kept his promises to the ordinary. He swept. He mended a button on his patched tweed. He wrote letters he did not send. Winston was slowly finding ways to make peace with his soul. But each morning the path to the hollow drew him like gravity.

The air had changed. He could not say how—only that the cold felt alert, as if listening. The sky's pallor seemed stretched too tight across the light. Even the snow had a new texture beneath his boots, not the squeak of bitter cold but a quiet hiss, like breath behind a door.

He and Asher crested the low ridge. The hollow lay below, a perfect bowl, wind-combed. Winston felt the pull in his chest and, with effort, did not quicken his pace. He descended, stood, and waited.

For a long time, silence had its way. Then the Seam appeared—not as it had before, bright and sure, but as a guess of light, a rumor, a nerve beneath skin. It widened the width of a hand—no more—and what rose through it with an answering radiance, a voice borne on light the way heat rides a stove.

"Winston Thornberry."

"I am here." He did not move closer. He did not reach. He remembered his vows: return, threshold, empty.

The light deepened, and with it came another presence—cold and crystalline, like frost upon glass: Arioth. Then returned the steady warmth that had often anchored him: Seraphiel. A gentler spark followed, bright with youthful hope: Lumen. Their unseen voices braided together in silent harmony, while Asher pressed close to Winston's leg, offering a soft, uncertain whine.

"You have kept company with our silence," Seraphiel said.

"You have practiced... This is good."

Winston swallowed. "Then—may I come?"

The Seam pulsed once, not assent but regard.

"*No, Winston,*" Arioth said, his tone not unkind. *"Not now, there are many things that you do not know and would struggle to understand."*

The refusal took the strength from Winston's knees more than the cold ever had. He steadied himself with one gloved hand on Asher's ruff.

"I thought I was nearer," he said, the admission shaming him with its naked hope.

"You are nearer," Lumen answered, quick and bright. *"Yet, nearness is not entry. Nearness is not yet readiness."*

He closed his eyes and let the words sit. When he opened them, the light within the Seam had thinned to the shape of a doorway drawn in air, only a finger's breadth deep. He saw then—beyond it, far inside—one white plane, the suggestion of another, the memory of a vaulted curve. Just enough to ache toward. Just enough to leave him on the threshold.

"What would you have me do?" Winston asked. He meant, how would you have me bear this? But he asked the smaller question, as he had learned to do.

"Attend to the pattern you carry," Seraphiel said. *"Let it alter your habits until the habits sing. Return. Threshold. Empty."*

"I have tried."

"We have seen." They let the assurance stand in the air like a lantern hung from an invisible nail. He felt its light without any increase of warmth.

"Then why call me?" he asked at last. "Why show me the door and teach me the word—and bid me remain outside?"

He had not meant to sound injured, only to be honest. His voice broke anyway, and the embarrassment of that weakness was its own sting. Asher leaned harder into him. The Seam's light steadied.

"Because your hour here draws to its close," said Arioth. *"And the closing must be given to you cleanly, or you will stay and be undone."*

"Undone?" The word came out as fog.

A new vibration entered the hollow—thin, almost metallic, as if some far wire had been plucked by a glove of ice. The snow at the rim took a different sheen, not green, not violet, not any color the aurora confers, but a faint smoke of shadow that refused to accept sunlight even when it touched. Winston felt the hair on his arms rise.

"There are watchers who do not wait to heal," Arioth said. *"Forces that take, not keep. They have learned to scent hunger and follow it. They circle this region. They come not for you only, but for any bright seam that can be made into a door they can own. We do not open to them. But your hunger is a torch in winter. It can draw what would use you to unmake what has been kept."*

A tremor moved through Winston that was not from illness.

"You told me once," he said softly, "that I am not the savior of the world."

"Yes," Seraphiel answered, tenderly. *"And therefore, we trust you."*

He let the sentence fill him. He found it could.

"Must I leave, then?" It hurt to shape the words. "Now?"

"Soon," Seraphiel said. *"Before your hunger is read as consent by those who stand outside our keeping."*

"Consent?" Winston whispered.

"No. No—Hunger becomes consent when it refuses refusal," Arioth said. *"You have learned to hear 'Not yet' and say, 'Then I will not hurry the hour.' Keep that learning intact. Protect it by departing."*

Some stubborn thing in him—old professor, old

father, old need—rose to argue and found no ground. He stood inside a silence that did not punish.

"And what of what I've seen?" His voice went small then, like a boy's. "What of the music in the stone, the written light, the—" He stopped. He had promised not to rattle doors even with the tongue.

The Seam brightened once, briefly, like breath on glass—and dimmed.

"*When you cross back into the latitudes that claimed you*," Seraphiel said warmly "*memory will thin like mist at noon. You will not grasp structures as you do now. The chamber will become a rumor to your waking mind.*"

Winston stared into the narrow radiance until his eyes watered. He could not help it. "And then what am I for?"

"*Intuition remains*," Lumen said, quick as a spring of water under snow. "*It will burn. It will guide. It will be enough—if you treat it as flame for bread, not for spectacle.*"

He nodded once, but the assent did not reach his bones.

"Limited recall," he said, to make it ordinary. "Strong intuitions..."

"*Yes. This is the way mercy travels when interference is forbidden.*"

"Forbidden." He tasted the word and heard, to his own surprise, no accusation in it. Only law, and the steadiness law confers.

"*We are observers and keepers of pattern*," Arioth said.

"*We are not permitted to unmake the field on which your kind must choose. If we displace the contest, we dishonor the freedom by which healing becomes possible.*"

A breath of wind crossed the hollow. In that breath Winston heard the smallest sound—Asher's growl, low and unwilling. He looked up. On the rim of the bowl, the snow filmed and refilmed with whirls of darkness, the way lamp-smoke gathers under a ceiling it wishes to stain. It did not enter, but it waited, learning the distances.

"Will they—" He could not finish. He placed his hand behind Asher's ear and felt the dog's life there, insistently present.

"They will test the door," Arioth said. *"That is what they do. Your leaving closes your part of it."*

A quiet fell that did not accuse him of cowardice. He wondered what Margaret would say of this—what Elizabeth would read in his face if she were to see him now: a man told he is trusted and told to go.

He lifted his eyes to the Seam. "What do I carry with me?"

The light drew itself into three slender strokes, almost too faint to bear meaning, and yet he knew them with that knowing that goes backward as well as forward: a circle, a doorway, a palm. Then the figures dissolved as breath dissolves off glass.

"Carry what you have been given until it changes you," Seraphiel said. "Give small tasks to those who seek you. Refuse to hurry the hour that would save you from yourself. Love without witnesses. And when the sky writes what we will show, you will know what to do next."

"And if I fail?"

"You will begin again," Arioth said in a supportive and fatherly tone.

"And if I am not believed?"

"Do not publish unbelief into spectacle," Seraphiel answered. *"Bake bread. Sweep floors. Teach listening. When it is time to speak, your obedience will have tuned your voice."*

He felt tears without drama. They warmed his cheeks and then cooled into the air. He did not wipe them away.

"Will I see you again?" He found, in asking, that he could bear the answer either way.

The Seam flickered, became only light, then less than light.

"In the manner permitted," Seraphiel said. *"We will come to you in what you call dreams and visions..." There was a slight pause. "And in a manner that will be enough."*

"What of Earth?" he asked suddenly, surprising himself, as if petition had been waiting for a lull. "What of our greed, our noise, our misuses? We do not seem ready."

"Few ever are," said Arioth. *"Readiness is found while walking, not before. The pattern heals one hand at a time: a man who will not take what is not his; a woman who mends without praise; a teacher who refuses spectacle for stewardship. When enough hands remember how to be hands, the world remembers how to be a world."*

Lumen's tone brightened, delicate and real. *"And when Earth's children awaken to the spark within, the wounds will begin to close. This is why we do not force the hour—we guard the conditions in which the hour can arrive."*

Something in Winston unknotted at last. It was not relief. It was the surrender that makes room for endurance. He bowed—not to the Seam but to the work.

"Very well," he said. "I will go. I will not hurry what would only harm by arriving early. I will keep what I can, and I will trust what I cannot keep to find me as intuition. I will love without witnesses."

As if in answer, the light narrowed to a filament and drew itself shut. No crack remained. The hollow was a bowl again, unremarkable as wind.

Winston stood for a long while in the whiteness. Asher leaned against his shin like gravity moved to pity. He did not feel abandoned. He felt consigned.

On the walk back to the cabin the sky performed one of its small mercies: a pale widening that suggested day to an eye that wanted reason to believe it. The cold felt cleaner, almost persuading. He kept his breath slow. He did not look back.

Inside, he did what he knew to do. He melted snow. He warmed broth and coaxed Asher to drink. He packed with attention, the way a man sets the table for guests he cannot yet see: journal, letters he would carry but not post, the chalk stub he had used to mark three figures in snow now somewhere far behind him. He mended the blanket where it had begun to fray. He swept again.

When he sat at the table with his pen, words came obediently, though he did not force them into proofs.

Journal entry, March 30, 2022

I have been told to depart. Not banished—entrusted. The Seam withdrew as a teacher draws a map and then folds it away so the student will learn the country by walking it. I am told memory will thin, intuition remain. This frightens me less than I thought. Perhaps proofs were my crutch. Perhaps intuition is the staff of this terrain. I am told watchers circle. I am told I am not the savior. I am told to love without witnesses. *I am told not to hurry the hour that would save me from myself. These are good instructions for any world.*

A soft sound at the window made him lift his head. There was no face there—no luminous visitor—but the moon had found a gap in the weather, and through it came a cold beam that silvered the table. He laid his hand in it, palm open. He felt foolish and then very much otherwise.

"Return," he said. "Threshold. Empty."

Asher thumped his tail once in his sleep.

The wind rose, then gentled. Something outside—something he would not name—moved on, as a patient hunter, denied, might move to other trails. He banked the fire to last the night, set the kettle on iron, and lowered himself to the cot with the heavy care of a man carrying neither triumph nor defeat.

He planned nothing beyond morning: a path to the station at the edge of the white, the knowledge of a supply plane that came on certain days when the weather took pity, the plain work of tying what must be tied and leaving what must be left. He would go down out of the latitudes with what he could keep and what would keep him. He did not try to picture the faces he had failed, nor the faces he might yet love rightly. He allowed them to stand at the edge of the room like witnesses who had decided to be merciful and wait outside.

Before sleep, he stepped to the door and opened it. The air burned clean, and above the ridge a faint aurora loosened its veil. For a single suspended breath, the light bent toward the shapes he knew—almost circle, almost doorway—and then surrendered its geometry back to river. He felt no anger at the almost. He felt gratitude.

"Not yet," he said, and heard in his own mouth the hard-won note of a man who will obey time.

He closed the door softly, as one closes a book in the middle and trusts the page will wait.

FOURTEEN

THE HORIZON

The morning broke without ceremony—no omen in the sky, no last flare at the Seam—only a pale light dilating behind cloud, the kind of light that tells you day has decided to arrive whether you are ready or not. Winston rose early, moving the way a man moves when he has already said his goodbyes. He banked the fire to a dull red, tied the twine around his journal, folded the letters he would not send, and slipped them into the inside pocket of his coat. Asher watched with the grave attention dogs reserve for departures and illness. When Winston knelt to loop the lead through the collar, Asher leaned forward and pressed his brow against Winston's sternum—a benediction of weight and warmth.

He stepped outside. The cabin stood hushed in the dawn, windows rimed in frost, the stove sighing its last embers. He let his gaze travel the narrow room one final time: the shelf with its shorthand of a life (tin, cup, kettle, a dog's brush), the chair with its repaired rung, the broom resting like a staff and the shortwave radio that worked only occasionally. Proofs would not come with him. The ordinary would. He touched the doorframe the way a man touches the shoulder of a friend.

He lingered there longer than he meant to, letting his eyes drift across the space that had held so much of him—notes scattered across the desk, the cold hearth still blackened from the last fire, the faint impression of his coat on the chair where he had spent too many sleepless nights. Every object seemed to watch him as he prepared to leave, quiet witnesses to revelation and regret alike.

"Well, my friend," he murmured, turning to Asher, who waited patiently by the door, tail thumping once against the floorboards. "It's time." He forced a faint smile. "You taught me to listen," he murmured. Then he closed the door.

The snowmobile sat outside half-buried under the previous night's drift, its metal frame glinting dully beneath the pale light. Winston brushed off the snow with deliberate care, as though uncovering something sacred. He secured the few belongings he still claimed as his own—the worn satchel, a bundle of papers, the remnants of his provisions. And last of all, he placed the Book inside its wrapping, stowing it beneath the seat as one might conceal a living heart.

Asher leapt onto the sled with practiced ease, curling atop the blankets. Winston adjusted his goggles and took one last look at the cabin. In its quiet walls, he saw not failure but completion. The man who had arrived here had sought to master truth; the man who departed now understood that truth had mastered him.

The engine coughed to life, its low growl shattering the silence. Snow flared behind them as the machine began to move, carving a solitary trail across the endless white.

The cabin grew smaller until it was only a dark fleck on the horizon—then nothing at all. Winston didn't look back again. The cold air cut against his face, sharp and cleansing, and for the first time in a long while, he felt the strange relief of motion. The wind rushed past, mingling with the hum of the engine, and for a moment he could almost hear another sound beneath it—soft, musical, as if the ice itself remembered his name.

He tightened his grip on the handlebars and pressed forward, the snowmobile gliding steadily toward the faint promise of the southern horizon. Somewhere ahead lay a landing strip, and a world that had forgotten him. Somewhere ahead waited the next chapter of his obedience.

The horizon gradually shifted from endless white to faint shapes—metal towers, fuel drums, and the skeletal outline of a windsock frozen in place. The sound of the snowmobile engine faltered against the low hum of generators. After nearly four hours of travel, Winston had reached the edge of civilization—a modest landing strip carved into the frozen plain, little more than a scar of dark gravel and corrugated hangars.

He slowed the snowmobile to a crawl, his muscles aching from the long ride. The air was brittle, sharp with kerosene and ice. A few figures emerged from a shack near the runway—bundled men in parkas and goggles, their movements brisk and practical. They watched as Winston dismounted, brushing frost from his beard, his posture stiff with exhaustion but steady with purpose.

"Where the hell did you come from?" one of them called, the words muffled by his scarf.

Winston hesitated, glancing back toward the horizon that had swallowed the cabin from view. "North," he said simply. His voice cracked from disuse, the syllables rough and foreign in the open air.

The man chuckled, exchanging a look with the others. "There's nothing north of here but death, old timer."

Winston offered a faint, almost wistful smile. "Then I suppose death was kind to spare me."

They laughed lightly, uncertain whether he was joking. One of them stepped closer, examining the snowmobile, the gear lashed to the sled, and Asher—whose steady gaze unnerved him for reasons he couldn't name. "You been out here alone?"

Winston nodded. "Not alone," he said softly, resting a gloved hand on the dog's head.

The man raised an eyebrow but said nothing. "We've got a plane heading south in a few hours," he finally offered. "You look like you could use a doctor and a hot meal."

"Yes," Winston murmured. "Perhaps both."

They guided him toward a small outpost building warmed by a propane stove. Inside, the hum of fluorescent lights felt too loud, too artificial. Winston sank into a chair, removing his gloves. His hands trembled—not from cold, but from the strangeness of being enclosed again, surrounded by chatter, radio static, and the mundane rhythm of the human world.

"You got papers?" the officer behind the desk asked, glancing up from his clipboard.

Winston reached for his satchel, then stopped. The Book was inside, bound and silent. He hesitated, then closed the flap again. "Not the kind that can be stamped," he said.

The officer frowned but said nothing. He scribbled something on a log sheet. "You're lucky to be alive."

"I suppose so," Winston replied, though his tone carried no conviction. Inwardly, he thought: *Alive. Yes—but to what end?*

Outside, Asher waited by the door, watching the wind sweep across the strip. Somewhere far below the surface of that ice lay the valley of light, and the beings who had judged him not yet ready. The thought struck him with equal parts sorrow and gratitude.

He leaned back in the chair, letting the hum of the heater fill the silence. For the first time since leaving the hollow, he whispered a prayer—not for revelation, but for patience.

"One day," he murmured to himself, "I'll be ready."

The officer glanced up. "You say something?"

Winston smiled faintly, shaking his head. "Just thanking God for small mercies."

Outside, the wind howled again, but to Winston it no longer sounded empty. It carried a low, familiar music, faint as memory—reminding him that the true journey was far from over.

Hours later, the plane arrived. Winston stood, looking at the plane. He no longer walked like a man chasing visions; he walked like a man entrusted with silence. The Cessna idled when he arrived, washing the air with a thin metallic insistence. The pilot—a woman with weather-wise eyes—tipped her chin, took Winston's pack, and helped Asher into the rear. No questions; the north cures people of needless talk. They lifted into the pale. The vastness fell away and then gathered, the way a sheet draws up when a hand lifts its corner.

Ten minutes into the climb, the pilot banked to skirt a low ceiling of cloud. The window caught the horizon and then the ground again—white, white, a braid of willow shadows—until, like a bruise blooming under skin, a dark thread unwound across the bright. Smoke.

He pressed a hand to the window, the cold seeping through his glove. The world beneath looked impossibly still—until a flicker of movement caught his eye.

At first, he thought it was dawn light reflecting off a ridge of ice. Then, slowly, he realized the color was wrong. Not the blue-white shimmer of frost, but orange—living, restless. Fire.

He leaned closer. A column of smoke unfurled upward, dissolving into the low clouds. It came from the direction of his cabin. He could almost trace the exact line of the ridge where it had stood. Now it was gone, swallowed by the blaze.

"Good Lord..." he whispered. His fingers trembled against the window. "The cabin—it's burning."

The pilot glanced over her shoulder, half-distracted, her voice steady over the roar of the engines. "Lightning strike, most likely... Happens all the time out here when the fronts collide. Nothing survives long on that ice."

Winston didn't answer. He kept staring, his reflection caught in the window—two images of himself merging: the man who had descended into the hollow and the one who had returned. The fire below seemed almost deliberate, cleansing. A fire, perhaps, for the man he had once been.

The pilot's voice came again, casual. "You left something there, doc?"

Winston exhaled slowly, the breath misting the glass. "Only everything I no longer need."

The pilot chuckled softly and turned her attention back to the instruments. Outside, the fire dwindled into distance, a fading ember swallowed by the storm.

Winston closed his eyes. Behind the darkness of his lids, he could almost hear the whisper of the Regal Ones—not in words, but in feeling: *The hollow must empty before it can be filled.*

When he opened them again, the horizon was clean and endless, the snow unbroken. The cabin, the valley, the fire—all had vanished into the quiet. Only the hum of the engine remained, steady.

Winston leaned back against the seat, weary but strangely at peace. The smoke on the horizon had become a kind of benediction—a visible release of the past. He turned once more to the window, murmuring to no one in particular:

"Let it burn. The light was never meant to stay in one place." The cabin had already lost its face; fire licked through the windows and fingered the seam where the door met the frame. Sparks rose, spent, rose again. The place where he had learned to be small, where he had been taught to listen, dissolved into hunger and light.

His throat closed. Asher, reading him through the tense rope of the lead, lifted his head and keened once—an old sound, thin with bewilderment. The pilot's eyes flicked to him and back to her instruments.

The plane leveled. Winston laid his hand against the window. The cold answered, clean and impersonal. What was burning was not only wood. What could not burn would have to prove itself.

He drew his hand back and tucked it into his coat for warmth. His fingers brushed paper, crisp and unfamiliar. He stilled. He did not keep loose slips in that pocket; the journal took that space, and the letters. This was smaller. Folded twice. He eased it out. Snow-dusk paper, mineral-brown ink. Four lines, no seal, no signature—written in a script he did not recognize and yet, impossibly, understood:

"Do not mourn what burns. Things do not merely happen—they happen justly.

Keep what cannot be taken."

His breath left him in a soft sound that was not quite a laugh and not yet a sob. He read the lines again, slower, as if the weight of each letter were its own instruction. Asher's head found his knee and stayed. Winston let his palm rest between the dog's ears and felt the certainty of living bone and warmth. He closed his eyes, and in that brief dark, the seams of the world held.

An hour later, Rankin Inlet's tower crackled its routine welcome. Snow broke in soft swells over the runway as they landed. The engine ticked into silence. The pilot gave him a nod—part farewell, part benediction. "Safe travels," she said.

"And to you," he answered.

In the small terminal—more warmed container than building—he sat with Asher at his feet, the room smelling of diesel, wool, and thawed rubber. A noticeboard offered a constellation of human needs: a used skidoo, a room to let, a lost glove awaiting its mate. The ordinary reasserted itself with gentle insistence.

He remembered then the phone, dead for weeks—a lump of glass and quarrel at the bottom of his pack. He had left it off for the same reason a man leaves his hat outside a sanctuary. Now, on this threshold between latitudes, he turned it over in his hands as if it might bite, and pressed the button.

The screen woke like an eye. A vibration. Another. Then the device became a trapped animal, shuddering with a backlog of the world: missed calls flowering in a column until the number was absurd; text messages in clusters—Margaret's name repeating, Elizabeth's, his department chair, a colleague who had once called him brilliant and then called him dangerous; unknown numbers; the university switchboard; a reporter he did not know; a neighbor from another life: Are you alive? The voicemails accrued until the mailbox declared itself full.

He scrolled without opening. Elizabeth's early text held; later, silence spoke for her. He placed the phone face down on his knee. He was not refusing the world. He was letting the world arrive at the pace of his obedience.

The southbound came on time, a larger plane that wore its scars with dignity. In the queue he nodded to strangers as if nodding were a language. He took a window seat because he could not help himself. Asher curled in the shadow of his boots and slept the way only the faithful sleep—completely.

The aisle rustled with coats and the small diplomacy of elbows. A young woman paused beside him, eyes widening. "Professor Thornberry?" she asked, disbelief softened into a smile.

He looked up, startled, braced against an old word—madman—that did not come. Her voice carried only warmth.

"I was in your seminar last spring—'Lost Civilizations and the Human Imagination.' I wanted to take another class, but they said you'd gone on sabbatical."

Her words hung gently, a reminder that a life still claimed him. Winston managed a nod; his throat cinched, then opened. "Yes," he said quietly. "I did step away." He studied her earnest face, so different from the ridicule he had grown used to. "And did you find the class worthwhile?"

"I loved it," she said, brightening. "You made us believe wonder itself was worth studying. I hope...well, I hope you'll be back."

She slipped into the row across the aisle, moving

with the ease of someone who had never learned to rush. Winston watched her stow her bag—an ordinary gesture, yet threaded with something extraordinary, a fragile thread of continuity he hadn't expected to find again. For a long moment he studied her profile, trying to place the echo that tugged at memory. Then it came to him: Clara. The quiet student with the steady eyes—the one who had asked questions no one else dared to ask.

A faint smile touched his lips. Asher, curled at his feet, nudged his hand, sensing the soft tremor of remembrance. Winston widened his smile despite himself. Fire had taken the cabin, yes—but what mattered most could not be burned.

They lifted into a light the color of bone. The land scrolled beneath them: ice pocked with black polynyas, a river held mid-gesture, a road insisting across the white. The phone buzzed again and he did not turn it over. He reached for the folded note instead, confirming its reality with his fingers. The sentence did not explain the fire; it lifted the ache into a grammar he could carry.

As the afternoon deepened, the sky unfurled its drapery. The aurora rose—pale at first, then poured green and violet veils. Winston leaned toward the glass as the light bent—almost circle, almost doorway, the briefest suggestion of an open palm—and then softened back to river.

"Not yet," he murmured, the words steady now. "I will wait."

He opened his journal and wrote a line with clean

edges; the size of a stone one might carry in a pocket: *The fire consumes the husk; what is true cannot burn.*

He added nothing, closed the book, and let it rest.

Clouds thinned. The sun, aloof for weeks, made a thousand small mirrors of the land. At the edge of sight, the aurora lay faint as a healed scar, not performing, simply being what it is when no one asks it to shape a word. He laid his palm open on his knee—empty, receiving.

"Then let it be just," he said—not to the sky, not to himself, but to the hour that had chosen him.

Asher stirred and pressed closer. Winston leaned back into the hum of the engine—note folded against his heart, phone at rest, journal closed, horizon no longer a proof to be won but a distance to be walked. Ahead waited roads and the slow labor of making amends without witnesses. Behind, a cabin surrendered to flame, giving back to the elements what it had borrowed long enough to teach a man how to listen. Between them, in the narrow country called now, he kept the only pattern that had not burned: return, threshold, empty. For he knew all too well that to ascend, one must first descend; to receive, one must be emptied; to live in truth, one must relinquish control.

As the plane droned southward, Winston felt the first tremor of that inward battle. The glow of revelation still lingered in him like embers under ash, yet already the cold air of the ordinary world was beginning to steal its warmth. Pride whispered softly, subtle as breath: *You have seen what no other has seen.* For a fleeting moment, he almost believed it. Then guilt followed swiftly behind, sharp and familiar. He turned to the window, watching the endless fields of ice recede beneath the wings, and whispered the words he could not forget—*Return. Threshold. Empty.* They sounded different now, not as command but as mercy. He understood that surrender was not a single act but a daily yielding, and that his greatest work would not be discovering the light—but learning how to carry it without casting his own shadow.

The hum of the engines filled the silence between thought and memory. Winston leaned his head back, eyes half-closed, still tasting the echo of the Regal Ones' command. Surrender was not an act of grandeur, he realized, but of gentleness—a softening of the will in the presence of grace. Yet even that was proving difficult.

A motion across the aisle caught his attention. Clara, the young woman who had taken the seat a few rows ahead. Something about her stirred a faint recognition. Of course, this was the quiet student who had once stayed after lectures, asking questions about the unseen, the impossible. He felt a strange warmth rise within him, something between nostalgia and gratitude. The world, it seemed, was already sending him reminders that his work was not finished. He watched in silence, humbled by the ordinariness of her presence—the way she existed without effort, without the hunger to prove or possess.

Asher nudged his hand, a gentle reminder. Winston smiled faintly. *This,* he thought, *is what I must learn again—to see without claiming, to love without naming, to teach without believing myself the teacher.*

Outside, the clouds thinned, revealing a soft wash of dawn over the horizon. The light touched the wing, pale and clean, and Winston closed his eyes, letting it fall across his face like a benediction.

FIFTEEN

RETURN TO FAMILIAR GROUND

The door parted with a mechanical sigh, releasing Winston into the damp night air. The smell of gasoline, rain-soaked pavement, and the babble of too many voices rose up to greet him. After months of silence and snow, the ordinary world pressed in close, heavy and restless. He carefully departed the plane, paying close attention to Asher who appeared disoriented, as he attempted to navigate unfamiliar surroundings. Asher hesitated as if waiting for Winston to lead the way.

"I know boy," he murmured to Asher, as if expecting him to understand. He smiled. "This is what we now have to look forward to..."

Asher looked at him, wagged his tail and followed his lead.

Winston shifted the weight of his worn satchel—heavier now, not only with papers and belongings but with the leather-bound volume that seemed to breathe in his keeping. Weary travelers rushed to greet waiting loved ones. No one waited for him. No familiar hand waved from the crowd; no eager voice called his name. That was how it had to be. The Regal Ones had been clear: walk softly, reveal nothing. Still, the emptiness of it tugged at him as he moved toward the taxi line. To his surprise, he heard a piercing voice that was all too familiar, calling out to him.

"Thornberry? Dr. Winston Thornberry?" the voice echoed from the crowd.

"Well, I'll be—!"

The voice, sharp and incredulous, cut through the noise. Winston recognized the voice and immediately turned to see Dr. Sherman Ellis, a colleague and nemesis of sort from the university, standing just inside the doors. His scarf was loose around his neck; his suitcase tilted on one wheel. Dr. Ellis had always been known as a busybody in faculty circles—the kind of man who thrived on scraps of gossip the way others thrived on food and air. He was a predator when it came sticking his nose in the affairs of others and was always on the prowl for tomorrow's chinwag. Dr. Ellis once smirked openly at Winston's lectures, whispering with others in the faculty lounge about "fairy tales" and "lost causes."

"Good heavens, it is you," Dr. Ellis continued, hurrying forward. Winston looked at Asher and shook his head from side to side.

"We all thought you had disappeared completely. Off the grid...they said. I suppose you know the rumors have been flying like crows since you left." He chuckled, though the sound was brittle. He paused, only long enough to catch his breath and continued with his usual mockery and sarcasm. "Honestly, Winston, you could have left a forwarding address."

Winston inclined his head slightly but said nothing. Dr. Ellis filled the silence.

"You've missed quite a show at the university. Three new hires since you've been gone—one already dismissed after a scandal with a graduate student. Wallace finally retired, though not before a shouting match in the boardroom. You would have relished it, Thornberry—though, of course, they'd never admit you were right about his mismanagement."

Dr. Ellis enjoyed the one-sided conversation and yakked on, as if there would be no further opportunities to engage Winston. His eyes narrowed. He cleared his throat, and continued looking for new fodder to feed his enormous appetite information.

"Look, I can understand if you don't want to talk about this...but I am just dying to know if..." There was a long pause, as if he struggled for the right words to express his thoughts. "I'm just going to come right out with it... Tell me, is it true you missed your daughter's wedding?" He paused and stared at Winston, who said nothing. "Some say you didn't even send a gift. And there were whispers—pardon me if this is tactless—that you and your wife finally called it quits, over the whole wedding fiasco. Is there truth to it?"

Winston met his gaze evenly. He hesitated, searching for words. Then he lifted his pointer finger in Dr. Ellis's direction and shook it from side to side, now displaying a mysterious expression.

"The world teaches us in many ways, Dr. Ellis...

Not all of them are meant for discussion in an airport lobby."

Winston spoke with eloquence and class. Dr. Ellis laughed, though uneasily.

"Yes, yes, of course. You've always been a private sort. Still—people wonder. You vanish for months, turn up looking, well—" He waved a hand vaguely at Winston's weathered face. "Like a man who's lived a different life. And you say nothing? Come now, Thornberry, you could at least give me something to take back." He echoed in something of a defeated tone. "Where were you? Some kind of extended holiday? When I asked old stuffy Morgan, he said you were on sabbatical doing some type of field research, and I should leave it as that?" He paused, and let out a long sigh, as if fearing the response. "You know some said you ran off with a grad student, after your marriage fell apart."

Winston studied him in silence.

"You got to tell me something or I am going to die trying to guess..."

But Winston's silence continued. Once, he would have seized this moment to defend himself, to insist upon the truth of what he had endured. But the warning echoed in his mind: *What you have seen is not for all eyes. What you have heard is not for all ears.*

The man's eyes darted over Winston, sharp and appraising. Dr. Ellis blinked at him, uncomprehending, then forced another chuckle.

At last, Winston offered only a thin smile.

"The world is larger than we think, Dr. Ellis," he

said in a gentle voice. "The only thing worth carrying back...is silence. That's all I'll say."

Dr. Ellis frowned, uncertain, then nodded slowly. He shrugged his shoulders.

"Perhaps...perhaps you're right." Dr. Ellis blinked, then gave a short laugh to cover his discomfort. "You haven't changed a bit...still the philosopher. Well, I'll let you be on your way."

Dr. Ellis gathered his luggage, muttered something about catching his ride, and melted back into the current of travelers. Winston looked down at Asher. He slowly turned away, his satchel steady in his grasp, and joined the line of taxis waiting beneath the buzzing lights. As he reached into his coat pocket for his ticket stub, his fingers brushed something he did not remember placing there—another folded scrap of parchment, small and brittle.

He glanced around quickly; no one seemed to be watching. Carefully, he drew it out and unfolded it. The handwriting was strange, the letters curling in a script both alien and familiar. Only one bold word stared back at him, stark against the paper. He turned the brittle scrap over in his hands, the words cutting into him more sharply than the chill of the night.

"Caution."

The warning coiled in his thoughts, refusing to settle. Did it mean Dr. Ellis? The faculty who had mocked him? The streets he once knew as home? Or was the danger less visible—woven into the Book he carried, or rising from within his own mind?

A chill cut through him deeper than the night air.

He folded the note quickly, slipped it back into his pocket, but the message lingered like smoke: a reminder that the journey he thought complete was still unfolding, and that some hidden presence, whether friend or foe, was already one step ahead of him.

Winston carefully climbed into the waiting cab, with Asher faithfully at his side. As the driver pulled away, city lights fractured in the window, gleaming and unstable. Winston pressed his hand against his satchel, reassured by the weight of the Book within. Yet it was the fragile presence of that folded note, whispering without explanation, that haunted him most.

Had his dance with destiny ended, or was it only just beginning? The question pressed against him like the hum of the engine, steady and unrelenting. He had touched mysteries that few men would dare imagine, yet now he found himself returned to the ordinary world of timetables, traffic, and passing faces. Could he slip back into the rhythms of lectures and faculty meetings, or would the memory of regal eyes and ancient voices forever draw him beyond the veil of the familiar? And if destiny was not finished with him, what shape would it take—revelation, danger, or a summons even greater than before? In the silence of his own wondering, Winston sensed that the true test was not survival in the North, but learning how to carry the weight of the extraordinary within the confines of the everyday.

As the taxi weaved in and out of traffic, Winston knew the dance with destiny was not finished and he had to be prepared to play his part. And, whether his dance with destiny led toward revelation or ruin, was a question that only time would reveal.

The taxi rolled slowly down the quiet, tree-lined street, the tires whispering against the wet pavement. The city felt different now—too small, too loud, too full of its own forgetting. Winston sat in the back seat, collar turned up, his hand resting lightly on Asher's head. The dog leaned close, silent as always, his presence grounding what little remained of Winston's certainty.

"This the address?" the driver asked, glancing at him in the rearview mirror.

Winston nodded. "Yes...you can stop here."

The cab eased to the curb. Through the windshield, the old house stood as if time had held its breath for his return. The curtains in the front window were drawn halfway, and the familiar golden light of evening spilled out onto the lawn. Inside, two figures stood close together—Margaret and one of the neighbors, Mr. Cavanaugh perhaps—talking quietly, their movements softened by the glass. Margaret laughed at something, tilting her head in that gentle, absent way that once belonged only to him.

Winston didn't move. He simply watched. The moment had a strange clarity—fragile, almost sacred. The ordinary rhythm of life had gone on without him, untroubled by his absence. He realized, with a sudden ache, that this too was as it should be. The world was healing, and his presence might only disturb what peace had finally settled. From the surface, it appeared as if Margaret had moved on, and it was not his place to introduce chaos into her new life.

The driver cleared his throat. "You want me to wait, mister?"

Winston hesitated; eyes still fixed on the window. He shook his head from side to side. "No," he said quietly. Then, after a moment: "Actually...yes. Take me to a hotel. Something nearby."

"Sure thing." The driver shifted the car back into gear.

As they pulled away, Winston glanced one last time at the house, the faint outline of Margaret still visible in the glow of the living room. He imagined what it would feel like to walk through that door, to be met not with joy but with questions, perhaps pity. The thought steadied him. *Return. Threshold. Empty.* The words rose again, patient and familiar. He understood now that crossing the threshold was not about reclaiming what was lost—but about learning to stand before it without reaching.

The cab stopped in front of a modest brick hotel a few blocks away. Winston paid the fare, murmured thanks, and stepped out into the cool night air. The city lights hummed faintly, reflected in puddles along the curb. He crossed the lobby with slow, deliberate steps, Asher trotting beside him, and accepted a key from the clerk who didn't bother to ask for his name.

Upstairs, the hallway stretched long and dim. He stopped before the door marked *217*, the brass numbers worn and uneven. For a long moment, he stood there, the key cold in his palm.

His reflection looked back at him in the dark window across the hall—older, thinner, softer somehow.

With a steadying breath, he slid the key into the lock. The click echoed faintly, a small sound carrying the weight of both an ending and a beginning.

SIXTEEN

THE HALLS OF ACADEMIA (THE VEIL BETWEEN)

Winston had begun to settle into his new life, though it bore little resemblance to the one he had left behind. The clutter of possessions—clothes he never wore, books he never opened, papers he would never read—had been given away or discarded without regret. He rented a quaint home near the university and vowed to live as a minimalist. He promised himself to keep only what he deemed essential: a small bed, a desk with lamp and oversized chair for comfort, a modest supply of clothing, journals, books, and supplies for Asher, including his worn leash hanging by the door. It was enough. More than enough, he reminded himself, for excess dulled the senses and weakened resolve.

Asher had adapted more slowly. The dog still prowled the apartment restlessly some nights, as though searching for the sharp winds and wide silence of the North. His ears would prick at shadows, his gaze following sounds Winston could not hear. He had grown calmer, yes, but remained uneasy, as if he sensed what others could not—that the ordinary world had not fully reclaimed his master.

This morning, Winston moved through the house in a faint fog, his thoughts hazy with restless dreams. Yet beneath the blur lay a quiet determination. The mandates of the Regal Ones still pressed upon him: *return, threshold, empty*. He had repeated these words like a vow, steadying himself whenever the temptation to speak weighed heavy on his tongue.

Today, he would need that resolve. His appointment with the dean awaited, a meeting that would determine his place in the academic order he had abandoned so abruptly. What would he say? How much would he reveal? Winston straightened his jacket, touched the satchel at his side, and exhaled. The day had begun, and with it, another test of his fidelity to silence.

Yet beneath the outward calm, another unease gnawed at him. The mysterious notes—appearing in pockets, tucked among papers, surfacing without explanation—had unsettled his every step since his return. He did not know who sent them, nor when the next would arrive, nor whether they carried warning or temptation. Each message was both anchor and riddle, a reminder that his solitude was not complete and that unseen eyes still followed his path. As he prepared to face the dean, he carried not only the Book in his satchel, but the burden of questions that no parchment could answer.

The old stone façade of the university loomed against the gray sky as Winston crossed the campus quad. Students hurried past, bundled against the wind, earbuds tucked in, lives buzzing forward without him. In some ways, the place had changed—new banners, new construction fencing—but the rhythm was the same. Beneath the fresh veneer, the cadence was unchanged—the same hurried steps, the same hurried minds, remained intact.

As he neared the building that had once been his second home, a tremor of awe stirred in him. Not awe of the stone or the halls, but of the strange symmetry of his return. He had left as an exile, branded eccentric, dismissed as a dreamer lost in unprofitable conjecture. Now he returned carrying a secret weight—proof not only of his theories but of something far greater, a truth luminous and terrible in its implications.

The question pressed hard upon him: how could he live with such validation burning in his chest? To speak it would shatter the silence imposed upon him, perhaps betray the trust of those who had chosen to reveal themselves. To conceal it entirely felt like a betrayal of himself, of the very integrity that had marked him as an outcast. Between silence and revelation, between obedience and confession, Winston walked a narrow line, each step on the campus stones echoing like the toll of an unseen bell.

Although it was not his intent to dwell on the past or what had led him to this point, he harbored a secret which served as complete validation of the theories and philosophies that got him labeled as the campus odd ball. How would he share that validation, remain true to the Regal Ones and keep intact his integrity?

He entered the faculty building quietly, but whispers traveled faster than footsteps. Heads turned. A pair of junior lecturers, barely old enough to remember his earlier reputation, watched him as if he were a ghost.

The heavy oak doors groaned as he pushed them open, the sound rolling through the entryway like a sigh from the past. Warm air washed over him, thick with the mingled scents of coffee, printer ink, and old paper—so ordinary, so unchanged. Students hurried across the tiled floor, clutching laptops and half-finished essays, their laughter rising in bursts that faded as quickly as they came. The chatter of colleagues spilled from the faculty lounge nearby, punctuated by the hiss of the espresso machine.

For Winston, the scene felt almost unreal, as though he had stepped onto a stage where every actor played a role they had performed a thousand times before. Nothing here hinted at the vast silence of the North, or the regal voices that had spoken to him in cadences older than language. Yet he carried their presence within him, a secret flame smoldering beneath the surface of ordinary days.

He paused by the staircase, running his hand lightly along the cool banister polished smooth by decades of touch. Once, this place had been his entire world—lectures, disputes, long nights in the library. Now, it seemed fragile, almost childlike, measured against what he had seen. Still, it was here he must return, here he must dwell, and here he must decide how to live between silence and truth.

A faint rustle drew his attention. Slipped among the notes he carried was another scrap of parchment, curling at the edges as though it had always been there, waiting. His pulse quickened as he unfolded it discreetly. In the same familiar hand, one word appeared, stark and unyielding: "*Careful.*"

The hallway seemed to tilt for a moment, voices dimming, footsteps echoing like distant drums. Winston folded the note quickly, pressing it into his pocket. Whatever awaited him in the dean's office, the unseen presence was already one step ahead, reminding him of the narrow line he must not cross. Only a few feet away stood the hub of campus gossip—the faculty lounge. His first instinct was to bypass it altogether and walk directly to the dean's office. Yet he knew avoidance was no answer. To reclaim his place here, he would have to step deliberately into the current of ordinary life, even as he labored to evolve beyond its trivialities.

The chatter spilled into the hall, bright and restless, and above it all rose Dr. Ellis's unmistakable voice, carrying tales of woe and intrigue with the ease of a man who had never learned silence.

Winston drew a slow breath and pushed the door open. Warmth and chatter spilled over him in a wave—laughter, the hiss of coffee being poured, the crinkle of newspapers, the low murmur of academic politics. The air was thick with the scent of burnt espresso and the faint tang of ink. Heads turned as he entered. Conversations dipped, then resumed, though now hushed and sharpened, words bent around his presence. Winston moved with quiet composure, neither hurried nor hesitant, as though he were walking through mist.

Inside the faculty lounge, Dr. Sherman Ellis was already holding court. Dr. Ellis, perched at the center of a cluster of colleagues, looked up and seized the moment.

“Ah! The man of the hour,” he called, raising his voice so that no ear could miss it. “At long last, Thornberry returns! And not a day too soon, judging by the state of our little kingdom.” A ripple of laughter spread around the room, some genuine, others nervous. Dr. Ellis leaned back in his chair, eyes glinting. “Need I tell you...that you’ve been the talk of the campus, Winston. Whispers in every corridor. Tell us, did you finally find that lost city you were always dreaming about? Or was it simply a long holiday in the snow?”

The others smiled, eager for spectacle, but Winston did not rise to the bait.

“We thought you were lost to the snows, Thornberry. Tell us—were you writing a new gospel up there, or just learning how to fish?”

Laughter rose, awkward and forced.

Winston set down his satchel and poured himself coffee without answering. The chatter swirled on around him: the scandal of the dismissed hire, a rumored lawsuit, petty debates over committee budgets. It all felt oddly small, like actors quarreling over costumes while the stage itself was on fire. Winston’s silence stretched, unsettling, until even Dr. Ellis faltered beneath it.

At last, Winston spoke, his voice even but edged with reflection.

"There are places the mind can travel that the tongue cannot follow. Better, sometimes, to leave the silence intact...huh?"

The room fell still for a moment, as if the very air had been checked. Dr. Ellis gave a short, awkward laugh, trying to rally the mood, but something in Winston's presence unsettled the rhythm. It was as though a shadow larger than the lounge itself had entered with him, and though unseen, it could not be ignored.

Winston sipped his coffee and set it down gently. He had no need to defend himself. The truth he carried was not for them, and perhaps not yet for anyone at all. Dr. Ellis, uneasy by Winston's response, realized that he was no longer the center of attention and found a way to ease himself out of focus.

"Until the next act, I bid you good people farewell..." He chucked to himself, as if harboring a joke that only he was privy to, then gathered his belongings and left the room. One by one, each faculty member followed, except for one woman.

Dr. Katherine Marlowe, a historian known for her measured voice, leaned forward, her expression neither mocking nor amused but genuinely curious.

"So, Winston," she said softly, her words carrying in the hush, "forgive me if this is too direct. But out there...in all that time away...did you find something?"

Winston held her gaze. The question was simple, but it pierced him like a blade. He thought of the cavern beneath the ice, the regal faces lit by a light older than stars, the mandates that still rang in his blood. He thought, too, of the notes—warnings appearing like whispers from invisible hands.

His fingers brushed the edge of the coffee cup, circling its rim as though tracing the boundary of what could and could not be said. When he finally spoke, his voice was low, reflective.

"Yes," he answered. "I found something. But not something I can name... Not yet."

The weight of the words settled heavily upon her. She leaned forward, unsatisfied, hungry for details, while shifting uncomfortably, as though wary of a truth too large for her ears.

"I see..." she said mysteriously. He looked on still sipping his coffee.

"You see, there are still some things in life we just can't explain..."

The mood shifted. Dr. Marlowe's lingered on Winston, thoughtful, as though she heard more in his restraint than in Dr. Ellis's noise. Winston lifted his cup, finishing the last sip in silence. He would not explain further. He could not. The truth he carried was not for this place, not for this moment—and perhaps, not for them at all.

Winston set his empty cup back on the saucer, the porcelain ringing faintly in the silence that lingered after his words. The room seemed to hold its breath, as though Dr. Marlowe waited for him to offer more. But he remained still, his calm presence a wall no curiosity could breach. He adjusted his chair slightly and felt something crinkle beneath it. Slipping a hand to the edge of the seat, his fingers closed around a folded scrap of parchment, brittle against his skin. He drew it up with practiced subtlety, concealing it in his palm as the woman looked on with curiosity.

Unfolding it beneath the table, he saw the same curling script he had come to dread and expect: *"Eyes are upon you."*

His pulse quickened. For a moment the air grew thin, the faculty lounge dimming around him. He folded the note swiftly, sliding it into his pocket. At that very moment, Dr. Ellis had returned to the room to retrieve a forgotten item.

"Still here children?" he called out lightheartedly. Neither Winston or Marlowe seemed to notice him. Neither gave the faintest sign that they had observed his return. Winston was too occupied with the unseen presence that shadowed him and had somehow managed to slip another note at the edge of his seat.

The dean was finishing a faculty meeting. Winston stood quietly outside the closed door as reports droned on about hiring freezes and departmental reshuffles. His gaze drifted to the narrow glass pane separating him from those inside. As he paced the corridor, waiting for the meeting to end, a slip of parchment peeked from his pocket—one he had not placed there.

His hand trembled as he unfolded it, reading a message he had not seen before. Three words, written in the same curling script as the others: *Guard the tongue.*

He folded the parchment carefully, slid it back into his pocket, and said nothing. It was the third warning he had received that day.

Shortly after the meeting adjourned, Dr. Ellis

approached Winston with a grin that lingered a moment too long to be sincere.

"Enjoy your meeting," he said, his tone light but edged with mockery.

Winston met his eyes, steady and unreadable. He cleared his throat and spoke in a soft tone of voice. "The truth," he said tenderly, "is not always meant to be written."

Dr. Ellis blinked, unsure whether Winston was jesting or deflecting, and then changed the subject to a rumor about the new dean. Winston let him talk, until he decided to end the one-sided conversation. The third note weighed on him like a large rock. "*Guard the tongue.*" It was not only a warning. It was a command and he was curious to see how that mandate would apply to his meeting with Dean Harrow.

The dean's office smelled of leather, polished wood, and the faint sting of ink. Sunlight strained through half-drawn blinds, striping the floor with slanted bars of pale gold. Winston entered quietly, the satchel heavy in his hand, its presence a reminder of all that could never be spoken.

Dean Harrow looked up from behind a desk stacked with folders, memoranda, and committee reports. His spectacles caught the light as he rose to shake Winston's hand. His grip was firm, perfunctory.

"Professor Thornberry," Dr. Harrow said, a hint of relief in his voice. "At last,... You've been gone nearly a year."

"More like six months or so," Winston said emphatically.

"The faculty, the students—even the trustees—have asked about you and your whereabouts. I trust you've returned with something to show for your time away?"

Winston met the dean's eyes, steady but unreadable. "Time away has its own lessons," he said gently.

The dean gestured for him to sit.

"Yes, yes. But you must understand, the university requires more than sentiment. Sabbaticals are meant for research, publication, some tangible contribution to the field. Your absence has already stirred its share of whispers. I'll be frank—we need to know whether you intend to resume your post, and if so, how you mean to reestablish your reputation."

The words fell like stones, heavy, pragmatic, stripped of wonder. Winston listened, his fingers brushing the clasp of his satchel, where the Book rested in silence. He could almost hear the regal voices: "*Guard the tongue.*"

A part of him longed to speak—to tell Harrow of the cavern beneath the ice, of faces crowned with dignity beyond time, of truths that would overturn every dusty lecture and narrow journal. It would silence the whispers, vindicate every scornful smirk, prove that he had not been the madman they believed. But he knew the cost. To reveal what was entrusted to him would be to betray the very beings who had given him sight. His integrity, his promise, his place in destiny—these were not his to discard.

"I have seen," Winston said slowly, "things that will shape my teaching, though they may never find their way into print. I intend to return, to guide students, not with answers, but with the courage to ask questions that reach beyond the walls of this university."

The dean frowned, tapping his pen against the desk. "That is...poetic, Thornberry. But you know the academy thrives on proof. The trustees will expect something concrete. A paper. A manuscript. Some form of output. Without it, your future here is uncertain." Harrow finally set the pen aside and leaned back, folding his hands. "You know I've always admired your...passion. You think big. You look for patterns where the rest of us see noise."

"I appreciate that," Winston said cautiously.

"But," Harrow continued, "passion isn't enough. The board's been asking questions. You've been on sabbatical for months, and, well—there's been no publication. No paper. No presentation. Not even a draft in circulation. You're aware what that means."

Winston's jaw tightened. "You're saying they want proof of productivity."

"They want scholarship, Winston. They want something measurable. You were granted an extraordinary amount of freedom—paid freedom, I might add—to pursue this...project of yours. But the longer you stay quiet, the more it looks like indulgence, not research."

Winston inclined his head, accepting the words as both truth and test. "Then let my presence be my proof. I have been tempered, Dean Harrow. What I carry cannot be reduced to ink, but it will make itself known in the lives I touch."

The dean studied him for a long moment, weighing

pragmatism against the strange aura that seemed to hang about him. Finally, Harrow sighed, pinching the bridge of his nose. "For God's sake, Winston, don't make this harder than it needs to be. I'm on your side, truly. But my neck's on the line too. I can't defend you to the provost without something—an abstract, a chapter draft, *something* that looks like scholarship."

"And if I can't?" Winston asked.

Dr. Harrow hesitated. "Then the committee will move to terminate your tenure review. You'd be free to continue your work independently, of course, but..."

The rest hung in the air.

Winston looked past him to the window, where the afternoon light fractured against the glass. "Independence seems to be the only kind of freedom left."

The dean softened. "You don't have to make this into martyrdom, Winston. Write something—anything—I don't give a dam what you write, as long as you give it some type of intellectual framework. Dress it in academic language if you must. You're too smart to throw your career away on mystery."

Winston rose, collecting his worn satchel. "Perhaps mystery is the only career left worth keeping."

Harrow exhaled through his nose, frustration tempered by pity. "You're a brilliant man, Winston. But brilliance doesn't mean much if no one can read it."

"Maybe not," Winston said quietly, hand on the doorknob. "But perhaps some things are meant to be understood before they are seen..."

"Very well. I'll allow you to return for the next term, but I must warn you—patience among the board is thin. Make your case with deeds, Thornberry, or the decision may be taken from both of us.”

Winston rose, shook the dean’s hand once more, and turned toward the door. Harrow sat for a long moment, staring at the closed door, then murmured to himself, “God help me, they’re going to crucify him.

Winston felt the folded note in his pocket like a brand against his skin: *Eyes are upon you.* As he stepped into the corridor, he knew the truth of it. His every move, whether in lecture halls or in silence, was being watched—not only by the academy, but by forces far beyond its reach.

SEVENTEEN

THE VEIL BETWEEN

The lecture hall was full. Students crowded into seats, some curious, others simply eager to see the professor who had disappeared for nearly a year. Winston stood at the podium, feeling the weight of their eyes.

The rustle of notebooks and shuffling feet stilled as Winston reached the lectern. He set his satchel gently on the floor, resting both hands on the wood, letting the silence stretch until the last whisper died away. For a heartbeat, the only sound was the steady hum of the lights overhead.

His eyes swept across the hall—rows upon rows of faces, some eager, some skeptical, some drawn by curiosity alone. He felt the weight of their expectation pressing against him, as though the entire room leaned forward, waiting for him to unravel the mystery of where he had been. He opened his lecture notes, and for a moment he froze. Another scrap of parchment lay atop the first page, as though waiting for him. His hand shielded it from view as he unfolded it. It said simply:

"Not yet."

The words pierced him more sharply than the others. His throat tightened. He looked out at the expectant faces—young, eager, unshaped. How could he not share? How could he hold back what he had seen, the truths that burned within him? Although filled with more questions than answers, he began to speak, his voice calm, deliberate. Winston cleared his throat, his voice low at first, but clear.

"I am sure many of you look at me now and see a man who has been away. And you are right. I have stood in places where silence is louder than speech, where questions echo long before answers arrive. I cannot tell you all that I have seen...not yet. But I can tell you this: knowledge is not only what we record in books or recite in lecture halls. It is also what reshapes us when no one is watching—when we are alone with the vastness of the world, and with ourselves." A hush deepened, students leaning forward, pens hovering above blank pages. He allowed a faint smile.

"So, let us begin not with what I know, but with what you are willing to seek. Let us learn not only from the pages we open, but from the silences we are bold enough to enter."

The words lingered in the air like a quiet invocation. In that moment, Winston knew he had not betrayed the Regal Ones's trust. He had given the students only an invitation, a door left slightly ajar. The truth, for now, remained safely veiled. What emerged was neither revelation nor explanation. Instead, the spoke of wonder. Of the vastness of the world, of civilizations long forgotten, of the human thirst to reach beyond the visible. The students leaned forward, captivated, hoping to hear more of what he had to share. For a long moment after he finished, the lecture hall remained hushed, as though his words had drawn a veil over the room. Then the rustle of notebooks resumed, pens scratching, but slower, more thoughtful than before.

From the back row, a young woman lifted her hand. Winston recognized her instantly—Clara Jennings, the former student who had once sat wide-eyed through his lectures on lost civilizations. The very same he had encountered on the airplane weeks before, her delight at seeing him alive, her curiosity sharper than most.

"Professor Thornberry..." she said, her voice steady, though softer than the silence she broke, "...you speak of silence as though it has a voice of its own. Did you hear something while you were away?"

A ripple passed through the hall. Students leaned forward, sensing the question beneath the question. Some smirked, others scribbled furiously, eager for any hint of revelation.

Winston's gaze met Clara's across the rows. He felt the folded note in his pocket, its words seared into him: "*Not yet.*" He let the silence stretch once more before answering.

"Yes," he said at last. "I heard the voice of silence. It does not answer directly, but it teaches us to listen—to ourselves, to the world, and perhaps to what lies beyond both." He cleared his throat, took a deep breath, and continued. "However, more importantly, it teaches us to remember who and what we were before consciousness began..."

Clara's eyes did not waver, though her pen stilled. For an instant, Winston thought she understood more than the others—felt the edges of the truth he could not yet name. He moved on quickly, shifting the lecture to safer ground: ancient texts, cultural myths, the long history of humanity's search for meaning. Yet the air in the hall never returned to ordinary. A spark had been struck, and its glow lingered in Clara's watchful eyes.

Winston continued his lecture, no longer giving weight to the hundred eyes staring across the room. His reflection in the narrow glass pane startled him—he looked older than when he had left. His hair, once neatly kept, now bore streaks of silver that caught the light like threads of frost. His face was leaner, weathered by northern winds, the lines around his eyes deepened into furrows of endurance rather than age. The tweed jacket he wore hung a little looser on his frame, but his posture remained upright, almost austere, as though held by something stronger than bone.

Beneath the surface, however, his composure frayed. His heart beat a rhythm of both dread and resolve. Months among the Regal Ones had carved new depths into him, and now he stood at the edge of a familiar stage made strange by his own transformation. He could not help thinking that to the students, he appeared as a spectacle, on trial for their examination.

He drew a steadying breath. Whatever questions they asked, whatever stories they demanded, he would have to walk the narrow line between silence and revelation. Winston knew that he was not merely a lecturer returned from sabbatical, but a man who had walked through fire and silence, carrying secrets too heavy for words.

His eyes continued sweeping across the hall—rows upon rows of faces, answering questions drawn by curious onlookers. He felt the weight of their expectation but he did not succumb to the pressure that sought to unravel mysteries he simply could not share. Instead, he cleared his throat, his voice faint, and continued to impart knowledge that enhanced the students' understanding of the world's vastness and mankind's understanding of itself.

"Professor Thornberry," a young man called out to him. "Can you tell us, with a yes or a no, if there really is or is not a lost civilization out there...watching us, maybe, giving us a chance to clean up our lives, the environment, and the world?"

"If we learn to let the silence guide us," Winston continued, "it will teach us to listen, to ourselves, world around us and perhaps what lies beyond both..."

He moved on quickly, shifting the lecture to the readings for the next class, just before ending today's session. He had successfully managed to skirt the edge of truth, never crossing the line. Every word felt measured against an invisible boundary. The Regal One's restrictions echoed in his mind, pressing against him like unseen hands.

When the lecture ended, a hush lingered in the room. Clara walked to the front of the class.

"Professor Thornberry," she said softly, "do you

ever feel like you've seen more than the rest of us?" Clara was determined to press the issue. She sensed that he was hiding something and she was determined to know exactly what he knew, once and for all.

For a moment Winston's resolve nearly broke. The truth trembled on his lips. But he remembered the note: "*Not yet.*"

He smiled faintly, while thinking of a skillful way to respond.

"I think all of us have seen more than we realize. The difference lies in whether we choose to notice." He paused. "Don't you think?"

Clara studied him in silence, her expression unreadable. Then, almost as an afterthought, a faint smile touched her lips.

"Maybe," she said.

The class filed out slowly, murmuring, eyes bright with speculation. Alone in the empty hall, Winston gathered his papers, the third note tucked among them. He felt both prisoner and guardian of something greater than himself. He slipped the note into the Book that was in his satchel. The very moment he touched the Book, he felt an incredible urge to reflect upon his encounter with the Regal Ones. The urge was overpowering. The veil between the ordinary and the extraordinary was thinner now than ever, a fragile membrane stretched taut across the fabric of his days. Each word he spoke, each silence he kept, felt like pressure against that veil, threatening to tear it open. He did not know how long he could hold it closed, nor what would spill forth if it gave way—the wonder that might enlighten, or the weight of truths too great for fragile minds. In the quiet chambers of his heart, Winston wondered whether he was guarding the world from revelation, or guarding revelation from a world unprepared to receive it.

He leaned on the podium, and continued cramming his papers into his satchel without order. His hands shook; the latch resisted and he cursed under his breath until it snapped closed.

The corridors outside were alive with students changing classes, their laughter and chatter grating like static in his ears. A pair of undergraduates spotted him at once. He was in high demand.

"Professor Thornberry—your lecture—what did you mean about silence?" one student called, wide-eyed, eager.

Another reached toward him, notebook in hand. "Will you publish something? Can I meet with you about—"

Winston brushed past, muttering something indistinct. He bumped shoulders with a faculty colleague who smiled too warmly, already prepared to ask for details about his sabbatical. Winston lowered his head and quickened his pace, their voices chasing him down the hall like ghosts he could not outrun.

The building itself seemed to narrow around him. Every fluorescent light hummed too loudly, every door opened into another demand. He all but shoved the front doors aside and stepped into the cold, gulping the air as though he had been drowning. Without waiting, without looking back, he hurried down the path and away from the campus, satchel clutched like a lifeline.

Nearly ten minutes later he was home, at the university operated faculty housing. Home brought no clarity, only relief. Asher bounded toward him the moment he stepped inside, tail thumping the walls, paws pressing against Winston's legs with unrestrained joy. Winston knelt, burying his hands in the dog's thick fur, trying to anchor himself in something solid, something simple.

"You wouldn't believe me, old friend," he whispered, forehead against Asher's. "Voices—voices from the Book itself. They told me why it exists, why I was chosen...and what I must do."

Asher only panted, his eyes bright, his presence steady. Winston drew in a ragged breath, the words spilling faster, more frantic.

"But how can I know it's real? How can I be sure I'm not mad? The mind can conjure anything when pressed hard enough—dreams, visions, delusions. What if I'm chasing shadows and all of this is nothing more than the fevered rambling of a tired old man?"

Asher whined softly, pressing closer, and Winston wrapped his arms around the dog as though clinging to the last certainty left to him.

The late afternoon sun slanted across the front yard of the modest faculty operated housing, gilding the stone walkways and bare trees with a thin, reluctant warmth. Winston walked slowly along the path, Asher trotting faithfully beside him, the leash loose in his hand. Students passed in clusters, laughing, bent under the weight of backpacks and bright futures. Few of them noticed the aging professor speaking softly to his dog.

"They think we've both gone mad, you know," Winston murmured, his voice barely above the breeze. "But then again, truth always looks a little mad at first." Asher glanced up, ears twitching, as if in agreement. Winston smiled faintly. "You see, my friend, they think the world ends at what can be measured. You and I—we know better, don't we?"

A pair of undergraduates slowed their pace, whispering as they passed, one stifling a laugh. Winston caught the sound, but only nodded toward them with a small, courtly bow, as though acknowledging an audience.

"They'll learn in time," he said to Asher. "Everyone does. Though most of us too late."

The dog nudged his hand, and Winston chuckled, a sound too gentle to be mistaken for bitterness.

"Yes, yes—you're right. Supper first, revelations later."

The two of them disappeared down the winding path, the murmurs behind them fading into the hum of the campus. To the passersby, he was only a lonely man talking to his dog. But to Winston, the conversation was sacred—one soul reminding another that belief, however quiet, still lived in the world.

Outside, the night pressed against the windows, vast and unknowable, while inside Winston trembled between revelation and ruin, wondering which one had truly claimed him. He sat on the floor beside Asher, his satchel still unopened at his side, the parchment burning like a hidden coal inside it. His body trembled, not from the cold but from the enormity of what he had just experienced. The voices seemed to linger in the corners of the room, fading but never gone, as though they had etched themselves into the very air.

He buried his face in Asher's fur, the dog warm, steady, and utterly untroubled. Asher's breathing was slow and rhythmic, an anchor against the storm that churned inside his master. Winston let the silence hold him there, his heart easing with each rise and fall of the animal's chest.

"Perhaps I am mad," he whispered, fingers tightening in the thick coat. "Perhaps it was only the voice of my own loneliness speaking back to me. But if it was real, then what am I to do with it, Asher? How can one man carry a world's warning?"

Asher whined softly, nudging Winston's hand with his muzzle as if urging him to stay present, here, now, with him. For a moment, Winston almost believed the dog's quiet loyalty was enough to tether him to sanity.

The room seemed to narrow, the silence collapsing in on itself. Asher pressed against his knee, steady, watchful, while Winston's thumb hovered over the screen of his phone. There were several missed calls. The world of voices and parchment, destiny and ruin, suddenly collided with the one message he had never expected but always feared. A simple message from Margaret, which simply said, "Let's talk."

The fire crackled, throwing ribbons of amber light across the bookshelves, the worn chair, the scattered papers of a man who had given his life to questions no one else would ask. He thought of the laughter in the lecture hall, of Margaret's silence, of Elizabeth's downturned eyes at the wedding. All of them, each in their way, had turned from him—not cruelly, but with the natural recoil of those who could not see what he had seen.

"Woman, I hope you are happy," he murmured, the words carrying no expectation, only the faint recollection of Margaret. He let out a hard sigh.

Only Asher had stayed. Only this faithful creature had followed him into the wilderness and back again without needing explanation or reward. Winston smiled faintly, stroking the dog's head. "If the world were half as loyal as you, my friend, heaven would be a crowded place."

The dog's tail thumped once against the floorboards, and the sound filled the small room with a warmth no fire could equal. Winston sat back, letting the silence stretch between them—not empty this time, but alive. Somewhere deep within it, he felt the faintest echo of the Regal Ones voice:

Faith that asks no proof is the first light of understanding.

Then his phone rang. The sound jarred the fragile calm, sharp and insistent. Winston pulled it from his pocket with reluctant hands, staring at the screen as though it had no right to intrude upon this sanctum. The name flashing there froze him. It was Elizabeth. The daughter whose wedding he had missed, the daughter whispered about in Dr. Ellis's gossip, the daughter who had once looked at him with admiration before it soured into hurt.

EIGHTEEN

RUMORS IN THE HALL

The corridors of the university buzzed with a new current the morning after Winston's lecture. His words, few and careful as they had been, had already multiplied in the mouths of students and faculty alike. What had he meant about "the voice of silence"? Had he confessed to a kind of madness? Or had he touched something vast and unspoken, something too large for ink or lecture notes?

Students clustered on the quad, recounting fragments of his talk as though they had witnessed an oracle. One insisted he had hinted at a lost civilization; another claimed he had dismissed centuries of scholarship with a single smile. Clara Jennings, seated apart from her peers, said little. She replayed his words quietly, sensing more in what he withheld than in what he revealed.

In the faculty lounge, the air was thicker still. Dr. Ellis presided over the conversation, leaning back in his chair like a magistrate delivering verdicts.

"He comes back from his so-called sabbatical, gaunt

as a monk, and gives us riddles instead of research," Dr. Ellis declared, his voice rising above the clink of coffee cups. "If Thornberry had anything worth sharing, don't you think he'd have written it down? Instead, he hides behind poetry."

Laughter rippled through part of the room, but not all. Dr. Katherine Marlowe, the historian whose questions in the lounge had unsettled Winston before, spoke quietly.

"Or perhaps he's seen something that can't be reduced to a paper or a lecture. We might consider the possibility that Thornberry is choosing restraint, not evasion."

Dr. Ellis snorted. "Restraint? That's a generous word for failure."

Winston entered then, his presence soft but immediately felt. Conversations dipped, then resumed with forced nonchalance. He poured himself coffee, each movement measured, and took a seat at the edge of the room. He did not glance at Dr. Ellis, nor at Marlowe, but the silence he carried seemed to shift the air. Dr. Marlowe approached after a moment, her voice pitched low.

"Winston, forgive me. But the trustees are restless. They want something tangible—an article, a manuscript, anything. You must know patience among them is thin. I don't think the dean can shield you much longer."

Winston inclined his head. "I know, but for Christ's sake, it's only been a few days." His voice was even, but behind it lay the weight of unspoken struggle.

When the faculty lounge emptied, Winston gathered his notes. As he slipped his papers back into his satchel, he felt a sharp edge against his hand. Tucked between two pages was another folded scrap of parchment. His breath caught. He unfolded it quickly, shielding it from view. The same curling script, stark as ever:

"*Truth will be tested.*" He folded it back into his pocket, the words burning hotter than Dr. Ellis's insults or the trustees' impatience. For the first time since his return, he felt the walls of the ordinary world tilt, as though the unseen had stepped directly into the halls of the university.

Leaving the lounge in silence, Winston walked down the narrow stairwell to his office. The room greeted him with dust and stillness, the kind that makes the ordinary world feel thin, as though something waits just behind the veil. He set the satchel on the desk and opened it. The Book lay within, its weathered cover etched faintly with shifting symbols. He lifted it out, spread it across the desk, and the silence broke—not with sound, but with presence.

No sooner than he could sit at the desk, it happened. Winston felt as though he was moving through a trance, each moment suspended between waking and dream. The familiar lines of the university blurred at the edges—the corridor walls seemed to waver, the windows shimmered as if holding more than their reflections. Ordinary sounds—the shuffle of papers, the echo of a closing door—took on a strange resonance, both near and impossibly far. He could not tell where reality ended and the surreal began, only that he was walking along the seam of both. His body moved with practiced ease, but his mind hovered elsewhere, drawn to unseen currents that whispered through the fabric of his surroundings. The world itself seemed to tilt, half-solid, half-vision, and he wondered whether he was the one haunting these halls, or whether they were haunting him. Out of nowhere, he heard whispers that sounded familiar.

"*We are the Seam, Winston,*" the whispers echoed.

The voices braided into his mind, not spoken but undeniable. They told him of the Book's origin, a record preserved across centuries, guarded in secret beneath the polar ice. It was not written by one hand, nor in one age, but assembled to heal humanity from its ruin: greed, destruction, division. The voices swelled.

"*You were chosen because obedience outweighs pride in you. You must tell them the truth: the world races toward its own undoing. Enlighten those whose ears are eager to hear. The time is short.*"

As the Book shook, a parchment slipped free, as though delivered by invisible hands. Winston unfolded it with trembling fingers. And, to his surprise, he saw coordinates, star maps, strange diagrams, and words that spoke of the hidden power of the human mind. A fragment that could be shared. A truth wrapped in remembrance.

The Book closed with a whisper, and Winston sat alone in the dim light of his tiny office, parchment pressed to his chest. The laughter from the faculty lounge still echoed faintly in his memory, but here was proof that their chatter was nothing against the weight of destiny. For the first time, silence was not only a burden—it was a trust. And he was no longer only a guardian of secrets. He was a messenger.

Later that evening, Winston sat on the floor beside Asher, his satchel still unopened at his side, the parchment burning like a hidden coal inside it. His body trembled, not from the cold but from the enormity of what he had just witnessed. The voices seemed to linger in the corners of the room, fading but never gone, as though they had etched themselves into the very air.

He buried his face in Asher's fur, the dog warm, steady, and utterly untroubled. Asher's breathing was slow and rhythmic, an anchor against the storm that churned inside his master. Winston let the silence hold him there, his heart easing with each rise and fall of the animal's chest.

"Perhaps I am mad," he whispered, fingers tightening in the thick coat. "Perhaps it was only the voice of my own loneliness speaking back to me. But if it was real, then what am I to do with it, Asher? How can one man carry a world's warning?"

Asher whined softly, nudging Winston's hand with his muzzle as if urging him to stay present, here, now, with him. For a moment, Winston almost believed the dog's quiet loyalty was enough to tether him to sanity. Then, suddenly, his phone rang. The sound jarred the fragile calm, sharp and insistent. Winston pulled it from his pocket with reluctant hands, staring at the screen as though it had no right to intrude upon this sanctum. The name flashing there froze him. It was Elizabeth, his daughter. The daughter whose wedding he had missed, the daughter who had once looked at him with admiration before it soured into hurt. It was her second call in as many days. His hand hovered above it, trembling slightly, caught between longing and dread. The last conversation had left him hollow, shaken in ways he could scarcely name. His mind was already a labyrinth of noise and half-formed visions; he wasn't sure he could endure another confrontation. For a long moment, he watched the light fade, the silence resettles, and told himself that waiting was not the same as refusing.

The room seemed to narrow, the silence collapsing in on itself. Asher pressed against his knee, steady, watchful, while Winston's thumb hovered over the screen. The world of voices and parchment, destiny and ruin, suddenly collided with the one call he had never expected but always feared.

NINETEEN

THE VOICES OF THE BOOK

The phone rang again the following morning, sharp against the stillness of Winston's home. The phone's shrill ring shattered the fragile quiet of the early morning, cutting through the thin veil of half-sleep like a blade. Winston jerked awake in his armchair, the blanket sliding from his shoulders. For a moment, he thought it might stop, but the sound pressed on, insistent, merciless. He knew who it was before he looked. His daughter again. That certainty lodged in his chest like a stone.

He sat frozen, staring at the phone across the room as though it were a serpent coiled and ready to strike. Each ring was a pulse, beating against the silence, pulling him closer to a moment he had long delayed. To answer meant stepping into her world of sharp questions and wounded silences, a world where no story of Regal Ones or sacred Seams could soften the edges of her pain. To ignore meant cowardice, a retreat that might seal the distance between them forever.

He rose slowly, his legs heavy, the floor cold beneath

his bare feet. He paced once, twice, trying to summon the courage that had carried him through storms of snow and fire, only to find that a single phone call could undo him more thoroughly than the elements. His breath came short, uneven. He whispered to himself, *not yet, not yet,* as though the plea might delay the inevitable.

But the phone would not relent. Its ringing filled the small house, louder with each cycle, echoing in his bones. Asher padded into the room and sat by his side, head tilted, as if urging him forward. Winston bent to rest a trembling hand on the dog's fur, grounding himself against the living warmth at his knee.

The ring cut again, sharp and final. He straightened, exhaled the breath he did not know he had been holding, and crossed the room with the slow resolve of a man walking toward judgment. His hand hovered above the receiver, every instinct screaming to delay a moment longer. But some truths, no matter how feared, demanded confrontation. With a weary surrender, Winston lifted the phone.

"Hello," he said, his voice breaking in the hush. There was a pause, heavy with distance and memory, before her voice broke through—familiar, yet edged with years of absence.

"Dad?"

His throat constricted. "Yes. I'm here." He paused. "How did you get this number?"

"Mom gave it to me." There was a deep sigh on the other end of the phone. "She said you sent it to her via text message. You sound...tired." A measured breath.

"I've called a few times...are you okay?" She appeared to struggle for words.

Winston closed his eyes, Asher's head pressing gently against his leg as though urging him to stay grounded.

"I'm managing," he said, though the words felt brittle.

"Managing," she echoed softly, with a trace of bitterness. "That's what you've always said, isn't it? Even when you missed my wedding. Even when you disappeared without a word. Just 'managing.'"

The accusation cut deeper than Dr. Ellis's gossip, deeper than any faculty doubt. This was the wound he had carried silently, the proof of his failures where love should have bound him strongest.

"I was wrong, Princess," he whispered in a broken tone. "About so many things... But never about you." There was silence on the other end, and Winston could hear only her breath, uneven, as though she was weighing whether to hang up or to press further. When she spoke again, her voice trembled.

"I don't want excuses, Dad. I want to understand. Where were you? What could matter more than walking me down that aisle, even if I said I didn't want you there?" She paused. "Surely, you had to know I didn't mean it..."

Winston's hand tightened on the phone. Behind her words, the Seam's voices stirred faintly in his mind, a warning that the time to speak—and to remain silent—was thinning. He bowed his head, caught between the weight of cosmic truth and the unhealed wound of his own family.

"Perhaps, this is a conversation we should have in person." He paused. "Maybe, over a cup of coffee or tea?" An awkward silence marked the moment before she finally interrupted.

"In due time..." she said firmly. "But, for now, I need to understand why you disappeared for nearly a year." She paused. "I don't think I am ready for a sit-down..."

"I deserved that," Winston said apologetically. Silence again filled the air.

"So, where were you? What was more important than my wedding day?" she said in a highly emotional tone of voice. "I want to understand..."

"I cannot tell you everything," he said at last, "but I can tell you this: I wasn't running from you."

"Then, tell me what you can...and what you *are* running from?"

"I was...called," he said hesitantly. "And what I saw has changed me forever."

Her voice cracked. "Called by what?" She spoke in an incredulous tone.

Winston looked down at the Book resting closed on his desk, the parchment still hidden within.

"By something that believes this world is on the edge of losing itself. And it chose me, though I never asked to be chosen." Another silence followed—this one not dismissive, but filled with something like fear, or wonder.

"Are you sure?" she said in a surprised tone.

Winston nodded, as if she could see him gesturing.

"Pretty sure," he said in a soft tone.

"Then if you're sure, Dad...are you safe?"

Winston exhaled, his hand brushing Asher's fur. "Not all safe. But safer because you've called."

"Then, trust the process and let go," she said in a calm and reassuring voice. "I forgive you, Dad. Goodbye."

She quickly ended the call.

Winston sat motionless, the phone still warm in his hand, as if reluctant to admit the call had ended. The silence that filled the house was vast and echoing, louder than any accusation she might have hurled. He had said so little—neither promises nor confessions—and yet the emptiness of what he withheld pressed upon him like a crime. Betrayal did not always arrive with action; it could live quietly in omission, in the unspoken truths that withered on the tongue.

What startled him most was not reproach but mercy. Her voice, fragile and steady, had carried something he had not earned: forgiveness. It slipped between his defenses like light breaking through storm clouds, leaving him exposed, humbled, and unsettled. He had braced himself for anger, for a wound that would at least confirm the distance between them. Instead, she offered grace—an unexpected gentleness that felt almost unbearable in its purity.

How had she chosen this path? What strength had enabled her to look past many months of absence, disappointment, and unanswered questions, when blame would have been so much easier, so much cleaner? He could not explain it, nor could he dismiss it. Her reaction felt less like human will and more like a mystery—something that reached beyond reason, beyond fairness.

Yet even as he tried to hold her forgiveness in his mind, he felt himself shrinking from it, afraid of what it required. To receive such a gift meant acknowledging not only her pain but his own failings, laid bare without excuse. It was miraculous, yes, but miracles often carried burdens of their own. He wondered if he had the strength to accept it, or if his heart would forever circle around it, unworthy, unable to comprehend its source.

Asher had curled beside him, chin on Winston's knee, his steady breathing the only rhythm in the room. Winston stroked the dog's fur absently, replaying his daughter's question: Are you safe? The words haunted him. Safe from what? The faculty's scorn? His own unsteady mind? Or the unseen forces who had marked him, who whispered warnings in folded notes and turned silence into command?

Night gathered. Winston drifted between exhaustion and unease, until at last he rose, turning on the desk lamp. The Book waited there, heavy and immutable, the parchment still tucked within its pages. He touched it hesitantly, his fingers tracing the strange symbols on its cover. The air thickened. A pulse—not sound but vibration—stirred around him.

"*We are the Seam, Winston.*"

The voices emerged again, layered and resonant, as though the Seam itself had opened in his study.

"*You waver, Winston,*" the voices whispered through the room. "*You speak half-truths when the hour demands clarity. You are tested by the bonds of flesh, yet called to the burden of spirit. You cannot serve both and remain whole.*"

Winston gripped the desk, his knuckles whitening.

"She is my daughter!" he exclaimed. "I have already lost so much—must I lose her too?"

The voices braided together, some stern, others tender, yet all insistent.

"Love is not loss. You cannot lose what already belongs to you... But your task is not hers to carry. Humanity fractures—greed consuming, divisions multiplying. The Book is not for your redemption, but for theirs. Through you it will speak, but only if you remain faithful."

The lamp flickered. The parchment stirred, edges curling as though touched by unseen wind.

"What you hold may be shared. The map, the constellations, the remembrance of the mind's forgotten power. This is your bridge between worlds—proof enough for the eager, protection enough for the truth. Guard the rest until the appointed hour."

Winston bowed his head, heart hammering. The words were both balm and burden. He longed to call his daughter back, to confess everything, but he knew the mandate was unchanged: some truths must wait.

Asher shifted, pressing closer against his leg. Winston exhaled and reached down, grounding himself in the dog's simple presence.

"At least you," he murmured, "require nothing but my hand."

The voices faded, leaving only the faint rustle of the night. Winston remained seated, the Book closed once more, caught between two worlds—one that demanded silence, and one that demanded love—and knowing that soon, he would have to decide which call he could answer without losing the other forever.

Winston pulled the parchment from the Book, smoothing it carefully across his desk. The symbols shimmered faintly in the lamplight, maps of stars interwoven with words in a language both familiar and strange. At first glance, it looked like astronomy; to the untrained eye, perhaps even myth. But to Winston, it was alive—coordinates that stitched the cosmos to memory, truths preserved through centuries of silence.

He reached for a fresh notebook, its pages blank, unthreatening. With slow, deliberate strokes, he began to copy fragments from the parchment. Not the hidden mandates, not the voices of the Seam, but the elements he was permitted to share: constellations charted with uncanny precision, notes on the mind's untapped strength, echoes of wisdom that would appear harmless in academic circles yet stir something deeper in those ready to hear.

Asher shifted, sighing in his sleep, and Winston paused to glance at him. The steady rise and fall of the dog's chest steadied his own. "One step at a time," he murmured, as if speaking both to the animal and to himself.

The night stretched onward, ink bleeding into paper, destiny translated into the language of men. Winston felt no peace, only the tension of a bridge being built—between silence and revelation, between ruin and hope. The test was no longer whether he could keep the secrets of the Regal Ones. It was whether he could share what was allowed in a way that would awaken, not destroy.

The day had been long. By the time he set down his pen, the first threads of dawn were unraveling across the horizon, pale light pressing faintly against the windowpanes. The lamp on his desk flickered, its glow paling against the encroaching day, as though it too knew its vigil was ending. Winston leaned back, every muscle taut with fatigue, the silence of the room pressing close around him. The parchment lay folded on the desk, small and unassuming, yet to him it was a covenant—one part confession, one part vow—sealed not by ink alone but by the weight of all he carried.

He closed his eyes, listening to the hum of the house, the slow settling of wood and stone, the faint rhythm of his own breath. It struck him then how little the world saw. Students hurried to their classes, colleagues sipped coffee, his daughter went about her life—and yet none could glimpse the invisible weight he bore. It pressed on him alone, sharp and unseen, demanding both silence and obedience.

Asher stirred at his feet and rose with a gentle sigh, padding to Winston's side. The dog laid his head against his master's knee, grounding him with the wordless fidelity that had carried them both through the most desolate hours. Winston's hand found the warm fur and lingered there, grateful for the steady presence that tethered him to the ordinary world.

He knew the road ahead would demand everything—his voice, his loyalty, perhaps even the fragile boundaries of his sanity. But as dawn widened, spilling gold across the window, he felt a flicker of defiance against despair. The past was closed, etched in memory like an unalterable script. To keep staring backward was to bleed from wounds that could never be undone.

He straightened, drew in a long breath, and allowed himself a thought that was neither certainty nor denial, but a fragile seed of hope: that one day this burden, unseen and unshared, would be transformed. Perhaps it would not break him, but shape him. Perhaps the weight itself was a refining fire, one that would teach him to endure until release came—not as escape, but as a freedom deeper than he yet understood.

Leaning forward, he pressed his palm against the folded parchment, whispering the words he could not yet give to anyone else.

"Let me be faithful. Let me not falter." Asher shifted closer, as if sealing the prayer with his silent companionship. And as the dawn fully broke, Winston rose from his chair, resolved not to look back upon the shadows that clung to yesterday, but to press forward into the uncharted day, carrying both burden and hope within him.

TWENTY

FRAGMENTS OF THE HIDDEN MAP

The lecture hall held its breath as Winston drew the constellation across the blackboard—a scatter of points that seemed ordinary until he connected them in a pattern none of them had seen before. The chalk clicked softly, deliberate as a metronome. When he stepped back, the figure hovered like a key against a door.

"Across civilizations," he said, "patterns recur. One can call it a coincidence, or one can ask whether we are remembering something we've been taught to forget."

A hand lifted near the middle—eager, earnest. "Professor, are you talking about diffusion? Like one culture spreading ideas to others?"

"Diffusion explains much," Winston replied. "But not everything. These star positions," he tapped the chalk twice, "match to within minutes of arc in traditions that never met, separated by oceans and centuries." He paused, eyes scanning the room. "So, either a messenger traveled farther and more faithfully than our timelines permit, or humanity was once more connected than we know—by a capacity we do not currently possess."

A few students laughed under their breath at that, uncertain whether to treat it as a provocation or a joke. Winston didn't flinch. He drew a second shape below the first, a curve intersecting the constellation at two points.

"Consider this arc—not an orbit you're taught, but a harmonic drawn from observation of the sky taken over generations. Some communities encoded it in story, others in stone. Either way, it's a memory disguised as myth."

A tall student in a worn baseball cap leaned back, arms crossed. "With respect, Professor, if these are so accurate, why haven't we heard about them in standard astronomy courses?"

"Because the modern habit," Winston said gently, "is to believe only what can be measured with instruments we already own. Anything that suggests a forgotten instrument—the human mind itself—locks the door from the inside."

Silence rippled outward like heat. Pens hovered; a few heads tilted, as if their owners were remembering something they couldn't name. Clara Jennings, midway up the left aisle, watched with her hands folded over a closed notebook, absorbing rather than annotating.

A hand went up near the front—soft-spoken, careful. "Are you saying people used to...think differently?"

"Yes," Winston said. "Not more magically, but more integrally. Less a matter of filing facts into drawers and more a matter of seeing the drawers as wood from a living tree."

The laugh this time was warmer, but it died quickly, replaced by a current of attention that made the room feel smaller. Winston reached for his notebook—the one copied from the parchment. He did not open the Book itself. He would not betray the Seam. But he allowed what he was permitted to share to cross the threshold.

"These notes," he said, tapping the notebook, "replicate ancient star positions you could verify with modern software. You'll find the precision uncomfortable." He allowed a faint smile. "Discomfort can be a teacher."

The same young man as before, wearing a baseball cap, lifted his chin. "Okay, say you're right. What does it matter? We already have telescopes."

"It matters," Winston said, "because if we accept that memory can outlast our tools, we might recover more than data. We might recover disciplines of attention—ways of seeing that knit our minds to the world rather than placing them above it."

A new voice from the rear—sharp, skeptical. "Isn't this all just a romantic gloss on ignorance? People told stories because they didn't have labs."

Winston nodded, conceding the tension. "Some stories conceal ignorance. Others preserve wisdom until there are ears to hear it. Confusing the two is how civilizations lose themselves."

Clara's hand lifted, then hesitated. Winston met her eyes, and the hesitation vanished.

"If memory is encoded," she asked, "how do we decode it without doing violence to it? How do we translate without flattening?"

Winston let the question breathe. "With humility," he said at last. "With the courage to leave some parts untranslated, and the patience to integrate what survives the crossing."

A murmur. More students leaned in as if a wind had shifted. Winston crossed to the side chalkboard and drew a tight cluster of points, followed by a line extending outward, and then another set of points echoing the first but at a different scale.

"Fractality," he said. "Not the mathematical kind alone—the contemplative kind. Patterns repeat across scales. A mind attuned to attention can perceive correspondences between the small and the vast: atom and star, river and vein, city and synapse. We've reduced this to a metaphor. Perhaps it is more than metaphor."

An engineering student raised his hand. "Are you advocating for...psychic phenomena?"

"I'm advocating for disciplined attention," Winston answered. "Call it what you like. I'm interested in what it reveals—and in how it transforms the one who practices it."

He could feel the edge he walked—the Seam's warning humming at the back of his throat: "*Guard the tongue.*" He kept to what the parchment sanctioned: coordinates, correspondences, and an invitation to test rather than a demand to believe.

"Try an experiment," he said. "Not mystical—practical. For one week, choose a patch of sky at the same hour each night. Observe without naming. Record only the changes you see: brightness, drift, cloud, the temperature on your skin, the noise in your own mind.

You'll discover the night is more articulate than you remember—and that your attention, when trained, becomes a tool that alters both observer and observed."

A philosophy major smirked. "So...phenomenology."

"If the shoe fits," Winston said, showing no emotion. "But bear in mind that phenomenology without wonder is taxonomy in a better coat."

Laughter again, but softer, complicit. Winston sensed skepticism thinning into curiosity—its better form. He glanced down at his pocket. The rough edge of a folded scrap pressed faintly against the lining. "Not now," he thought. "Please."

A hand halfway up on the right—nervous, earnest. "Professor, you said 'ears to hear.' Are you implying that some people can't—"

"Not can't," Winston said. "Won't... The difference is hope."

Clara's voice rose again, steadier. "If we start to remember—if attention changes us—what's the ethical obligation? To share? To protect? To...wait?"

The question reached behind his ribs. In the back of his mind, the Seam's cadence whispered: *This you may share. Guard the rest.* He felt, as he had all week, the thin membrane between offering and betrayal.

"Our obligation," he said carefully, "is to speak in a way that awakens without wounding. To share what strengthens the capacity to see, without shattering the protections that mystery provides."

"So, there are protections?" someone asked. "From what?"

"From ourselves," Winston said, taking a slight pause to clear his throat. "From the speed at which we demand answers. From reducing wonder to content." He erased a section of the board and drew a simple circle.

"Imagine this is the known. We assume progress is always pushing outward. But there is another trajectory," he marked a narrowing inward spiral, "which is depth. Some truths grow dangerous when spread too wide too quickly. Others lose power when hoarded. The art is in the timing."

A hand shot up—Baseball Cap again, sharper now. "With respect, who decides timing? You?" The room went still. Winston nodded once, accepting the challenge.

"No," he said. "Timing is discerned, not decreed. Communities of attention—patient, rigorous—decide together what can be borne."

"Communities like...this class?" someone joked.

Winston smiled, but the weight of it did not lift. "Perhaps. If we can learn to listen."

He moved toward the chalkboard and pointed to a copied diagram: a lattice of points overlaid atop a map of the northern sky. He traced a line with his finger—not quite touching the diagram.

"This," he said, "appears in four traditions that share no language. Each assert that when attention is trained upon this region—not merely observed but steadied—something in the observer aligns. Call it prayer, or focus, or resonance. The word is less important than the practice."

"What happens?" a student breathed.

"You sleep differently," Winston said passionately. "Dream differently. Remember differently."

"Is that...safe?" another asked.

"Nothing that changes you is entirely safe," he answered. "But neither is remaining unchanged."

He felt the room move, but this time toward him, the way a ship moves toward the wind. He stared at the chalkboard and stepped away, palms open, as if to show he held no contraband—only questions.

"Your task is not to believe me," he said. "Your task is to test your attention in the world and record what happens to your perception, your memory, your courage. If nothing changes, discard the exercise. If something changes, ask why."

Clara's hand lifted once more, but she didn't wait to be called on. "And if what changes leads us to a door, we're not ready to open...what then?"

"Then wait outside the door," Winston said, his voice low but unyielding. The fire in his eyes was not the flicker of performance but the steady blaze of conviction. To any witness—even the most skeptical—it was unmistakable: he believed every word he spoke. Either he was a man possessed by a truth too deep to deny, or he deserved the laurels of a stage great enough to rival kings. But in that instant, it did not feel like theater. It felt like faith made flesh. He stared into the audience and continued, now showing greater fire in his eyes.

"And you learn the discipline of patience."

The clock in the back ticked into the end of the

hour. Chairs creaked. A few students began to pack up, sheepish, as if they had broken a spell. Winston nodded dismissal without saying the word, and clusters formed instantly—whispers, bright-eyed arguments, a huddle around Baseball Cap who now seemed less certain of his own certainty.

Clara lingered in the aisle, then approached the lectern. "Professor," she said, voice low enough not to carry, "I don't think you're hinting. I think you're protecting something."

Winston held her gaze. "Protection is not always concealment," he said. "Sometimes it's hospitality. Making sure a guest arrives at a room warmed and lit."

Her eyes softened. "Then thank you for the light." He inclined his head, and she stepped away, leaving the compliment glowing like a coal under ash.

Shortly after the class ended, a line formed in the hall outside of his office—office hours without an appointment sheet. At least he had managed to stir a hunger in the students that could only be satisfied with answers only he could provide.

Questions came fast:

"Is this related to ancient navigation?" one student asked with morbid curiosity.

"Can I run the coordinates through Stellarium?" yet another jumped in before he had an opportunity to respond.

"Are you proposing a cognitive discipline?" the guy in the baseball cap asked.

"Would that be replicable in a study?" a student from the back of the line asked abruptly.

"What texts should we read beyond the syllabus—something with rigor, not just...mystical poetry?" Baseball Cap added.

Winston was overjoyed by the degree of interest he managed to stir. For years, he tried to make his class enjoyable, but it was hit or miss how the students would respond. However, this day was different, and he knew what the driving force behind it all was. He tried to answer each question in measured increments, offering references he trusted, practices that asked much and promised little: night-sky journals, contemplative field notes, cross-cultural star lore vetted by linguists, not merely anthologized by enthusiasts. Each response felt like a bead placed upon a string that must not be pulled too tight.

When the last student drifted out, the hall exhaled. Winston stood alone, the chalkboard a group of lines that seemed to vibrate in the empty air. He felt simultaneously emptied and brimming, as if he had poured from a vessel that was being refilled from a source he could neither see nor fully endure.

He reached for his coat. As he slid his hand into the pocket, his fingers found what he already knew would be there—a fold, a rasp of old parchment against wool. He closed his eyes, steadying himself, then unfolded the note.

"The eager will ask. You must choose how much to answer."

He stared at the words until the black ink seemed to thicken. Somewhere, a door clicked shut. The building's old bones settled. Winston folded the scrap and slipped it back into his pocket, feeling the Seam draw tight like a wound stitching closed.

"Choose," he murmured to the empty room, as if the walls themselves were listening. "Yes. But not alone."

By the time the last student's voice faded down the corridor, Winston was alone again, suspended in the hollow echo of his office. A haze settled over him, as though the room itself had slipped backward in time—lamps humming faintly, weary of their own glow, chalk dust lingering in the air like the residue of unanswered questions. He rubbed the bridge of his nose, eyes raw with strain, grounding himself in the present after a day of relentless inquiry that had left his thoughts muted and thin.

The hours had been unyielding—students hounding him with riddling questions, colleagues lingering after meetings, whispering of rumors. They pressed him not about coursework but about the *other matter*: the strange symbols in his notes, the whispered account of a half-seen map. He had answered with careful vagueness, yet their eyes betrayed unease. Curiosity, once awakened, was not easily silenced.

At last, silence reclaimed the building. Winston gathered his papers, but as he reached for his satchel, another scrap of parchment fluttered loose, spiraling to the floor. He bent to retrieve it—and froze.

It was no ordinary page. The fragment was brittle and uneven, as though torn violently from a greater whole. Its surface bore not words but faint, interlaced lines: a curve, a constellation, a coastline—shapes that seemed to shift the longer he stared, as if reluctant to be known.

The moment his fingers brushed it, a warmth surged up through his skin. Not the warmth of paper, but of something alive—something that pulsed faintly, like a heartbeat. He recoiled, then grasped it again, compelled. The lines upon the fragment glimmered faintly, as though inked in fire that remembered how to burn. He turned it over. Blank. Yet the warmth clung to him, burrowing into his palm.

A sound stirred in the corridor—a slow creak, the shuffle of weight. Winston stilled. His breath caught. He listened, heart hammering, but when he opened the door, the hall lay empty, its shadows long and unbroken. Only silence. Only waiting.

He shut the door with deliberate care and leaned against it, the fragment clutched to his chest. The lamp in the corner flickered once, twice, as if the room itself had noticed. Winston slipped the fragment into the inner pocket of his coat. Its heat seeped against his heart, steady, insistent. It was almost as though it wanted to remain there.

"Not yet," he whispered, the words half vow, half plea. "But soon."

He gathered his notebook, buttoned his coat, and stepped into the corridor, where the air still carried the faint scent of chalk and questions. Outside, the winter sky had deepened to a color that was not yet night, but no longer afternoon—a seam of its own. Winston breathed it in and walked toward the threshold, a messenger permitted to carry fragments, a guardian of what he could not yet name, and a teacher preparing a room he hoped would be warm when the appointed hour finally arrived. Somewhere deep within the silence of the building, something shifted—too faint to name, too present to ignore. Thus ended the day: not with answers, but with a fragment that breathed and waited, a piece of a map unwilling to remain hidden.

TWENTY-ONE

THE BREAKING POINT

The call came again two days later. This time, his daughter's voice carried no hesitation—only steel. Gone was the gentle tone of forgiveness that had softened their last conversation.

"*I forgive you, Dad...*" The words still echoed in his memory, fragile and luminous, a promise he had clung to like a lifeline. He had let himself believe that her call marked the beginning of repair, that grace—once spoken—could not be withdrawn. But what reached him now was urgency sharpened into demand.

There was a long, uneasy silence before Elizabeth's voice broke through, trembling with restrained fury.

"You owe me some straight answers."

Winston flinched at the force behind the words. He drew breath to reply, but she cut him off, her voice rising, raw and commanding.

"Don't you dare hang up on me!"

The sound tore through him like a lash, severing the delicate thread that had still bound them. Gone was the tender daughter who had spoken forgiveness; in her place stood someone harder, wounded, unreachable. Winston sat frozen, the receiver pressed to his ear, his pulse hammering. Something inside her had shifted—something beyond his reach—and he knew, with a helpless certainty, that no defense or reason would bridge the distance between them now.

Her anger did not erupt; it gathered. What followed was not so much accusation as a careful reshaping of the past, memory pressed into the shape that pain required. She did not need Winston's agreement. She only needed him there.

"You weren't there when it mattered," she said evenly. "Not once."

She paused, as if consulting something long settled. "Not at my wedding. I walked down that aisle alone because you had a conference you said couldn't be postponed."

The words did not rush. They landed one by one. "You broke Mom's heart. You broke mine. And after that, you disappeared into your work, as though we were marginal notes—necessary for reference, but never central to the argument."

She looked at him then, her expression steady, almost tired. "Every failure in this family, every fracture that split us apart, leads back to that choice."

A final pause. "You never chose us. You chose your obsessions. Every time."

The words came like hammer blows, unrelenting, each one striking where he was weakest. Winston's breath faltered. In his mind, he saw her wedding day, the empty chair that should have held him, the bitterness in her mother's eyes. He saw all the moments when silence had been easier than confrontation, when research and pursuit of hidden truths had seemed safer than the chaos of home. His throat constricted, guilt pressing hard against his chest, yet no answer rose to his lips. He wanted to tell her she was wrong—that his absence had been a sacrifice, not neglect—but even he could no longer untangle where duty ended and failure began.

At last, the silence cracked.

"Enough!" Winston's voice thundered into the receiver, harsher than he intended, breaking under the weight of everything unspoken. "Take some responsibility. You are the one who decided that you did not want me at the wedding. You think I wanted it this way? That I chose riddles and shadows over you?" He paused, his voice now filled with emotion. "Every day of my life I've carried the cost of those choices—your mother's pain, your anger, my own exile." He hesitated to clear his throat. "Do you think that doesn't tear me apart? You see neglect. I see the only way I knew to keep you safe."

His hand shook as he gripped the receiver, the words tumbling out half-confession, half-defense. His breath caught, and for a moment, he thought he had said too much. The line went quiet, her anger paused by his sudden outburst.

"Safe from what?" she whispered, her fury giving way to a trembling demand. "I'm sure that's just another one of your cop outs...when you can't deal with it, you run or throw in some esoteric propaganda that can't be verified. Huh?"

Winston closed his eyes, feeling the gulf between them widen. He had revealed too much already. He hesitated, as if pondering the right words to soften the urgency of the direction the call had taken.

"I love you," he said, voice breaking. "But some truths aren't meant for you. Not yet." He paused. "Goodbye, Princess."

Before she could speak again, the line went dead. He had ended it.

The silence that followed pressed in on him like a weight, heavier than her accusations. Winston lowered the receiver slowly, setting it into its cradle as if it were a fragile relic rather than a simple phone. His hand trembled. Her words lingered, unshakable—accusations of absence, betrayal, and obsession. And the cruelest truth was that every charge carried its echo of truth. He pressed his palms together, knuckles whitening.

"Forgive me, Elizabeth. If only you could see the whole of it—the danger, the burden. If only you could understand why I had to choose shadows over home," he whispered softly. But explanations would not soothe the wound. She wanted presence, not riddles. And he had given her neither.

The room darkened. The air shifted, and once again the regal figures—those luminous beings who had begun haunting his solitude—emerged at the edges of perception. They were silent, watchful, their eyes filled with a gravity that stripped away all pretense. Winston's pulse quickened. He wondered if they, too, had heard the call, if they judged him now as harshly as his daughter had.

"Why do you come to me now?" he whispered into the stillness. "Do you come to condemn me as well?"

But no answer came—only their steady, inscrutable presence, like living statues cut from light and shadow.

Then—KNOCK.

The sound shattered the stillness. A heavy, persistent pounding at the door, startling in its urgency. Winston flinched. His heart lurched as dread coiled tight in his chest. Elizabeth. The thought struck him like lightning. Had she come all this way? Had she followed the trail, determined to force the truth from him in person?

The knock came again—louder, insistent. KNOCK. KNOCK. KNOCK.

His jaw clenched. Annoyance sparked within him, cutting through fear. Whoever it was had no right to intrude, not now, not when the veil between worlds felt so thin. He longed to remain still, to let the knocking fade unanswered, to hide from both daughter and destiny. But the pounding would not cease.

Reluctantly, Winston rose, every step toward the door heavy with dread. He opened it a crack—then froze.

Dr. Katherine Marlowe stood on the threshold. Her face, pale and drawn, carried not accusation but urgency. Her eyes burned with something raw—fear mingled with recognition.

"Winston," she said, breathless. "Please forgive me for not calling." She hesitated, as if struggling for words. "I need you to listen. I know you think I doubted you before, but I don't...I can't. Because...I've seen the Book myself."

The air between them thickened.

"You—what?" Winston's voice was a rasp. Her gaze darted past him, as if searching the shadows of the room.

"I thought I was losing my mind," she said in a low whisper. "Visions. Whispers. Pages are appearing where no pages should exist. I dismissed it at first—chalked it up to exhaustion, to grief, to stress. But last night...last night the Book came to me. And I realized everything you've said, everything you've carried, wasn't madness. It's real. And it's happening to me too."

The Regal Ones lingered silently behind Winston, their forms flickering faintly at the edges of vision, as though acknowledging her words. He gripped the doorframe for balance. His annoyance gave way to awe, his fear to something far more unsettling: recognition. At last, he was no longer alone.

"I'm sorry...please come in," he said.

Dr. Marlowe stepped over the threshold as if crossing into a different gravity. Her coat slipped from her shoulders and pooled at her feet; her hands trembled, but her eyes were relentless. She did not look like someone who had come to accuse. She looked like someone who had been pushed through the same darkness and had come back with a story that would not let her be.

"I thought you were like the others," he said softly.

"What do you mean?"

"You know...thinking I was mad?" he added lightheartedly.

"Hardly," she said, voice low and urgent. "I thought I was losing it. I thought I had made it all up after nights of too little sleep and too many regrets. But it started up again—last week—after you returned to campus."

Winston closed the door and led her to the small lamp by the desk. The Regal Ones hovered near the far wall, their presence a slow, luminous hush that neither of them mentioned. Marlowe sat, fumbled in her bag, and withdrew a small, coffee-stained notebook. She opened to a page and flattened it on his desk. There, in her cramped clinical scrawl, margins crowded with arrows and underlines, were notations that made his chest tighten: sketches of a symbol he had seen in the Book; a time recorded in the margins when she said she'd heard a voice whisper something like a line of a sentence that had no business being in anyone's head.

"I thought the notes were a coincidence," she said. "A misremembered lecture. Then the lights started. Not electric—not exactly. The air itself would hum, like someone tuning a string you could not find. At my lab one night, the fluorescents dipped, and the whole room smelled of rain on hot metal. The paper moved on its own. Not pages blowing—pages rearranging." She smiled then, but it was the smile of someone who had watched a thing unravel. "I watched the page order change. I watched a single sheet slide against the stack until a sentence I hadn't seen before was there, clear as bone." She looked up at him. "The Book is alive, Winston...it finds people." She stared at him with an earnest expression. "I thought it came for those who wanted it, but I quickly realized that *it* came for those who needed it."

Winston looked on with a puzzled expression but remained silent.

"It came to me while I was working on grant proposals. It laid against my hand like a living thing." She added in a mystical tone. Dr. Marlowe's words hung in the air between them. "You're not alone, Winston. I've seen them too—the tall ones... And I've read from the Book."

The air seemed to thin. Winston's hand froze halfway to his face. For a long moment, he stared at her, uncertain whether this was happening. His mind reached for reason, for a foothold, and found none.

"You—what did you say?" His voice barely rose above a whisper.

"I've seen what, maybe, you've seen," she said again. "And I believe you."

The words should have brought him comfort, but instead they split him open. His pulse pounded so loudly it seemed to fill the room, an unwelcome intruder in his own thoughts. He had confided in almost no one—certainly not like this—and the sound of his own admission now echoed back through her. Relief came first, sudden and intoxicating, followed by a sharper edge that tasted of fear.

What if this was all part of a clever ruse? What if this was a trap, a quiet test from the university—a way to bait him into confirming what they already suspected? The thought chilled him. His stomach tightened.

He drew back slightly, choosing silence as his armor, and studied her face—the steadiness in her gaze, the tremor in her hands. She looked neither calculating nor cruel. If this was deceit, it was masterful. And yet, beneath his doubt, a spark of something else flickered—recognition. The kind that comes when one soul stumbles upon another shaped by the same fire.

He waited, unwilling to betray himself too soon. Better to let her speak, to reveal her intent, while he listened from the narrow borderland between faith and fear.

"I wasn't supposed to tell you," Marlowe continued, her voice trembling now, "but I couldn't keep silent any longer. I think...they want us to find each other."

Her confession fell into the quiet like a stone into water—small, unassuming, but destined to ripple outward, altering everything it touched. Better to let her speak, to reveal her intent, he thought to himself, while he waited in the stillness between trust and suspicion. Dr. Marlowe looked at him, sensing his unease and decided to continue in her efforts to convince him that she was a friend and not a foe.

"Last night I woke to music," Marlowe continued, as though she were racing to get the words out before they fled. "A rhythm under the floor, three beats, then a long note. When I went to the kitchen, there was a folded paper on the counter I hadn't left there. A sentence I know I didn't write: '*Remember the first turning—do not read aloud.*' I hadn't read it aloud. I hadn't opened it. But I felt something watching the back of my neck like a presence waiting to be acknowledged."

Her hand brushed the lamp, and the light guttered, then steadied—a small mimicry of the thing she described. The Regal Ones in the corner stirred, their forms bending like reeds in a windless field.

Winston reached out and picked up her notebook. “May I,” he asked politely. She gave a nod of approval. He slowly opened the book and saw many familiar sketches. They were crude but exact: concentric runes, a tiny notch on the top right of one symbol that he, too, had seen. He turned the page and found, tucked loosely between sheets, a fragment of paper with a single sentence scrawled in a frantic hand:

“There is a time for all things.”

Marlowe’s voice was almost a whisper now. “I didn’t tell anyone because the truth is...I didn’t want to be the sort of historian who walks into mythology. But then I found pages from the Book in my office drawer while working on a very intricate proposal. Not the whole thing—a single leaf, damp at the corner. It vanished by morning, but the words stayed with me.” She closed her eyes. “I think I was supposed to share this with you...to let you know that you are not a man cornered by obsession...” She hesitated. “You are not the only one.” Winston felt something like a door unlatch inside him. Part of him wanted to laugh with incredulous relief, part of him braced to answer a charge.

“Will you tell me everything you saw?” he said finally. His voice had the brittle steadiness of someone who has practiced self-control until it becomes a thin armor.

She told him—the nights of dreams shaped like cartographic lines, the sensation of being watched not by eyes but by attention, the sudden certainty that language folded differently near the Book. She described a woman in a market who had stopped and bowed her head as if acknowledging something no one else could see; a child whose drawing matched a glyph from Marlowe's notes; the way the edges of pages sometimes shimmered, as if ink were a membrane between two kinds of air.

When she spoke of the Book sliding across her kitchen counter, she reached into her bag and produced something else: a scrap of vellum, browned and softened, smaller than a hand. Winston's breath hitched. He had seen leaves like this, the tactile shock of paper that carried the wrong light.

"I didn't come looking for you," she said. "I came because I didn't want anyone else to be alone in this madness. I thought I might be able to call it clinical—attribute it to sleep apnea or stress. But it's not clinical. It's not simply neurological. Something else is learning to speak through pages. And—" She leaned forward, lowering her voice, "—and last night, when the air hummed in my study, I heard a voice behind the words. Not a language I knew. But it understood my fear. It told me: 'Prepare the reader.'"

A coldness threaded his spine. The Regal Ones at the wall were unbecoming statues no longer; their posture softened into something like attention. Winston felt the room contract, like the moment before a tide turns. Marlowe's hands were steady now. Her look was that of a clinician who had ceased to believe in neat diagnoses and instead believed in whatever intelligence reached past the rules.

"I believe you," she said simply. "Not because I want to, but because I have seen it. Because I felt it. Because the Book touched me." She paused, searching his face. "We need to be careful. We need to be deliberate. And we need to read it together—not to pry, but to understand what it is asking for. If it can change the order of pages, if it can speak through paper, then it can change what we remember, what we fear, what we choose."

Winston folded the scrap of vellum between finger and thumb, feeling its odd coolness. He thought of Elizabeth—of forgiveness turned to fury—and of the cost the Book had already exacted from his life. He thought of the narrow, terrible relief of not being the only one anymore.

"Why me?" he asked, not for the first time. The question was quieter here, threaded with a lifetime of questions.

"Maybe it is not why you," she replied, "but why now." She pushed a breath into the space between them. "I don't know if it chooses or simply reveals. But it surfaces where things are fragile. It surfaces where people have already begun to look away. It finds seams."

In the small lamplight, her face looked older and younger at once—older from nights stolen by the Book, younger because relief had lifted a weight not of her making. Dr. Marlowe stood then, the fatigue of confession trailing her like a shadow.

"We don't have to do anything tonight," she added. "But we must not pretend this is nothing. If the Book is teaching someone—or teaching something through someone—we need a plan. We need witnesses, rules, and someone who will keep a record of everything exactly as it happens."

Winston thought of his daughter. He imagined Elizabeth's fists, her accusations, her forgiven softness now hardened into an urgency he could not ignore. He imagined how fragile that forgiveness had been—a reed that had been bent and might snap. He imagined, too, the Book's strange appetite. Outside, a wind sighed against the cabin, on the fringes of the North Pole. The Regal Ones bowed as if in agreement. Winston set the scrap down between them and looked at Dr. Marlowe. The room felt smaller and fuller at once, crowded with possibility and peril.

"Very well," he said. His voice was steady in a way that surprised him. "We begin carefully. We document everything. No reckless reading. No solo experiments. We keep a record, and we keep each other honest."

Marlowe nodded.

"And if—" she hesitated, searching for a word that wouldn't sound like prophecy or paranoia, "—if it asks for more than words, we do not let it have them without understanding the cost."

He met her eyes and saw the same mixture of terror and resolve that lived in him. For the first time since he had discovered the Book, Winston felt the scale tip—not toward relief, not yet, but toward a shared burden. They stood in the lamplight, two small figures against a vast and waking mystery. Behind them, beyond the thin domestic walls, the world hummed with a patience that was not quite benign. A single, low note seemed to thread the air—not music, not speech, but an intake of breath from somewhere.

Winston's chest tightened. He wanted to scream, but instead he sat in his oversized chair replaying the brutal exchange that had taken place between him and his daughter. He took a few deep breaths and sat there trying to regain his composure.

"I am not mad?" he whispered, while Asher looked on quietly.

The room stilled. He stared at Dr. Marlowe, who sat quietly, her gaze steady on Winston, her face now drained of color.

"Winston, about two years ago, I received a message that supernatural beings had invaded Earth and were living somewhere on this planet at an unknown location." Her voice remained quiet but unwavering. "These beings originally landed approximately one hundred years ago and were here watching the inhabitants of this planet to study our progress."

Winston looked on, displaying a curious expression.

"Go on," he said softly.

"During their habitation, they were imparting fragments of the Book to various individuals whom the council had selected to help impart knowledge to the masses regarding their ascension to a higher plane."

"How do you know this?" he asked in a curious voice.

"Because everything communicated to me in these dreams has over time become true," she said poignantly. "Earth is a fallen planet, separated from the rest of the cosmic system due to a spiritual rebellion that happened many centuries ago. As a result of the fall, Earth did not complete its planetary ascension and has been isolated from the rest of the universe to avoid contamination... Yet, the supreme rules are trying to save Earth from its own destruction and are seeking to impart knowledge to the masses to implement self-healing."

"Is healing possible, given man's thirst for money, sex, power, greed, and all manners of evil that have literally destroyed all traces of morality?" Winston asked tenderly.

"That is the question that we wrestle with." Dr. Marlowe replied with conviction. "But, as educators, we have the best chance of reaching young minds and imparting information that will help them sow seeds of love, forgiveness, healing, and knowledge that can help us save ourselves from ourselves." She paused, now staring at Winston. "I don't have all of the answers, but I feel that there is more. I've only encountered fragments of information that spoke of a seam between worlds. I dismissed them, at first. But then I heard the voices too. They weren't mad. They were...something else."

He sat frozen, torn between chasing after reality and hidden truths from an unknown world. Asher pressed tighter to his leg, a silent reminder that the line between revelation and ruin was razor thin.

"Do you ever feel that you are caught between skepticism and fear?" he asked at last.

Dr. Marlowe's eyes met his. "All the time..." she said softly, while displaying a brief smile. "More importantly...I think something out there is trying to tell us that we are enough."

TWENTY-TWO

KINDRED SHADOWS

The house was quieter after her confession, but not with peace. The silence pressed against her skin, alive with the echo of things spoken that could not be recalled. Dr. Marlowe lingered on the porch, the night air cool against her flushed face, her hands clasped tightly as though holding herself together. She felt lighter—unburdened, even—yet a flicker of dread gnawed at the edges of her relief. Had she given too much away? Was it folly to lay bare her visions, to admit she too had seen the Book and the Regal Ones who moved like sovereign shadows over the fate of the world? A part of her longed to believe honesty had forged an ally; another part feared she had surrendered something she could never take back.

Inside, Winston sat slumped in his chair, Asher curled faithfully at his feet, the rhythm of the dog's breathing the only anchor in a room still vibrating with aftershocks. The conversation with Dr. Marlowe replayed in fragments, each admission a shard that pierced more profoundly the silence he had tried so hard to protect. She had seen the Book. She had known the Regal Ones. The burden he thought was his alone had shifted, lightened in one sense but grown heavier in another. If she carried the same knowledge, then the danger was no longer his to shield from others—it had spread. For the first time in years, he was not alone, and yet the company brought no comfort. Instead, it summoned a darker question: what had been set in motion the moment she chose to confess?

Dr. Marlowe continued to delay her departure from the house long after the door had closed behind her. Had she betrayed them? The Regal Ones had never set their covenant in plain speech, but she had felt its weight nonetheless—an unspoken bond, a sacred restraint. To speak of them was to invite their gaze. To reveal the Book was to tread on ground not meant for ordinary feet. She had crossed that line. She had told Winston.

And yet—her heart flinched at the idea that silence would have been mercy. He had sat there hollow-eyed, questioning his sanity, crushed beneath a burden too significant for one man. How could she have withheld the truth when it might be the only thing that kept him from breaking? Compassion, not defiance, had moved her. Still, compassion could also be rebellion.

The wind shifted. She thought she felt eyes on her again—not hostile, not condemning, but steady, as though the Regal Ones weighed her decision in a silence older than words. She turned back to the door, hesitated, then knocked softly. Once. Twice.

Inside, Winston stirred. Asher barked once, then

quieted, as though recognizing a familiar presence. Winston opened the door. His eyes were rimmed with fatigue, but his expression softened when he saw her.

"Dr. Marlowe," he said quietly, stepping aside. "I didn't think you'd come back."

"I shouldn't have," she murmured, stepping inside, her voice trembling with both relief and dread. "I had no right. Perhaps no permission. But I couldn't leave it there—not when you... Not when you looked as if you doubted your own mind."

He gestured toward the chair opposite his own. She sat, her coat gathered in her lap like a shield.

"Katherine," he said, voice low, "you've given me more than I could have asked for...and yet you seem burdened. What is it?"

Her eyes flicked to the corner of the room where the Regal Ones still lingered—dim outlines of radiance, watching without judgment. Her chest tightened.

"I wonder," she whispered, "if I have broken something between them and me. If speaking aloud what they chose to show was a trespass. I've carried their presence like a covenant—never written, but binding nonetheless for the better part of two years. And now I've spoken it to you." Her hands trembled as she clasped them tighter. "Did I betray them?"

Winston leaned forward, his own weariness softened by tenderness. "No. You showed mercy. If these beings are what I think they are—keepers of truth, watchers of mankind—then they too must know that silence can destroy as surely as a sword. You did what was human. And maybe what was divine."

Her throat caught, and for a moment, she could not speak.

"Still," she said at last, "I wonder if they will call me to account." She glanced again at the radiant shadows, her eyes wide with both awe and fear.

"Perhaps they already are."

The air in the room seemed to hum, subtle but undeniable, like the faint resonance of an unseen chord. The Regal Ones neither moved nor spoke, yet their presence deepened, filling the space with a solemnity that pressed on both of them. Dr. Marlowe reached across the edge of the chair, her hand trembling as it touched Winston's.

"If they take me to account, let them. But I couldn't watch you walk alone into madness. You needed to know it was real." His hand closed gently around hers, his eyes wet with a gratitude he could not name.

"And I needed you to say it. Whatever comes, Katherine—we face it together. For each other. For them. And for mankind. We must become what we teach...tonight, you showed mercy."

The lamp flickered. The Regal Ones bowed their heads, not in reproach, but in something like acknowledgment—whether of a broken covenant or a fulfilled one, neither could tell. The silence that followed was not empty but thick with mystery, mercy, and the first fragile thread of trust.

Winston leaned back, his hand still resting over hers, the silence stretching between them like a veil. He did not dare break it quickly; the presence of the Regal Ones demanded patience. At last, he spoke, his voice a low murmur. "You've seen them too," he said, his gaze flicking toward the figures in the corner. "Then you know—they are not here by accident. Their watchfulness has purpose. And if they have allowed us to glimpse the Book, to feel the weight of their nearness... it must mean something is coming."

Dr. Marlowe shivered. "I've thought the same. But what kind of plan binds itself in riddles? If they desire mankind's good, why not say so plainly? Why not speak as we do, so there is no fear of error?"

Winston's lips pressed tight, his mind reaching for words he scarcely trusted himself to say.

"Perhaps plain speech would destroy us? Perhaps revelation in full would break the mind of man. So, they give us fragments, like notes in a melody. And it is left to us to listen carefully—or misstep." He looked at Dr. Marlowe and then quickly turned away. "There is a time and season for all things; maybe, we must cultivate patience and wait for the duly appointed hour."

She exhaled, her shoulders sinking. "That's what terrifies me. What if we mishear? What if we mistake their mercy for judgment? Or their plan for salvation as something we twist into ruin? I confessed tonight because I feared silence would cost you your sanity. But what if my words were premature? What if I've led us both into disobedience?"

Her eyes glistened, the conflict tearing at her. Winston reached across the space again, his voice steady, tender.

"You are not alone in that fear. I have asked the same questions every night since they came. But perhaps the greater trespass is not to speak, but to hide. Perhaps what they want most is not blind obedience, but faithful courage." The air seemed to pulse gently, as though the Regal Ones themselves acknowledged his words. The lamp flickered, twice, before settling into a steady glow.

Dr. Marlowe's voice softened, almost breaking. "Then their plan is not only for Earth—it is for us. To test whether men and women will carry truth with mercy."

Winston nodded, his eyes wet with both awe and dread. "Yes. And if we fail, mankind may not survive the weight of what is written."

They sat in the lamplight, two trembling figures bound not only by their humanity but by the mystery that had claimed them both. Beyond the house walls, the night stretched silent and vast, as if the world itself held its breath.

At last, Winston whispered, "Then we must not falter. For them, for the Book, for whatever covenant still holds. Whatever comes—we walk it together."

And for the first time since the Book had entered his life, the burden felt not lighter, but shared.

A faint and mysterious message whispered to both of them from the Regal Ones, indicating that Dr. Marlowe's sharing was approved because they instilled in her the desire to share with Winston, who was losing his grip on reality.

The lamplight flickered again, not with the hesitation of weak flame but with the cadence of something unseen moving through the room. The air grew thick, resonant, as if the house itself had become a vessel. Winston and Marlowe both stilled, their hands linked across the table, eyes drawn instinctively toward the Regal Ones.

They had not moved. And yet—something stirred among them. It came not as a sound carried through the ear, but as a whisper woven directly into the marrow of their bones. Faint, steady, undeniable.

"Do not fear. It was placed within her to speak. What is shared between you is not rebellion but design. Mercy is the covenant."

The words brushed their spirits like breath across glass, fragile but searing. Winston's chest heaved; tears gathered at the corners of his eyes. Dr. Marlowe trembled, her hand tightening around his as though anchoring herself to the only reality she could still trust.

The Regal Ones stood in stillness, luminous silhouettes, their silence carrying the weight of eternal assent.

Dr. Marlowe's lips parted, her voice breaking into the hush. "Then it was not disobedience...it was obedience of another kind."

Winston's gaze remained fixed on the radiant shadows. "They placed it in you. To save me from the madness of silence."

The air throbbed once more, softer this time, like the closing of a great book. The presence receded, but the echo of the words remained, written not on parchment but in the hollows of their souls. Winston released a long breath; his hand still entwined with Dr. Marlowe's. The fear that had hunted them both was stilled—not gone, not conquered, but bound by the assurance that what had been spoken was meant to be spoken.

They sat in the quiet, two fragile human hearts

steadied by mercy older than the stars. The lamplight shivered once more, shadows lengthening along the walls until the air itself seemed to vibrate. Then it came—not through the ears, but through the soul. A whisper, faint yet thunderous, threading into both of them:

"Do not fear. It was placed within her to speak. What is shared between you is not rebellion but design. Mercy is the covenant."

The words pressed into Winston like a balm and a blade at once. His breath caught, chest rising sharply as though he had been pierced. Tears blurred his vision. For months, he had carried the torment of secrecy, doubting whether his silence protected or destroyed. Now, in a single echo, the burden shifted: his daughter's fury, his long loneliness, his fear of madness—all had been met by mercy. He bent forward, pressing his hand to his brow, the other still clutching Dr. Marlowe's as though it were the last tether to sanity.

She gasped, her body trembling as though the voice had passed directly through her bones. She bowed her head, clasping Winston's hand tighter, tears slipping silently down her cheeks. Relief mingled with awe. She had feared betrayal, feared she had trespassed against beings she could barely comprehend. Yet the message was clear: it had not been disobedience, but a planting. The very impulse to confess had come from them. Her chest loosened, the gnawing guilt dissolving into something like reverence.

She lifted her face, eyes shimmering. "Winston… they knew. They placed it in me. I wasn't betraying them—I was obeying them."

Winston met her gaze; his own face streaked with tears. His voice shook, but it carried a steadiness born of certainty. "Then you saved me. They used you to pull me back from the edge."

The Regal Ones stood unmoving, luminous in their silence, yet their stillness carried the weight of assent. The air pulsed once more—softer this time, a closing benediction. Then the presence thinned, leaving behind not emptiness, but a charged quiet that felt like the pause after a vow.

They sat together in that silence, hands still entwined, two fragile mortals steadied by a mercy older than the stars—bound now not only to each other, but to the covenant they had both heard.

TWENTY-THREE

THE WEIGHT OF WITNESSES

Several weeks later, Winston and Dr. Marlowe still found time to meet and discuss their mutual interest.

The house had settled into a hush—the slow new rhythm of a place that has been remade by heat and fear. Today's fire had dwindled to a faint glow, its light barely touching the corners of the room. The hearth kept a bed of dull coals that threw one or two reluctant sparks up like small, embarrassed confessions. The air smelled of char and ash, the kind of scent that clings to cloth and memory and will not be hurried away.

Winston sat forward, elbows on his knees, as though the posture might steady him against thoughts that wanted to tumble free. His face was etched with exhaustion; the pale lines at his temples had deepened as if mapping the strain. His hands rested, callused and unsteady, on his knees. On the low table between them, the Book waited—silent, immovable, like a judge presiding over their words. In the thin light, its cover seemed to drink and hold what little brightness there was, making its small surface feel both common and terrible.

Dr. Marlowe remained upright in the armchair opposite him, her posture as steady as her gaze. Shadows sharpened the planes of her face so that she looked carved, but her eyes were alive—watchful, haunted. She had spoken her truth, and in doing so tethered herself to his fate in a way that made retreat impossible. There was a gravity to her presence that the room seemed to honor; when she spoke, it sounded as if she had been rehearsing both the words and their consequences.

"We can't ignore this anymore, Winston," she said, her voice quiet but firm. "The Seam doesn't choose at random." She hesitated and took a sip from a large mug. "It marks those who can endure its weight...those who can serve as bridges. But bridges are not meant to stand alone. You've carried this burden in isolation too long. That is dangerous—for you, and for what the Book contains."

Winston rubbed his temples, a long breath escaping him. His hands trembled slightly as he spoke. "Dangerous, yes. But involving others—" He gestured vaguely at the Book, as though even pointing at it might trigger its power. "It feels like betrayal. The Regal Ones warned me. They imposed limits. Boundaries... I fear what happens if I overstep them."

Dr. Marlowe leaned forward, her face lit by a thin band of firelight. "Boundaries exist to protect. But protection can suffocate if never tested. Look at me. I kept silent for years. I convinced myself that burying my memories in scholarship was fidelity to the Seam's command. But in truth, it was cowardice. And what did my silence bring? Loneliness. Sleepless nights. Regret." Her voice cracked. She pressed her hands together tightly, as though to keep from unraveling. "I will not let you make the same mistake."

Asher rose and padded softly across the floor. He pressed his nose against Dr. Marlowe's hand, and she allowed her fingers to rest on his head, steadying herself with the dog's warmth. Winston watched the scene in silence, feeling the stirrings of gratitude—and guilt.

For a moment, the sight blurred into another memory: Elizabeth, twelve or thirteen, crouched in the old yard as their family's husky pressed into her hand in the very same way. Her laughter, bright and unguarded, rang out in the cool evening air, a sound of simple trust and delight. That memory cut deep against the bitterness of her voice in their last call. He swallowed hard, guilt pressing into him. The innocence she once carried had hardened into accusation, and he could not escape the thought that his absence had played its part in the change.

At last, he said, "Then what do you propose?"

"We begin," she answered. "By cataloging what can be spoken. Fragments. The safe truths. Coordinates, constellations, patterns that awaken attention without exposing the Seam itself. Practices of observation that anyone can attempt. Enough to ignite curiosity, but not enough to endanger."

"And the rest?" Winston asked, his voice barely above a whisper.

Dr. Marlowe met his eyes without hesitation. "The

rest waits. Until the Seam commands otherwise. Until the world proves ready, or until others—others like us—rise to share the burden."

Winston leaned back in his chair, staring up at the beams overhead. Shadows stretched across the ceiling like ribs, enclosing him in both safety and confinement. "You speak as though there is a plan. As though we are only pieces in something larger."

"Isn't that what you already know to be true?" she asked. Her words cut through him like a bell tolling in a cathedral—deep, undeniable. Winston bowed his head, the firelight catching in the lines of his face.

"I know," he admitted. "But knowing and accepting are not the same."

Dr. Marlowe leaned forward, her eyes blazing with urgency. Her voice was low but fierce, each word cutting through the silence. "Accept that you were chosen because you listen when others laugh... Accept that the Book has not destroyed you, though it could have... Accept that silence may no longer be obedience but disobedience."

Her words struck the air like hammer blows, but Winston did not flinch. He sat rigid in his chair, his jaw tightening, his breath unsteady. For a long moment, he said nothing, and then his voice broke the stillness, rough with the weight of restraint.

"You don't understand, Katherine," he said, each syllable measured, iron beneath the fatigue. "I was given a mandate on that ice, in the heart of the North Pole, where no man should survive. They made it clear: what was entrusted to me was not for the eyes of the world. Not yet. Not until they declare it so. Do you think I could stand before them—those who are older than empires, who see further than any prophet—and tell them I chose to break their command because I thought I knew better?"

He rose then, pacing, his hands trembling at his sides. His voice grew stronger, the frustration sharpening into anger. "You call silence disobedience, but I call your urging a kind of blasphemy! Do you not see? To publish what I have seen, to spread what they have revealed—it would not be courage. It would be treason. Against them... Against the very covenant that has preserved my life. Against the mercy that has carried me through madness."

Dr. Marlowe tried to interject, but he raised his hand sharply, his eyes burning now. "No, hear me! You speak of persuasion, but I hear only temptation. I will not—" his voice caught, then hardened again. "I will not be the one who squanders their trust. I would sooner die nameless, forgotten, than lift a pen against their command. If silence damns me, then let it damn me. But I will not betray them...I will not."

He turned from her, chest heaving, the room heavy with his refusal. For a moment, he stood like a sentinel at war with himself—torn between the plea of human compassion and the weight of a covenant carved in fire and frost.

"Then accept..." Dr. Marlowe said, her voice firm now, almost commanding. "Accept that you were chosen! Admit that silence may no longer be obedience but disobedience."

Winston looked down at the Book, its cover gleaming faintly. For a moment, he thought he heard the low hum again—the Seam whispering, testing. He reached out but did not touch it, his hand hovering above the surface.

"What if obedience to the Seam means disobedience to my family, my students, the very world I live in?"

"Then you must decide which world you serve," Dr. Marlowe said softly. "But hear me, Winston—you are not alone in that decision. I am here. I carry part of it with you now."

The silence that followed was not heavy, but profound, as if the walls themselves listened. Asher curled at their feet, his presence bridging them in quiet solidarity. At last Winston exhaled, his shoulders slumping under the weight of it all.

"I can't make a decision of this magnitude without first seeking clarity." He paused, eyes fixed on Dr. Marlowe. "Let us begin, first by seeking wisdom and clarity…and trusting the Regal Ones to lead us to a place of safety."

Dr. Marlowe nodded, her eyes unwavering. The fire guttered, casting its last sparks. The Book remained closed, but both of them knew the true work had only just begun.

TWENTY-FOUR

RIPPLES ON THE SURFACE

By the end of the week, Winston's lecture was no longer confined to the classroom. It had spilled into the corridors, seeped into the dining halls, and lingered in the hushed aisles of the library stacks like incense after a liturgy. Students whispered about it in corners, their voices sharp with curiosity, as though speaking too loudly might invite the very mysteries he had suggested. Scraps of paper passed from hand to hand, covered in hurried sketches of the constellations he had traced across the blackboard—crooked stars, incomplete patterns, but glowing with a kind of borrowed significance.

"Did you hear what he said about the Seam?" one student muttered, his eyes darting nervously toward the hallway as though the word itself might be overheard. Another scoffed, though her fingers betrayed her, tracing the outline of Orion in the margin of her notebook.

"It's not an actual seam, it's a metaphor. He wants us to think beyond what we can see," another student continued, trying to make sense of it all.

"No," a third whispered, leaning forward so that even the dim light in the library barely caught his face. "I swear he wasn't talking in metaphors. There was a moment...it was like he knew something—something no one else should know."

The speculation followed Winston like a shadow. In the dining hall, trays clattered and conversations rose in the usual din, but clusters of undergraduates bent earnestly over half-eaten meals, debating his words as though explaining scripture.

"If even half of it is true," said one, pale with sleeplessness, "then history is smaller than we thought."

Her companion laughed, tilting back in his chair. "Or maybe he's just an eccentric old man who reads too much folklore. You all want prophets, so you turn the man into one."

Later, in the corridor outside his office, Winston stumbled upon a small knot of students waiting like parishioners at a confessional. Their notebooks were clutched to their chests, faces lit with the kind of eagerness that made him ache with both pride and dread.

"Professor Thornberry," one of them began, a tall boy with ink stains across his knuckles, "the constellation you drew—the one with the broken line—I couldn't find it in any star chart. Was it...was it something new?"

Winston hesitated, the answer hovering like a fragile truth on his tongue. He saw again the ice-lit cavern, the ceiling of uncharted stars that no chart dared claim. He could almost feel the cold breath of that place. But he forced the memory back, pressing his voice into the steadier cadence of a lecturer.

"Not new," he said carefully. "Only overlooked. Sometimes our eyes grow accustomed to patterns that no longer serve us. And so...we miss what is already there."

The students exchanged looks—excitement, suspicion, wonder. Another leaned in, her voice soft but urgent.

"Is it true, then, what they're saying? Have you seen something? That the Seam...chose you?"

The word *Seam* on her lips was a knife of temptation. Winston's chest tightened. He thought of Dr. Marlowe's warning, of the regal command carved into the marrow of his conscience: silence until the time appointed and a symbol in the sky. And yet here were his students—the young, the questioning, the very ones he had always believed worthy of more.

He straightened, hands clasped behind his back to still their tremor.

"What I have seen, and what I have not seen, is less important than the questions you are willing to ask." His gaze swept across them, softening. "The constellations are patient. They will wait for your eyes to find them."

It was not an answer, and yet it was more than silence. The students scribbled his words with the reverence afforded oracles, while Winston turned back toward his office, the weight of their voices following him down the hall. He felt it then—gratitude for their hunger, and guilt that he could not feed it. For he knew that knowledge was a fire, and fires did not stay contained for long.

That evening, Winston sat in his study with his

own fire reduced to a glow, the room thick with the silence that follows too much conversation. He had tried to busy himself with papers, but the students' voices trailed after him, insistent as echoes: "*Is it new? Did the Seam choose you?*" Their wide eyes haunted him, their eagerness mingling with Elizabeth's voice in memory, accusing him for all he had withheld.

When Dr. Marlowe arrived, she found him pacing, his notes scattered across the desk in restless patterns. Asher lifted his head at her entrance but did not move; even the dog seemed subdued by the heaviness in the room.

"They're beginning to ask questions," Winston confessed before she had even sat down. His voice was low, as though the walls themselves might conspire to betray him. "Not idle ones," he said tenderly. "Serious ones… They repeat my words as if they were scripture. Some even draw the stars as though they were maps waiting for destinations."

Dr. Marlowe removed her coat slowly, folding it across the arm of a chair, her eyes never leaving him. "You knew this would happen… Words are seeds, Winston. You've scattered them—now you cannot command what grows."

He stopped pacing and turned to her, his face etched with a mixture of pride and dread. "Do you think I do not know that? Their hunger…it is a mirror. It reminds me of my own, when I first traced those impossible constellations. But their questions…" His hands opened helplessly. "They demand answers I cannot give without breaking the covenant. If the Regals meant silence, then I am already standing too close to the edge of disobedience."

Dr. Marlowe stepped closer, her voice measured, but her eyes burning with urgency. "And if silence itself becomes the disobedience? Have you considered that? Perhaps the Regals never intended for you to hoard what you have seen, but to learn when the time for witness arrives. And maybe," she leaned forward slightly, "the students' questions are that time knocking, which will be followed by symbols in the sky."

Her words landed like flint on dry tinder. Winston felt his chest constrict, torn between awe and terror. He turned away, staring into the last dim glow of the coals.

"Do not tempt me, Katherine. You do not understand the cost of defiance. To them, treachery is not measured in words but in eternity. And yet..." His voice faltered, and he pressed a hand to his temple. "And yet the students' faces—the way they looked at me today—I cannot banish it. They believe I hold something worth their faith. And what if I am wrong to keep it from them?"

Dr. Marlowe moved to his side, her tone gentler now. "You are not wrong to fear. But fear must not be the author of your choices. Let us seek wisdom together. Not rashly, not in arrogance, but with care. Perhaps the Seam has given you the students as your measure—to test whether you can bear the weight of witness without breaking."

For a long moment, Winston said nothing, only listening to the fire's final sigh as another coal collapsed into ash. At last, he whispered, "If they are my measure, then I fear I am already failing them."

Dr. Marlowe reached out, letting her hand rest lightly on his arm. "Then do not carry it alone." The words lingered, soft yet immovable, until even Asher shifted closer, curling at Winston's feet as if to confirm the truth: the burden, whatever its weight, was never meant for one man only.

By week's end, Winston's words had escaped the classroom. His students whispered them like contraband, scribbling sketches of constellations on margins of homework and the backs of receipts. Some spoke of revelation, others mocked in parody, but none remained indifferent. It was in those whispers that Winston first felt the danger of his own teaching—those ideas, once loosed, no longer belonged to the speaker. They became witnesses in their own right, stubborn and impossible to silence.

In the library, a cluster of students huddled around a round oak table. One, a philosophy major with wide eyes, insisted that since following Winston's night-sky experiment, her dreams had sharpened.

"I can remember colors now," she whispered. "Deep reds, greens I can't even name. And there's a pattern—I know it means something."

A skeptical engineering student scoffed. "It's just a suggestion. He planted it in your mind, and your brain ran with it."

But another leaned in, lowering his voice. "What if it's both? What if expectation is part of the process? Maybe that's the point."

The debate grew heated enough that a librarian hushed them twice, but none left their seats.

Elsewhere on campus, a satire column in the student paper mocked him under the headline: *Professor Draws Stars, Declares Humanity Forgotten Itself.* The piece quoted students—some anonymous, some not—laughing at his metaphors and calling him "Professor Paradox."

Yet by the next day, copies of the paper had been clipped and posted on dorm bulletin boards, circled and underlined with notes that read:

What if he's right?

In the residence halls, late-night gatherings spilled onto the lawns as students tried the 'experiment' themselves, staring at the sky in small, intent groups. One freshman journaled obsessively, convinced she had seen a star shift places. Another wrote a poem about the silence of the night speaking louder than his own thoughts. Skeptics mocked, but even they joined in, unwilling to be left out of what had become a quiet craze.

The faculty, however, was less charitable. Winston heard fragments when he passed the lounge—snatches of ridicule delivered with the practiced sneer of those too careful to be fully quoted.

"Gone mystical, has he?" one colleague muttered.

"Should've stayed in the north—fewer ears to corrupt up there," another jumped in. "Students are impressionable. This could turn into a scandal."

Dr. Ellis's voice rose above them all, predictably, spinning gossip into performance. "I heard he's writing a manifesto. Says he's got a map that proves humanity's forgotten how to think. Next thing you know, he'll be founding a cult." The room erupted in chatter and laughter, though Winston noticed not all were smiling. Some turned away, as though unwilling to join in the mockery.

But the whispers reached higher ears too. By Monday morning, Winston received a neatly folded note slipped under his office door:

Assistant Dean Hargrove requests a word—today, at your earliest convenience.

The dean's office was a vaulted room of dark wood and older portraits, the kind of place where silence seemed curated and intentional. Books lined the shelves, their spines immaculate, as though untouched by honest inquiry. A tall window let in a shaft of pale autumn light that fell directly across the dean's desk, illuminating a spread of papers already waiting when Winston entered.

"Professor Thornberry," Dean Hargrove said with the kind of measured warmth that always seemed to precede an admonishment. "Please, sit... This is just a friendly conversation, nothing official that should concern you."

Winston obeyed, lowering himself into the chair with the faint creak of leather. He folded his hands in his lap to still their tremor.

"I've heard," the dean began, tapping one paper with an elegant finger, "that your recent lectures have been...well, let us say, memorable. Students are speaking of little else. Constellations redrawn, patterns that no astronomer seems to have published, and curious references to—what was it?" He glanced at the page. "A Seam?"

Winston inclined his head, his tone neutral. "I encourage my students to think beyond the rigid frameworks of standard star charts. The Seam is a metaphor—a boundary between what is known and what is overlooked."

The dean smiled thinly. "A metaphor. Of course... that makes perfect sense to you and me." He leaned back, steepling his fingers. "The trouble, you see, is that students are not always adept at distinguishing metaphor from proclamation. They are young, impressionable. When they believe a professor is handing them secrets, they tend to grow...excitable. And excitable students can become disruptive."

"I assure you," Winston said evenly, "my intent is not disruption. Only illumination. Academic rigor remains the cornerstone of my teaching." He paused to clear his throat. "But we must find ways to stimulate curiosity and inspire young minds to ask thought-provoking questions..."

"Rigor," the dean repeated, as though tasting the word for sincerity. "Yes, well. You've always been an inspired lecturer, Professor Thornberry. But inspiration must be handled with care. The Board expects sound scholarship, not...folklore." His eyes narrowed slightly, voice softening in that dangerous way of men who prefer velvet sheaths for their knives. "Tell me honestly—do you believe what you are teaching?"

Winston hesitated. For a fraction of a second, the memory of the ice cavern flared—uncharted stars, the Seam's low hum, the command of the Regals. His throat tightened.

"I believe," he said carefully, "that education should challenge the boundaries of perception. That is all." Winston gazed at him with a wily expression. The dean studied him in return, silence stretching like a blade across the desk. At last, he nodded.

"Good. Then I trust we will see your next lectures return to firmer ground. Astronomy, anthropology, and comparative mythology—fields our curriculum recognizes. Leave the wilder...seams...to literary classes that encourage students to explore fiction."

"I understand," Winston said, rising to his feet. His voice was steady, but inside he felt the weight of every syllable being cataloged, filed, and prepared for use against him.

The dean smiled once more, polite but sharp-edged. "Excellent. We are, after all, guardians of young minds. We must not let them wander too far into shadows, eh?"

Winston inclined his head, murmured a polite farewell, and left the office with the unnerving certainty that the conversation had not been closed but only suspended—like a gavel held aloft, waiting for the moment it would fall.

Outside the university, the ripples spread wider still. A podcast run by two undergraduates replayed his chalkboard demonstration with breathless commentary, describing it as "half astronomy, half mysticism, but strangely compelling." A graduate student in anthropology emailed him a long letter, half skeptical, half pleading for more information.

And Clara Jennings often lingered after class, her

questions sharper, more personal, her eyes steady with a recognition Winston had begun to fear. She no longer asked for clarification but for implication. During her last meeting with him, she had asked several thought-provoking questions. He could still hear her voice and her previous question lingered with him:

"If observation changes us," she pressed one afternoon, "doesn't that mean you're responsible for what happens to us if we take this seriously?"

The words unsettled him more than Dr. Ellis's gossip, more than the dean's measured warning. Clara was listening too closely—he could see it in her gaze, feel it in the silence that followed her questions. Her words lingered long after the conversation ended, circling in Winston's mind with the persistence of a bell that would not stop tolling. She had spoken with the earnestness of youth, declaring that knowledge should never be buried, that truth must be carried into the open air no matter the cost. At first, Winston resisted her conviction, bristling at the confidence with which she dismissed boundaries that had cost him blood and silence. And yet, beneath his resistance, her voice pressed into him with a strange familiarity—it echoed his own secret ache. Had he not once believed the same, long before the Regals laid their command upon him? Had he not built a career on drawing veiled patterns into the light and handing them to his students as gifts?

Reconciling her declaration with his own vows left him raw. He wanted to affirm her hunger, to encourage the spark that made her see more than her peers. But behind that desire lay the covenant of ice and fire, a charge delivered in a realm no student could imagine. To betray that trust would be to undo the very mercy that had spared him. His heart strained between the two poles—Clara's bright insistence that knowledge must breathe, and the Regals' solemn decree that some truths must sleep until the world is ready.

As he walked back through the dim corridors, Winston felt both pride and unease. Pride that his words had awakened something real in the young, but unease that their awakening might summon storms too soon. The weight of it pressed harder with every step. Later that evening he would meet with Dr. Marlowe, and already he dreaded the fervor he knew he would find in her eyes. She was eager to go public, eager to scatter fragments into the waiting world. And though part of him longed to share her fire, another part recoiled, afraid that once released, their knowledge of the Regal Ones would become a flood neither of them could hold back.

He and Dr. Marlowe continued to meet in stolen hours, chasing threads of meaning and mapping questions that refused to rest. At night, they lingered in his study, the lamplight trembling against shelves heavy with silence, while the Book lay between them like an uninvited sovereign, its presence shaping every word. With cautious hands and measured voices, they drafted fragments—truths thinned into metaphor, coordinates disguised as parable, patterns veiled in allegory. Yet beneath the careful craft Winston felt the swell of something vast and inevitable. He had cast a single stone into the stillness, and now the water no longer remembered calm; the ripples had become waves, and the waves a tide that threatened to claim his body and soul.

Dr. Marlowe dipped her pen, pausing above the paper. "If we say too little, they'll dismiss it as whimsy. If we say too much, we risk betraying the Seam. Where is the middle ground?"

"The middle ground," Winston murmured, his gaze fixed on the Book, "is a fiction. One either stands inside the command or outside of it. These fragments," he gestured at the scattered drafts, "are already a dangerous compromise."

She studied him, her voice soft but edged with urgency. "Then why keep writing with me at all, Winston? If every word is betrayal, why not burn the papers now?"

His jaw tightened, and he leaned back into the shadows. "Because silence itself feels heavier than treason. The students look at me as though I owe them the world. I cannot give them what I have seen...but I cannot leave them starved, either."

Dr. Marlowe lowered her eyes to the page, her hand trembling slightly as she wrote.

The Milky Way—students think of it as a scatter, a spilled jar of light. But to the ancients, it was a river. The river above us does not flow toward an ending, but circles like a vein carrying life. The ones who follow its current do not arrive, they return.

She looked up. "A river suggests travel. Return suggests...home."

"Or judgment," Winston muttered. They both sat in silence for a while before Dr. Marlowe continued.

"What of the dark spaces between stars?" she asked softly.

Winston's brow furrowed. "Students call them voids. But the Seam taught me that absence is its own kind of fire. A flame that burns unseen."

She pressed ink to paper and continued writing:

The heavens are full of unlit fires. To eyes that seek only brilliance, they appear as nothing. But to those who wait with patience, and seek only truth, the dark is not empty—it is fuel awaiting spark.

Winston leaned back, the words weighing on him. "Would you not agree that...statement alone could bring more questions than answers." As the clock chimed, Winston rubbed his temples. "One more. Not stars this time. Earth."

Dr. Marlowe raised her pen. "The ground beneath us listens," she said softly. "Every step, every vow. We pretend it is deaf rocks, but the ancients knew otherwise."

Her hand trembled as she wrote:

The soil is not mute. It remembers. Each path we tread presses into it a word, and the earth reads it in silence until the appointed hour. When the reckoning comes, it will not be the sky that testifies, but the ground we thought dumb beneath our feet.

She laid the pen down, staring at the page, before turning to Winston. "This one...this one is dangerous..."

Winston closed the notebook gently, as though to muffle the words. "Dangerous, yes. But truer than the rest."

"Then perhaps these fragments are not compromise," she said slowly, "but preparation—a way to teach them to listen before they hear, to see before they are shown."

Winston closed his eyes, the tide of her words colliding with the weight of his vow. Somewhere deep within, he wondered if the Regals would judge his silence as obedience...or cowardice. He looked at Dr. Marlowe and displayed a slight nod, as if assenting to her statement. But Winston could feel the tide rising. He had cast a single stone into the water—and now the ripples were swelling into waves, threatening to drag him under.

As the fire in his study dwindled to an amber glow, Winston felt a strong desire to share with Dr. Marlowe what he had not told another soul. The Book lay between them like a silent arbiter, its presence pressing upon every syllable he spoke.

"Katherine," he called out to her. "Since we are being open about things, there is one student," he hesitated, his voice shaky and filled with uncertainty, "who causes me great concern."

Dr. Marlowe looked on with great curiosity, waiting for him to continue.

"It's Clara Jennings..."

"How is it that Ms. Jennings is a cause of concern for you?"

There was a long pause. "There is something about her that I cannot put my finger on. She lingers after class, asking questions no textbook could have planted. At first, I thought it was harmless curiosity, but now..."

He hesitated, his hand tightening around the arm of his chair. "Now I see something in her eyes I once recognized in my own. A dangerous recognition of hidden truths."

Dr. Marlowe leaned forward, her expression unreadable but her interest unmistakable. "Dangerous in what way, Winston?"

"She no longer asks me what the constellations mean," Winston said, his voice roughened by the admission. "She asks what they imply. And today, she pressed further. She asked me if observation changes us, whether that makes me responsible for what happens to them if they take my words seriously." He shook his head; his eyes fixed on the dying coals. "That question has followed me all day. It unsettled me more than Dr. Ellis's silly gossip, more than the dean's warning."

Dr. Marlowe's lips curved faintly, not in amusement but in recognition. "And does it not prove your point? That truth, even in fragments, awakens those who are meant to hear it?"

But Winston did not share her satisfaction. He reached into his coat pocket and withdrew a folded scrap of paper, laying it on the table between them. Dr. Marlowe's eyes flicked down to the Seam's message scrawled in that otherworldly hand:

"Guard the fire from those who come only to warm their hands."

He drew a second note, creased from being carried too long:

"Not all eager are ready."

"Do you see?" His voice was strained now, urgent. "The Seam itself warns me. Clara listens too closely. She is eager, yes—but eagerness is not readiness. What if she is the spark that turns the fire against us? What if the very attention we long for is the ruin they foretold?"

Dr. Marlowe's eyes stayed fixed on the scraps of paper, but her voice was steady. "Or perhaps the Seam warns you not to fear her hunger, but to guide it. To guard, not to withhold. You mistake vigilance for prohibition, Winston. The young will come whether you invite them or not. The question is whether they find you willing to lead."

Her words deepened his dread. For though part of him wanted to believe her, another part feared that in guiding Clara—or anyone—he might betray the Regals themselves. The silence stretched long between them, filled only by the soft crackle of the fire and the weight of knowledge neither could set down.

Dr. Marlowe lifted the slip of paper, her eyes tracing the Seam's words as though weighing their meaning in her own balance. When she looked up, her gaze burned with urgency. "Clara Jennings," she repeated softly, as though testing the name. "You call her dangerous because she listens. But Winston, isn't that precisely what you have long prayed for? A student who refuses to be lulled by comfort, who hears beyond the lecture into the truth?"

Winston stiffened. "And what if she hears too much? What if her hunger outruns her wisdom? I have seen what eagerness can destroy. The Regals warned me that not all are fit to bear the fire." He gestured at the scraps. “Their words are not suggestions, Katherine. They are commandments.”

But she leaned forward, her hand flattening beside the Book. “Or warnings meant to temper you, not silence you. Have you considered that the Regals chose you not simply to carry secrets but to discern who might carry them next? Perhaps Clara is not your threat, Winston. Perhaps she is your test.”

His jaw tightened, the weight of her words pressing hard against his vow. “No. To invite her in would be to betray them. I will not draw her into a covenant she cannot comprehend. If I stumble—if I misjudge—then I have not only doomed her, I have doomed us all.”

Dr. Marlowe’s voice dropped to a whisper, but the whisper was sharper than any shout. “And if your silence dooms her instead? If she is meant to rise, and you smother her calling out of fear... What then, Winston? Whose betrayal would that be?”

The words struck him like a blow. He could not answer.

Asher stirred and pressed his nose against Winston’s hand, grounding him in the ordinary moment while the extraordinary threatened to consume him. At last, Winston forced himself to speak, his voice ragged. “I cannot risk it, Katherine. Not yet. The Seam is watching; the Regals are watching. You ask me to gamble with destinies I cannot even name.”

Her eyes flashed with a mix of frustration and compassion. “I am not asking you to gamble, Winston. I am asking you to trust—that perhaps the regals have already woven Clara into the Seam’s design, and that is your test." She paused and kept a steady gaze in his direction. "Perhaps, your refusal to see this with clarity is the true danger."

The fire guttered then, casting both of their faces into fractured light and shadow, as though the room itself refused to choose sides. Winston sat in silence, the fragments and warnings spread between them, and felt the dread swell: that Dr. Marlowe would not cease until his silence broke, and that Clara's voice had already begun to tip the scales.

The following afternoon, the lecture hall emptied in its usual shuffle of chatter, notebooks closing, and chairs scraping the floor. Winston lingered at the blackboard, his chalk marks half-erased, when he noticed Clara still seated near the front, her books closed but her gaze unbroken. She did not fidget like the others. She waited.

"Miss Jennings," Winston said, his tone deliberately casual, though his pulse quickened, "is there something unclear in today's material?" She rose, gathering her things slowly, and moved closer rather than toward the door. Her voice, calm but intent, carried none of the reverence of the other students.

"No, Professor," she said with a hint of hesitation in her voice. "I understand the material. That's not what troubles me..."

Winston set the chalk down, the faint dust clinging to his fingers. "Then what does trouble you?"

Clara's eyes narrowed slightly, as if measuring how much she dared. "You spoke today of constellations as if they were more than patterns. You said they carry memory. That when we look at them, we are not just observers but participants." She paused, the silence stretching. "So, I need to ask—if that's true, then who first entrusted that memory to us? And why?"

The question struck him with more force than she could know. For a moment, he thought of the cavern under the ice, of the Regals' voices thundering in silence, of the Seam itself shimmering like a wound in the sky. His throat tightened. He could not answer without betraying them—and yet to dismiss her would be to betray himself.

"You press hard, Miss Jennings," he managed at last, keeping his tone level. "Memory, meaning, myth—they are the scaffolding of civilization. We inherit them, but we must also interpret them. That is all."

Clara tilted her head, unsatisfied but undeterred. "And if our interpretation awakens something greater than us?" she asked softly. "What then? Do we stop listening?"

Winston's heart clenched. The words mirrored Dr. Marlowe's challenge from the night before, almost verbatim, as though the Seam itself had found another mouth to speak through. He steadied himself, adjusting his papers to avoid her gaze. "That is not a question I can answer for you," he said, the weight of the half-truth heavy in his chest. "Only you will know when listening becomes danger."

She studied him a moment longer, then nodded, though her eyes held both disappointment and determination. Without another word, she slipped out, leaving the room echoing with her absence. Winston stood alone at the desk, the chalk dust still on his hands. He could feel the Seam's warning notes burning in his pocket, and Dr. Marlowe's voice rising again in memory: "*Perhaps Clara is not your threat, Winston. Perhaps she is your test.*"

The thought chilled him. For if Dr. Marlowe was right, then the Regals had already woven Clara into his path—and his silence might not be obedience at all, but the beginning of betrayal.

TWENTY-FIVE

THE CIRCLE TIGHTENS

By Monday morning, the whispers had hardened into action. Winston returned to campus to find a sealed envelope waiting in his mailbox, stamped with the dean's crest in deep blue wax. The sight of it sent a shiver down his spine. Inside, a single sheet bore the clipped formality of official language:

The Faculty Review Committee requests your attendance to discuss recent reports concerning your lectures. Attendance mandatory. Tuesday, 3 p.m.

The words blurred for a moment, his breath catching. He had seen such summons before—colleagues summoned, questioned, humiliated. Some returned diminished, others never returned at all. Academic freedom had its limits.

The corridors felt different that day. Conversations faltered when he entered; laughter shrank into whispers. Students who had once leaned forward eagerly in his lectures now looked away, as though choosing sides too openly might cost them something. On the quad, two undergraduates debated loudly.

"He's brilliant—he's saying what nobody else dares," one insisted.

"He's dangerous," another snapped. "We're not here to buy into a cult."

In the faculty lounge, the tension was sharper. Winston paused by the half-open door and heard Dr. Ellis's voice cutting above the murmur.

"Mark my words," Dr. Ellis said, "the man's unraveling. First, it's stars and cryptic notes, next it'll be robes and chanting. The committee won't let this stand."

Chatter broke out—thin, brittle, too loud. Winston turned away before they saw him, his stomach churning.

The following afternoon, Winston entered the dean's boardroom. The long oak table gleamed under fluorescent light, its surface polished to a harsh perfection. At its head sat Dean Ashcroft, Dean Hallow, and Dean Hargrove, flanked by three members of the Faculty Review Committee. Their faces wore masks of civility, but their eyes glimmered with judgment.

"Professor Thornberry," Ashcroft began smoothly, "we've received several troubling reports. Students describe your lectures as...unconventional. Some praise them as transformative. Others feel misled, even manipulated. We must ask: are you advancing scholarship, or indulging mysticism under the guise of teaching?"

Winston folded his hands, willing them not to tremble. He spoke slowly, carefully. "I teach my students to observe. To notice what has always been there. The stars are not my invention, Dean. They have shone above us since the beginning. I merely remind them to look."

A committee member leaned forward, adjusting her glasses.

"But you imply more than observation. Students say you speak of hidden truths, of humanity forgetting itself. These claims border on theology, not Archeoastronomy and Comparative Mythology."

The words struck the rawest part of his fear. He swallowed hard. The Regal Ones' warning echoed within him: "*Guard the tongue*".

"I remain within the bounds of scholarship," he replied, his voice steady. "Comparative Mythology, by definition, is a discipline that opens itself to myths and folklore. Let's face it, before man wrote upon clay or papyrus, he wrote upon the sky." Winston took a deep breath. "Every dawn was a revelation...every constellation a chapter in a vast celestial text." He paused, looking carefully around the room at each of the onlookers. "The ancients did not merely *look* at the stars—they *listened* to them. They saw stories written in light: gods who rose, fell, and returned; worlds reborn in fire and flood." Winston cleared his throat and displayed a brief smile. "When we speak of *Archeoastronomy and Comparative Mythology,* we are not engaging in superstition, but in memory—the memory of humanity's first theology, its first science, its first art. The heavens were the classroom, and mankind the attentive student. The tragedy is not that we once looked to the stars for meaning...but that we have forgotten how to look."

Ashcroft's gaze narrowed. "See that your teaching does not slip into indoctrination," he said, showing some resentment.

"I am simply exploring healthy ways to inspire thought and keep the students engaged." Winston let out a loud sigh. "If students draw a larger meaning, maybe I am doing my job by forcing them to think and question things that are not clear."

"The university cannot risk scandal," Ashcroft said. "I suggest that you consider this your first and only caution."

The meeting ended with polite handshakes, but Winston walked out with the air of a man carrying a sentence not yet delivered.

That evening, the rain had set in, tapping against the windowpanes of his study. Winston sat hunched in his chair, with Asher close by, the Book resting closed on the table, its presence heavy as iron.

The house was still, its silence amplified by memory of the committee's words.

Dr. Marlowe arrived without ceremony, shaking the water from her umbrella. She studied him in silence for a moment before speaking.

"They've begun their tightening, haven't they?"

He nodded. "A review. A warning. One misstep, and I'm finished."

Dr. Marlowe removed her coat and sat across from him, her gaze sharp, steady. "Then you must decide whether to retreat—or to hold the line."

His voice cracked under the weight of it. "Every word I say feels like betrayal. If I speak too much, I risk exposing the Seam. If I say too little, I look like a fraud. My daughter thinks I'm mad. My colleagues mock me. Even the dean watches me like a suspect on trial. How long can I walk this line before it swallows me whole?"

Her eyes softened but did not waver.

"That is the burden of witnesses. We are trusted with truths too heavy for the world. Silence preserves, but silence also erodes. It gnaws at the soul until nothing remains but fear."

Winston leaned back, his chest tightening.

"And what if obedience to the Seam means exile from everyone I love? What if telling the truth destroys every relationship I still have?"

She reached forward, her hand hovering above his.

"Then you decide whether truth is worth the exile." She paused. That is a question that only you can answer."

For a moment, the only sound was the crack of the fire. Winston stared at the Book, its cover gleaming faintly in the shifting light. He thought of the notes that kept appearing without explanation—cryptic, insistent, alive. Almost as if the Seam itself were reminding him that he had no choice in being chosen.

"Sometimes I think I'm losing my mind," he whispered.

"You are not losing your mind," Dr. Marlowe said firmly. "You are losing the comfort of certainty. That is not madness. It is awakening."

Her words pierced him, leaving him both comforted and condemned. He slipped a hand into his pocket, almost unconsciously. His fingers brushed some folded paper. Heart pounding, he drew it out. Under the lamp's glow, the message revealed itself:

"Storms strengthen roots."

Winston closed his fist around the note, the paper

crumpling as if sealing the command within him. The storm was no longer distant. It was here—pressing in from the university, from his family, from within his very soul. And now, there was no turning back.

That night, the study appeared to glow faintly with a dim lamplight, as the fire hummed with a deliberate hush. The Book lay where it always did, occupying the center of the table like a presence neither of them invited, yet both obeyed. Winston sat hunched, his hands pressed against his brow, as though the weight of the day had finally tipped into something unbearable.

Dr. Marlowe watched him in silence until at last he spoke.

"On another note," Winston said, his voice low, "Clara Jennings stopped by the office again. She asked me questions I cannot escape."

Dr. Marlowe leaned forward, her expression keen. "What questions?"

He exhaled, the weight of exhaustion finally finding its way out. "She asked who first entrusted us with the stars' memory. And why. And when I faltered, she pressed further—asked what happens if our interpretation awakens something greater than ourselves. Tell me, Katherine, how is it that her words sound like yours?"

Dr. Marlowe's lips curved, not with triumph, but with recognition. "Because the Seam speaks to those who are willing to listen. You hear it in the cavern of ice, I hear it in the fragments we draft, and Clara—she hears it in your words. Don't you see? She is already marked."

Winston stiffened, his hand curling into a fist. "Marked? No. She is a student. A child, in comparison to what we carry. If I allow her to believe she is chosen, I risk shattering her. Or worse—I risk shattering the covenant."

"The covenant," Dr. Marlowe countered, her eyes blazing, "was never meant to calcify into silence. It was meant to guard the flame until others could bear it. Perhaps Clara is one of those others. Perhaps the Seam is giving you what you fear most: a successor."

The word pierced him. Successor. He thought of Elizabeth's laughter in the yard, of Clara's unwavering gaze, of the Regals' warning in the freezing dark: "*Guard the fire.*"

His chest tightened with dread. "Katherine, do you not see the danger?" His voice cracked with desperation. "If I misjudge her readiness, if I mistake hunger for calling, the fire will consume her. And the blame will be mine."

Dr. Marlowe's tone softened, but her words pressed closer.

"And if you misjudge the Seam by refusing to see its choice? What then, Winston?

The study seemed to narrow, shadows thickening around them. Asher stirred at Winston's feet, sensing his turmoil, while the Book lay between them, silent, inscrutable.

Winston closed his eyes. In the darkness behind them, Clara's voice rang again: "*Doesn't that mean you're responsible for what happens to us if we take this seriously?*"

He opened his eyes again slowly, his face pale, his voice barely audible.

"If that is true...then God help me, I am already responsible."

TWENTY-SIX

UNRULY SEEDS

By Thursday night, the lawns of the university looked less like quiet green squares and more like scattered observatories. Blankets stretched across the damp grass, notebooks and sketchpads splayed open, students craning their necks toward the stars. Clara Jennings lay among them, her dark hair spread across the blanket like an ink stain, her journal steady in her lap. She drew slow, deliberate lines, mapping constellations as if they might rearrange themselves under her gaze. Around her, two classmates debated in hushed tones whether the exercise was absurd or profound. Clara said nothing. She had no interest in debate. She was listening—for the silence, for the pattern beneath the pattern.

Others were less quiet. A group near the fountain laughed as one of them pretended to "hear voices in the stars." Another claimed he had dreamt of light pressing through his eyelids all night. Some treated it as a kind of performance art. Yet even their laughter had an edge of nervousness, as if mocking it was safer than admitting curiosity. By dawn, photographs were appearing online—grainy shots of star maps scribbled in margins, captions reading *Thornberry's Map* and *Find the Seam*. A student-run blog carried a post titled *The Thornberry Effect: Why Students Are Sleeping Under the Stars*. It described "a movement" forming—half academic, half mystical, entirely intoxicating.

When Winston arrived for class the next day, the room hummed with expectancy. Students leaned forward before he spoke, notebooks poised, eyes sharp with hunger—even those who had previously dismissed him now watched with wary fascination. Clara sat in the front row, her gaze direct, unwavering, as if she had already decided this was no ordinary class but a crossing.

He began with caution, reciting historical references, weaving the safer fragments of observation. But midway through, Clara raised her hand.

"Professor," she said, her voice clear and steady, "if attention changes what we see, doesn't that mean you've already changed us by showing us where to look?"

The question hung in the air. Students shifted in their seats, pencils suspended.

Winston felt the Seam's hum like static in the back of his mind:

"Guard the tongue."

Yet Clara's words demanded more than silence. He cleared his throat. "Perhaps. But change does not always mean control. To see differently is not to be mastered—it is to be invited."

A murmur rippled across the room, pens scratching furiously as though his words might contain an equation.

Clara tilted her head, her eyes narrowing with a mix of wonder and challenge. Winston felt the weight of her attention like a hand pressing against his chest.

After class, Clara lingered again. Winston felt the pull of her presence before he even reached the door.

"You didn't answer me," she said quietly.

He stopped, weary. "Some questions aren't meant to be answered quickly."

"Or at all?" she pressed.

Her voice wasn't hostile—it was intent, almost pleading. Winston saw in her the dangerous mix of youthful certainty and unshakable curiosity. He wanted to tell her everything and nothing in the same breath. Instead, he shook his head. "Be careful, Clara. Curiosity is a gift—but it can also be a fire."

She studied him for a long moment, then smiled faintly. "Fires bring light, too, Professor."

With that, she turned and walked away, leaving Winston unsettled, her words echoing in his ears.

Later that evening, Winston overheard Dr. Ellis in the faculty lounge, relishing the commotion. "Have you seen them?" the man crowed, his voice pitched high enough to draw a small circle of colleagues in the faculty lounge. "Students sprawled on the grass like druids, scribbling charts as though the heavens would deliver their exams. Thornberry's turned the campus into a carnival." The laughter that followed was sharp and gleeful, like glass breaking. A few professors shook their heads; others smiled behind their coffee cups.

Again, not everyone laughed.

Dr. Khan, younger than his colleagues, his eyes

shadowed from too many late nights, muttered just loud enough to be heard: "Say what you will—he's got them thinking. That's more than most of us manage." He paused. "Most of us are lucky if the students bother to show up, but I hear that Dr. Thornberry's classes are packed, every day, and students are literally showing up half an hour early just to get a seat." "He must be doing something right to get that kind of' turnout and, from what I hear, one hundred percent participation."

Dr. Ellis ignored him, struggling to regain control of the conversation by fanning the flames with fresh rumor. "Next week it'll be rituals, mark my words. And when the committee hears about students chasing visions in their dreams, they'll have no choice but to shut him down." A murmur rippled. Some professors exchanged uneasy glances. Others smirked, eager to see the drama play out.

One older lecturer, Dr. Morgan, spoke with weariness rather than malice. "There's a line, Dr. Ellis. We're meant to expand minds, yes, but not to untether them from reality. If Thornberry's work tips them toward obsession, then maybe—just maybe—you're right. We owe it to them to step in." Dr. Morgan paused. "However, if he is on to some new teaching technique that opens the students' minds to critical thinking, then, maybe, just maybe we owe him an apology...?"

Dr. Khan straightened at that, his voice cutting in more firmly now. "Or maybe the handwriting is on the wall, and we owe it to them to trust that hunger for knowledge isn't a disease. What are we so afraid of? That they might ask questions we can't answer?"

A silence fell, heavy, broken only by the hum of the vending machine. For a moment, it seemed the weight of Dr. Khan's words might hold. But Dr. Ellis scoffed, breaking the spell.

"Afraid? No. Amused. Thornberry's feeding them poetry dressed as science, prophecy dressed as scholarship. And when they fail their exams or worse—when one of them goes mad chasing his fictions—it won't be amusing anymore."

Outside, the campus bore out both sides of the argument. On the central lawn, clusters of students hunched over notebooks, chalking constellations onto sidewalks, comparing fragments of phrases passed from hand to hand. Some whispered as though guarding sacred truths; others laughed and doodled caricatures of Winston on their pages, mockery disguised as wit.

Clara stood at the center of a small circle, her notebook open, her voice low but fervent. "They're not symbols. The patterns are alive. If you let them, they change you. That's what he's teaching us."

A boy across from her rolled his eyes. "Change us? You sound like a convert. Next, you'll be saying Thornberry's a prophet."

"Not a prophet," Clara shot back, her tone sharpening. "A witness..."

The word landed with force. Some in the circle shifted uneasily; others leaned closer. Another student, softer, asked, "But what if Dr. Ellis is right? What if it's just words? We're building towers out of fog."

Clara held their gaze, her voice steady. "And what if it isn't? What if the fog is the doorway, not the distraction? Don't you feel it—when you trace the patterns, when you speak the fragments? Something greater is pressing on us, waiting to be recognized."

The debate swelled, voices overlapping. Accusations of fanaticism clashed with cries for freedom of thought. What had begun as classroom curiosity had blossomed into something unruly, uncontrollable—a seed scattered on soil no one could measure. And somewhere, watching from the library steps, Winston felt both pride and dread twist together in his chest. Pride that the hunger was real. Dread that it might devour them before they were ready. He remembered the Seam's warning: "*Not all eager are ready.*" And he wondered, as the laughter of skeptics tangled with the chants of believers, whether the actual test had finally begun—not of knowledge, but of discernment.

That evening, Winston's study felt smaller than usual, its walls pressing inward as though echoing the voices he had overheard on the lawn and in the faculty lounge. The Book rested between them, still and terrible, its silence more commanding than speech. Winston poured a measure of tea but did not drink. His hand trembled as he set the cup aside.

"They're no longer whispering," he said at last, his voice low. "The campus is divided—students shouting across the lawn, professors trading barbs in the lounge. Dr. Ellis crows like a rooster every chance he gets, mocking them as druids. And yet...Clara stands in their midst like a flame that will not be put out."

Dr. Marlowe leaned forward, her eyes catching the lamplight. "Then the fire has caught. What you feared is now upon us. But Winston—don't you see? This is not disorder. This is the Seam pressing outward, breaking through the walls you tried to build around it."

He shook his head, running a weary hand across his brow. "Pressing outward, yes—but not with order. It's chaos, Katherine. Half mock, half worship. Some are sketching constellations in the dirt, others are laughing at them as if they were children playing at prophecy. The faculty grows restless. The dean watches. If this continues, I will be discredited entirely."

"Discredited to men," Dr. Marlowe countered, her voice taut, "but not to the Regals. What does their judgment matter if the Seam itself is moving?"

Her words cut deep, but Winston pressed back, his voice hardening. "It matters because the Seam warned me: *Not all eager are ready*. If I fail to guard the fire, then I am complicit in their ruin. What happens if Clara or any of them mistake hunger for readiness and burn themselves on truths they cannot bear?"

Dr. Marlowe did not flinch. "Then you teach them how to bear it. That is the call, Winston—not silence, but shepherding. Not hoarding, but guiding. The Seam entrusted you with fragments, not to bury them, but to scatter them. You are afraid because you cannot control how they grow. But seeds were never meant to be controlled." Her voice softened. "You call it chaos. I call it awakening. The world is straining toward what has been hidden. If you refuse to lead them, they will follow their hunger blindly. But if you stand before them, the fragments will find their true shape."

Winston's chest tightened as he remembered the

students sprawled on the grass, Clara's voice rising above them: "*Not a prophet—a witness.*"

He whispered, almost to himself, "And what if I am not worthy to lead them?"

Dr. Marlowe's reply came without hesitation. "Then the Seam would have chosen another. But it chose you."

The words hung between them like a verdict. Winston sat in silence, the fire guttering low, feeling the weight of inevitability settle upon him. Outside, the campus murmured with restless voices, and he knew that whether he wished it or not, the tide was turning. He slipped a hand into his coat pocket and felt the crinkle of paper. Another note. He unfolded it beneath the glow of the fire.

"*Seeds grow whether sown or scattered. Tend with care.*"

The words chilled him more than they comforted. For the first time, he felt the truth of what Dr. Marlowe had warned: "*once loosed, some truths could not be contained.*" The students had taken his fragments and turned them into seeds. And already, the ground was restless.

TWENTY-SEVEN

FAULT LINES

The article found her before he could. His daughter texted a link without preamble—photos of students on blankets under a hard winter sky, headlines calling it *The Thornberry Effect* as if curiosity were a contagion. Beneath it, a message:

"We need to talk. Tonight."

She arrived at dusk, the air brittle with cold and the smell of snow held somewhere in the clouds. Asher barked once, then settled, tail wagging with cautious hope. Winston opened the door and stepped aside, also feeling hopeful that old wounds would be forgiven quickly.

Elizabeth pushed her way into the house and immediately started in on him.

"It's everywhere," she said, removing her gloves with careful fury. "Your students. The blog. People at work sent it to me like a joke."

He gestured toward the living room. "Come in. Please."

She shook her head, hovering at the threshold. "Are you doing this on purpose?"

"Doing what?" he asked softly.

"Becoming a spectacle." The word broke on her tongue. "If this is a cry for help, then say it. If it's not—then what the hell is it?"

He searched her face and found the child he had failed: the crooked brow when puzzled, the set of her jaw when she fought tears. The sight pierced him.

"I am not trying to be anything," he said. "I am trying to teach...the only way I know how to."

She let out a short laugh—too sharp to be amused. "Teach? The campus thinks you're starting a movement. Mom says you're starting a cult." She smirked. "So exactly what are you doing? Is Mom right? Are you starting a cult?"

"Your mother is entitled to her opinion," he replied, and winced at his own stiffness.

She stepped past him at last, into the room he kept too tidy when he was afraid. Her eyes landed on the desk, on the neat stack of notebooks beside a closed, old book whose presence seemed to deepen the light around it. Asher pressed his head against her knee, and she stroked him reflexively. "You missed my wedding," she said, not looking at him. "You vanished. Now you're everywhere for strangers. Where was this for me?"

The question struck like a thrown stone, but he did not dodge it.

"I missed your wedding, young lady, because you made it pretty darn clear that you didn't want me there!" he snapped back at her. "I vanished, as you say, because you made it clear that you didn't want me around. I have no defense that doesn't sound like an excuse. You can take it or leave it...but the truth is I was called away, and what I saw changed me."

She turned then, eyes bright with anger and something else—a trembling glaze of fear. "Called by what? You keep saying that...the Seam? The Book? Dad, listen to yourself." She swallowed. "What does all of this mean?

Winston folded his arms and began pacing by the fireplace.

"And you're breaking your silence now by—what? —recruiting freshmen to stargaze?"

He exhaled and continued pacing back and forth, as he was known for doing when truth threatened to spill.

"I am giving them what I can without breaking what must be kept. A way to attend. A way to remember."

She stared at him as if through glass. "Do you hear yourself? You talk like someone who's gone too far and can't come back. You might as well be speaking in riddles."

"Maybe, that's what you believe, but I am trying," he said, the words rough. "I am trying to come back without lying about where I've been."

Asher whined softly. Snow began to tap at the windows, the sound a faint brushing, as if the night was trying to wash them clean. Elizabeth was now pacing in front of the mantle too, before she stopped abruptly.

"People at my office are sending me memes, Dad... Friends call to ask if I'm okay. Do you know what that feels like? To be the punchline for someone else's enlightenment?"

Winston stood. "I don't want you to pay for my choices."

"But I am, *again*." She drew a breath, steadying herself. "I came here to ask you to stop. Withdraw from the class for the semester. Tell them it was an experiment you regret. Let this die."

He felt the words as a door closing. Behind it, a life he could step back into if he disowned the path he had already taken. His chest ached with the temptation.

"I can't," he said at last. "I can be careful. I can be slow. But I cannot un-know."

Her face went still, then hardened. "Then you are choosing them over me."

"I am choosing," he said, voice barely audible, "what I believe I was given to carry."

For a heartbeat, he thought she might strike him. Instead, she looked at the door, then at him, then at Asher, as if deciding which goodbye belonged to which creature. "If you won't save yourself," she said, "save your students. They are not ready for whatever you think you found."

She reached for her coat and he stepped forward, hands open, palms empty. "I want to see you," he said slowly. "But, maybe outside of this. Coffee... A walk. Say when..."

"After the headlines stop," she answered. "After people stop saying your name like a warning." She tugged her sleeve free of Asher's nose, then bent to kiss his head. "Be good for him," she whispered to the dog, then added in a broken tone, "He's made his choice."

The door closed with a softness that hurt more than any slam. The snow's tapping filled the space she left. He stood a long time, the room blurring at the edges, then returned to the desk. The Book waited. He did not open it. He pressed his palm against the cover as if to test whether warmth rose from it or sank into it.

A knock startled him. For a moment, he thought Elizabeth had reconsidered. But when he opened the door, Dr. Marlowe stood on the stoop, hair dusted with snow, eyes taking everything in with a single sweep.

"Bad time?" she asked.

"Always," he said, but he stepped aside.

She entered, ungloved hands red from the cold. "I saw the latest article," she said. "Students are planning an all-night watch this weekend. A hundred, perhaps more."

He closed his eyes. "Unruly seeds."

"Seeds do not ask permission," she said gently. She studied his face. "You've been crying."

He shook his head, then gave up the pretense. "My daughter. She wants me to stop."

"And can you?"

"No." He paused while walking over to a nearby chair. "She doesn't know what she is asking of me."

"Then you must decide how to protect her from what you cannot stop," Dr. Marlowe said. She sat, leaning forward. "And protect the students from themselves." She paused. "You are capable of doing all of it, you know..."

"How?" he asked. "The dean circles. Dr. Ellis

circles. My family breaks. The students gather as if on pilgrimage. What am I supposed to do—issue a press release from the Seam?"

He was shouting now, displaying his defeat in the situation.

Dr. Marlowe's mouth tilted, almost a smile. "No. But you can name boundaries. You can teach them what not to do."

He laughed once, bitter as iron. "You suppose they'll listen?"

"They listened when you pointed at the sky," she said. "They may listen when you point at the edge."

He rubbed his eyes. "The edge?"

She nodded. "Yes. The line between attention and obsession. Between seeing and seeking to control. Between humility and hunger." She paused. "Invite them to the first line and warn them of the second."

He thought of Clara's face, bright and unyielding. "Some will cross anyway."

"Some always do," Dr. Marlowe said. "But you will have done your part. And if you do it publicly—clearly—the university will have less ground to claim harm."

Winston sat back, the shape of a plan forming like frost on glass—delicate, temporary, but visible.

"A public statement," he said. "Guidelines, not gospel. And a change to the syllabus: observation as discipline, not as promise."

Dr. Marlowe watched him with something like relief crossing her features. "Good. We'll draft it tonight."

They worked in near silence, only the scratch of pens and the crackle of the fire counting time. Asher shifted from Winston's feet to Dr. Marlowe's and back again, making small, contented sounds as if satisfied that the room had found its shape.

Winston wrote: *Observe without naming. Record without interpreting. Share without persuading. Rest before repeating. Stop when the work makes you proud.*

Marlowe added: *No solitary vigils. No sleep deprivation. Pair observation with practical care—water, warmth, returning to the body.*

They debated terms, softened blunt edges into invitations, and sharpened vague cautions into clear ones. Outside, the snow thickened, the night brightening with the slow fall of light. When they finished, Dr. Marlowe set her pen down. "This won't satisfy the wolves," she said, meaning Dr. Ellis, the committee, the hungry anonymous crowd. "But it may save a few lambs."

Winston folded the page. "And perhaps save me from myself." A silence followed—not empty, but full, as if the house approved. Then Winston, almost absently, slipped his hand into his coat pocket. His fingers closed on another small folded note he did not remember placing there.

She saw the change in his face. "Another?"

He nodded, unfolding it with a care that felt like prayer. The script curled darkly across the paper, the letters like tracks left in new snow.

"Not all storms are weather."

He read it twice, then passed it to her. She held it

as if it might burn, then set it gently on the table between them.

"What will you do?" she asked.

"Tomorrow," he said, "I will call the dean and share the guidelines before the students announce their watch. I will ask for a room, chairs, hot tea—anything that makes it civilized instead of clandestine."

"And your daughter?"

He swallowed. "I will write to her tonight. Not to convince her. To tell her I know the cost."

They sat until the fire sank to a red seam, the room thinning into its late-hour hush. When Dr. Marlowe left, the snow had stopped, and the streetlights turned the world to glass. Winston stood at the door a long time, the cold coming in like a truth he could bear. He returned to the desk. The Book remained closed, a dark island in the woods. He did not open it. He pressed his hand to its cover the way one might lay a palm against a sleeping animal, aware of the power under its skin.

"Asher," he said softly, "stay."

The dog settled with the sigh of one who had heard this command and obeyed it through many storms.

Winston turned off the lamp. The room held its breath, then released it. In the quiet that followed, he felt the fault lines of his life—family, work, calling—shift, then settle, not healed but aligned, for now, along a single intention: to tend without feeding the fire. To speak without breaking the Seam. To hold.

TWENTY-EIGHT

THE CHARGE TO SPEAK

Winston drifted in his chair, head bowed against the weight of exhaustion. Around him, the study was quiet, though beyond the walls he sensed the campus pulsing with unrest—students gathering, faculty whispering, reporters prowling. His breath slowed, and the glow of the fire blurred into darkness until he no longer felt the floor beneath his feet.

The cold struck him first—that old, biting cold that belonged to the ice at the top of the world. He opened his eyes and found himself once again at the edge of the Seam, its vast chasm glowing faintly, pulsing as though alive. The air thrummed with a resonance he had not felt since that first encounter.

He knew he was dreaming, but the dream carried the weight of command.

From the Seam came voices, woven into harmony:

"You have guarded. You have resisted. You have feared. But the hour has ripened. Speak."

The light within the Seam swelled, spreading across

the ice, illuminating Winston's form until he trembled beneath it.

"The Book was not given for silence. It was entrusted for preparation. A century it has waited, its truth guarded by watchers, its purpose obscured by time. Now, as the world staggers in confusion, the seed must be sown. Tell them: the Book is not of human invention, but of higher trust. It bears the story of their origin, their destiny, and the way of progress that is not power, but service. Speak to them, Winston. Speak as witness."

The vision seared into him, filling his chest with both awe and dread. He opened his mouth but found only two words: "Why me?"

The Seam's reply was like the tolling of a bell across endless miles of ice.

"Because you listened when others mocked. Because you bore silence without surrender. Because you are not its owner, but its servant. Now share. Guide. Prepare."

The light folded back into the Seam, and Winston gasped awake. His study returned—fire low, Asher curled at his feet, the Book silent but humming faintly beneath its cover. He sat motionless, the echo of the command still vibrating through him.

Outside, the tide had turned. Students filled the quad, their voices not divided but unified now, signs and petitions raised high:

"LET HIM TEACH."

"TRUTH IS NOT TREASON."

"WE CHOOSE TO LISTEN."

Their chants rolled like waves against the administration building, strong enough to drown the mutters of faculty dissent. Yet inside, jealousy brewed. Dr. Ellis moved through the corridors with sharp words and sharper eyes, muttering of cults and chaos, telling anyone who would listen that Thornberry's folly was unworthy of the honor it was receiving.

Dr. Khan, by contrast, stood quietly at the edge of the crowd, his arms folded, watching with a strange half-smile. "Say what you will," he murmured to his colleague, Dr. Morgan, "but this is what awakening looks like." He laughed briefly. "The campus is alive."

And above the crowd, cameras lifted on tripods. Major news stations had arrived; the hungry mouths of the world pressing in to devour or defend. Satellite vans lined the streets. Reporters shouted questions no one could answer. The quad had transformed into an impromptu amphitheater. Students pressed shoulder to shoulder, their signs swaying above the crowd like banners at some forgotten festival. Faculty lingered at the edges, some curious, some hostile, others uneasy with the spectacle. The media's cameras loomed over it all, red lights blinking, microphones bristling like spears.

When Winston stepped onto the stone steps of the administration building, a hush spread, rolling outward until even the birds seemed to hold their flight. He stood for a long moment, his hand resting on the rail, his breath steadying. The Book lay against his chest, not as an ornament but as a burden.

"I did not come to seek this," he began, his voice low, yet carried by the strange stillness that had fallen. "I am a teacher, nothing more. But sometimes teaching leads us into places we never wished to go. Sometimes it shows us doors that cannot be closed once opened."

A murmur rippled through the students, but they listened.

"You've asked what this Book is. You've whispered about its origin, its power, its danger. I will tell you what I can." He lifted it slightly, the leather gleaming in the camera lights. "It is not new. It did not come to me first. For a hundred years, it has been kept, guarded, waiting. It was entrusted to men and women long before you and me, not for ownership but for safekeeping. Its purpose is not to make prophets, nor kings, but servants."

He paused, searching the sea of faces, seeing Clara among them, her eyes alight with both hunger and fear.

"This Book bears a story greater than ours—the story of where we came from, and where we are meant to go. It speaks of a universe alive with order, not chaos; of life that stretches beyond our small world, of a destiny that is not random but entrusted. It tells us that greatness is not in conquest but in service, not in domination but in cooperation. That the measure of a civilization is not its wealth or weapons, but its ability to love, to heal, to lift its weakest without hesitation."

The crowd was silent, the cameras clicking like distant rain. Winston's voice grew steadier, as though carried by something beyond himself.

"I was told to guard it, and I did. I was told to keep silent, and I obeyed. But now the command has changed. I was told: *Speak*. And so, I will speak. Not everything—not yet. But enough to show you that we are not abandoned wanderers in a cold universe. We are children of a vast design. And though we stumble in ignorance and pride, the hand of mercy has not withdrawn."

He lowered the Book slowly, his voice quiet now, though it struck with greater force than before.

"If you remember nothing else, remember this: the truth is not given to make us powerful, but to make us faithful. We are not its owners. We are its witnesses."

For a long moment, silence blanketed the quad. Then, as if on cue, the students erupted—not in chants this time, but in applause, raw and thunderous, breaking against the walls of the campus and carrying out into the waiting streets.

Dr. Ellis, standing with his arms crossed at the edge of the crowd, muttered curses under his breath. Dr. Khan closed his eyes, a quiet smile tugging at his lips. And Clara stood motionless, her notebook clutched tight against her chest, her face pale but burning with something Winston recognized all too well: recognition. From the steps, Winston felt the air shift. He knew this was not the end—perhaps only the beginning. Yet for the first time, the weight in his chest felt less like a chain and more like a commission.

The applause still rolled across the quad when the first microphones surged forward. Reporters pushed through the students like hunters in a crowd, shouting questions in rapid succession.

"Professor Thornberry, are you claiming divine revelation?"

"Who gave you this Book? Is it authentic history or invention?"

"Do you fear disciplinary action from the Board?"

Winston did not answer. His words had already been spoken; the rest belonged to their echoes. He lifted one hand in quiet acknowledgment of the students, then turned and descended the steps, Asher trotting close behind.

By the time he reached the archway, headlines were already being written.

Campus Prophet or Academic Fraud?

Thornberry Defies Silence.

Ancient Book Sparks Modern Uprising.

The glow of camera lights made the evening air feel like a storm of fireflies, frantic and merciless. In the faculty lounge, the mood fractured like glass under strain. Dr. Ellis slammed a newspaper against the table; his face flushed with triumph and outrage.

"This is it. The man's lost his mind—and now he's dragged the university into his circus. Cameras on the lawn, students chanting like zealots—he's turned scholarship into spectacle. Do you not see the danger?"

Dr. Khan spoke softly, but his words cut through the noise. "I see danger, yes. But I also see hunger. Tell me, Dr. Ellis—when was the last time students fought to be heard because of your lectures?"

The room stirred with uneasy laughter, some siding with Dr. Ellis, others with Khan. Dr. Morgan, leaning heavily on her cane, shook her head.

"You're both wrong. This is not about lectures or fame. This is about a wound that's been opened. Whether it heals or festers depends on how we tend it."

Dr. Ellis sneered. "Poetic nonsense. The only

tending we should do is to excise Thornberry before he poisons the whole institution."

Outside, the students had already chosen their side. They swarmed the library steps, holding vigils with lanterns, copying fragments of Winston's words into notebooks and across the screens of their phones. Some sang. Others argued. But all remained.

Clara stood among them, her eyes still alight from his speech. To her peers, she whispered, "Did you hear him? We are not owners, we are witnesses. Do you see what that means? It means the story isn't his alone—it belongs to all of us." Her voice carried, and those nearest wrote her words as quickly as they had written his. Within minutes, they were already circling the crowd, spreading like wildfire:

Not owners. Witnesses.

From his study window, Winston watched the lanterns flicker in the darkness, each one a fragile light against the night. Dr. Marlowe sat across from him, her expression fierce with conviction. "You see it, don't you?" she said. "They are no longer yours to hold back. The Book has leapt from your hands to theirs. And that, Winston, was always its design."

He said nothing, only pressed his palms against the table to steady himself. For though her words rang true, he also remembered the Seam's warning: "*Not all eager are ready.*"

Between the chants of devotion outside and the threats of derision within, he felt the narrow path closing in around him. And yet, deep in his chest, the echo of the Seam's voice endured: "*Speak. Guide. Prepare.*"

It was both command and comfort, and though fear still clung to him, Winston knew the time for silence had ended.

TWENTY-NINE

THE TRIBUNAL OF LIGHT

The summons arrived on university letterhead, crisp and cold:

Dr. Winston Thornberry is to appear before the Academic Review Committee at 9:00 a.m. in Administration Hall.

Winston read it in silence, the paper trembling in his hand. He had known this was coming—the dean's warnings, Dr. Ellis's fury, the headlines splashed across newspapers and screens had all led to this moment. Still, the words landed with a finality that weighed on his chest.

That morning, the halls of the administration building pulsed with voices. Students lined the stairways and spilled out onto the quad, holding lanterns and notebooks, fragments of his speech scrawled on signs:

"WE ARE NOT OWNERS, WE ARE WITNESSES."

"LET HIM SPEAK."

"TRUTH IS NOT TREASON."

Their chanting rose in waves, muffled through the heavy wooden doors as Winston entered.

Inside, the committee chamber was stark—a long oak table, portraits of former chancellors staring down from the walls, and seven professors seated like judges in a tribunal. Dean Hargrove presided at the center, his expression polished into neutrality. Dr. Ellis sat further down, his face flushed with anticipation, his eyes bright with malice.

Winston took his seat at the opposite end of the table. His hands rested on the Book in front of him, its leather cool beneath his palms.

"Professor Thornberry," the dean began, his voice measured.

"You are here because concerns have been raised regarding your lectures, your influence upon the student body, and the recent public disruptions. This committee has been convened to determine whether your teaching has strayed from academic rigor into dangerous territory."

Dr. Ellis leaned forward, unable to restrain himself. "Dangerous is too mild a word. He's turned scholarship into superstition. The students speak of visions and revelations, not astronomy or history. He encourages them to see him as some prophet. It is unbecoming of this institution."

The dean raised a hand to still him. "We will hear from Professor Thornberry first."

Winston rose slowly, his voice steady but carrying the weight of sleepless nights. "I never sought to be a prophet," he said. "I am a teacher. I pointed to the stars and asked my students not to memorize them, but to see. To wonder. To ask what lies beyond the charts we inherit. And they responded—not with rebellion, but with hunger. Hunger for meaning, hunger for truth. Is that dangerous?"

Winston smiled faintly, not with scorn but with the quiet sadness of a man who has lived too long with misunderstanding.

Murmurs stirred among the professors.

Dr. Ellis slammed his hand on the table. "You gave them more than wonder—you gave them the illusion of revelation! You let them believe you possess a secret truth."

Winston met his gaze. "I did not give them illusion. I gave them fragments entrusted to me. Fragments meant to remind us that we are not wanderers in chaos but participants in a greater design. That our measure is not in conquest, but in service. That truth, wherever it appears, is not to make us powerful, but to make us faithful." His voice grew stronger, rising above the chamber. "If that is dangerous, then perhaps it is only dangerous to our pride—that we must admit the universe is larger than our syllabi, that mystery cannot be locked in a curriculum, that wisdom sometimes comes as a gift, not achievement."

The room was silent, every eye upon him. Even the portraits seemed to lean closer.

Then the meeting was interrupted by a telephone call.

The dean frowned and answered it.

"I asked you to hold my calls during this meeting," he said. The waiting guests looked on. "What?" The dean's hands began to tremble. "I see..." He ended the call abruptly. "Now, where were we?"

Winston gave him a mysterious look and slowly placed a hand on the Book. "I was told to guard it, and I did. I was told to keep silent, and I obeyed. But now I am told to speak. Not everything—not recklessly—but enough to awaken those who are ready. Not as prophet, not as master. As witness."

He looked down the long table, his eyes sweeping from professor to professor. "So, I ask you—what is the purpose of this institution? To train minds to repeat what they are told? Or to give them courage to face truths that unsettle them, truths that might lift them beyond themselves?"

His words lingered like incense. No one spoke for a long time. Even Dr. Ellis's mouth hung half-open, his fury robbed of its force. Then from outside the chamber came a sound—students' voices rising in chorus, their chant carrying through the stone walls:

"We are not owners! We are witnesses!"

The committee members shifted, some visibly shaken. The dean cleared his throat, his mask of neutrality faltering for the first time.

"This matter," he said, his voice less steady than before, "requires deliberation. We will recess."

And, just like that, the meeting was over.

Winston bowed his head, his hands still resting on the Book. He knew this was not the final word. But something had shifted in the air—not victory, not yet, but a recognition that truth had spoken, and could not easily be silenced.

"I hope you know this isn't over," Dr. Ellis said, displaying his frustration.

Winston stared at the man for a moment before speaking. "The tragedy," he said finally, "is not that we once looked to the stars for meaning—but that we've forgotten how to look."

Silence reclaimed the room as Dr. Ellis lowered his eyes.

Winston exhaled, his heart steady, and whispered inwardly: "*Speak. Guide. Prepare.*"

CHAPTER THIRTY

AFTERMATH OF THE TRIBUNAL

The committee recessed, but the hush they left behind did not feel like silence. It felt like breath held too long.

Outside, the chant continued—"We are not owners! We are witnesses!"—not frantic now but steady, as if the students had discovered a cadence that could outlast threat. Lanterns bobbed in the daylight like improbable stars. Winston stepped through the doors into their brightness and felt the world tilt: cameras pivoted, microphones rose, and yet his eyes went first to his students—their faces alert, unafraid, expectant. Clara stood near the front, not shouting, only watching him with that unsettling calm that saw past his words into the vow beneath them.

"As you were," he murmured, a hand lifted, and a soft ripple of relief moved through the crowd. He did not stay to feed the cameras. The speech had already been given; anything more would be repetition, and repetition would cheapen the charge. Inside the antechamber, the committee divided into murmuring constellations.

Dean Hargrove removed his glasses and polished them with unnecessary care. "We cannot appear to endorse mysticism," he said, "but I cannot ignore the fact that the school has received over two hundred and fifty million dollars in pledges and donations since all of this started."

Dr. Morgan—older, tired, keen—folded her hands on the table. "We need not endorse it," she replied. "We can recognize integrity when we see it."

A younger member, Dr. Sato, spoke carefully, as if each word might be subpoenaed. "He meets his classes. He assigns readings. The disruption originated in the response to his teaching, not its absence. If we censure him for awakening them, we censure ourselves for sleeping." He paused. "That is not scholarship!"

Dr. Ellis could not remain seated. He stood, the edge of his folder biting crescents into his palms. "Awakening? To what? To his private gospel? You heard him—'entrusted fragments', 'greater design'. This is not instruction; it is evangel."

"It is witness," Dr. Morgan said, surprising herself with the gentleness of the word. "And witness, unlike doctrine, admits it is not the source."

Dean Hargrove set his glasses down, a small surrender. "We will reconvene with a draft—guidelines for extraordinary instruction." He glanced toward the doors where the chant seeped under the wood like an insistent tide. "In the meantime, no suspension. Not yet."

Dr. Ellis's jaw worked, the verdict sticking like a fishbone in his throat.

On the lawn, Clara moved among clusters of students as if threading beads onto a single cord. "Tonight—no grand gestures," she told them. "No bonfires. No trespass. We keep vigil, we study, we help one another understand what we heard." She held up a notebook. Written on the open page: *Witness over ownership—service over spectacle.*

A first year with ink-smudged fingers asked, "Clara...what if this is a spectacle? The cameras, the chants. What if we're just...noisy?"

Clara considered. "Noise passes. Vows remain. We make vows—small, concrete. To study, to serve, to tell the truth when it costs us. If this ends as performance, it ends as nothing."

They nodded, and the phrase—*vows remain*—began to circulate, copied into margins and message threads, an anchor against the storm of attention.

Dr. Ellis crossed the quad with the purposeful stride of a man who has mistaken bitterness for backbone. He drew alongside Dr. Khan at the library steps.

"Enjoying the revival?" Dr. Ellis asked, voice bright with caustic cheer.

Khan didn't rise. "I'm watching students read on a Friday afternoon. It's unnerving. And, frankly...it's freaking beautiful."

Dr. Ellis's smile thinned. "There will be a reckoning. I will not let the discipline I have spent my life protecting be traded for incense and riddles."

Dr. Khan's eyes followed Clara as she knelt to explain a star map to two first-years. "Perhaps what you call incense is the breath we've been missing."

Dr. Ellis turned away, but not before Dr. Khan saw the thing he kept hidden beneath wit: fear. Not of heresy. Of irrelevance.

At dusk, the cameras receded and the lanterns returned. Winston's study was filled with the twilight hush that always made the room seem larger, like a lung readying for breath. Dr. Marlowe sat at the table with him, the Book between them, the leather dulled by handling into a kind of soft, obedient sheen.

"They did not silence you," she said.

"Not yet." He rubbed the bridge of his nose. "Hargrove will craft a narrow path and call it mercy."

"Mercy is still mercy," she said. "Even when it comes as policy."

He almost smiled. "The students have made a covenant with one another." He described Clara's phrase—*vows remain*—and felt a peculiar loosening in his chest. "They took the message where I feared to go."

"As they must," Dr. Marlowe answered. "You were never asked to control the tide. Only to announce it."

He looked down at the Book. "In the dream, the charge was simple. Speak. Guide. Prepare. I am startled by how little and how much that is."

Dr. Marlowe reached to the margin of a blank page and wrote, in a small, steady hand:

Preparation is the grammar of revelation. She slid the page toward him.

"Tomorrow, you begin a seminar. Limited seats. Open notes. No spectacle. Let those who are willing to serve, learn to listen."

Winston listened to the quiet between her words and found in it the shape of assent.

Night fell without ceremony. On the quad, students formed circles with their lanterns and read to one another—not only Winston's fragments, but histories, poems, and the incredible clarity of charts.

Clara spoke last. "No one owns this," she said, voice carrying just enough to reach the edges. "We are keepers, not claimants. If we cannot serve one another, we have misunderstood everything."

They answered not with applause but with stillness. The crickets resumed their liturgy. Above, the sky opened like a meticulously folded letter. Clara closed her notebook, slid a scrap inside without looking at it—one she had found tucked beneath her dorm door at dusk, ink unfamiliar, the phrasing not quite human:

"Guard the fire by giving it purpose."

She did not show anyone. Not yet. But when she raised her eyes to the constellations, something in their arrangement felt less like scattered fact and more like promise.

Later, alone, Winston stood at his window and watched the lanterns dim. The day had rounded off its sharpest edges; the tribunal's words no longer scraped, and even Dr. Ellis's face had receded to the size of a solvable worry. He should have felt triumph. He felt instead a rightness that was not triumph—like, a tool returned to the hand that knew its use.

"Asher," he said softly, and the dog lifted his head. "We are being lifted into something we did not design."

He thought of the North—the Seam like a wound

and a door—and of the voice braided from many: "*Because you are not its owner, but its servant.*"

He rested his palm on the Book. It was cool, and he realized the hum he had sometimes feared was not warning but welcome, like a boat's hull answering a river's current.

"Very well," he whispered, not to the Book, not to the night, but to the One who had authored both. "I will prepare."

Outside, a single cheer rose—brief, ordinary, affectionate—and then the campus settled into the softer noise of pages turning and friendships being made. In a world that demanded spectacle, stillness had chosen them. It would be enough.

Tomorrow he would announce the seminar. Tomorrow, he would draft the vows. Tomorrow, perhaps, the committee would return with guidelines meant to bind him and find, to their surprise, that he had already bound himself to something higher. But, for now, this moment was enough.

For now, he allowed himself one more look at the lantern-lit circles, at the students who had taken his burden and made it a banner without triumphalism, a service without servility. He closed his eyes and saw again the Seam's light pulsing in the ice, not conquering, not consuming—simply steady.

Witness over ownership. Service over spectacle. Preparation over power. The grammar of revelation.

He slept without dreams.

THIRTY-ONE

WITNESS

Journal of Winston Thornberry

I do not know who will read these words. Perhaps no one. Maybe only the Seam itself, listening through the silence of the page. But if another should one day find them, let this be clear: I was never the keeper of the Book. I was its servant, its witness.

What began in a classroom grew into something far beyond my measure. I thought of myself as only a lecturer, a man who drew constellations on chalkboards and asked tired students to look up. Yet in that looking up, something broke open—a seam, a door, a voice. I resisted. I guarded. I doubted. But in time, I obeyed.

The obstacles were many—mockery, suspicion, envy, even my own fear. I see now that they were not hindrances, but proving grounds. Each one asked me a question:

Will you guard the fire? Will you trust the timing? Will you remain faithful when silence seems safer?

And in the end, the answer was not found in eloquence or triumph. It was found in obedience. To speak when commanded. To guide when permitted. To prepare when entrusted. Nothing more.

The Book has waited a century in silence. It will outlast me and all who rage against it. Its purpose is not to make prophets or kings but servants—servants of truth, of love, of mercy. It is a reminder that we are not owners of revelation but participants in a design greater than we can comprehend.

What is that design? Not conquest. Not power. But service. To lift one another. To guard one another. To see in every life the spark of a universe that will not abandon us.

If I leave behind any testimony, let it be this:

We are not wanderers in chaos. We are children of a vast order. And though mystery surrounds us, mercy accompanies us. The hand that wrote the stars has not withdrawn.

Clara will carry her vow. The students will carry theirs. Elizabeth will find hers, Dr. Marlowe, in her fierce way, has already carried more than her share. And I? I will continue to prepare until preparation is no longer required.

To those who mocked, I offer no rebuttal. To those who feared, I offer no defense. To those who believed, I offer only this counsel: guard the fire not with walls, but with purpose. For fire must give light, or it dies.

And to the One whose voice I heard in the Seam, whose command shattered my silence and steadied my fear: I have spoken. I have guided. I have prepared. The rest is yours.

—W.T.

EPILOGUE

The campus returned to its rhythms, but the rhythms were not the same. Students still crossed the quad with books and backpacks, but in the evenings, they gathered under the open sky, their lanterns circling like constellations fallen to earth. Some studied astronomy with sharper eyes, others poetry with deeper hunger. Yet in all of them lingered a sense that knowledge was no longer merely information—it was invitation.

Dr. Ellis, bitter though he remained, could not silence what had begun. Dr. Khan smiled more easily now, as though the fire had thawed something long frozen. And Clara walked among her peers with a notebook always in hand, her words less argument than reminder: vows remain.

As for Winston, he kept teaching. Not louder, not grander, but steadier. He no longer feared that mystery would undo him; he knew now that mystery had carried him all along. In his study, the Book remained closed when it must, open when it could, alive always with the hum of a Seam that never slept.

What began with whispers in a lecture hall had become something greater: a covenant carried not by one man, but by many. The fire had leapt, not to consume, but to illuminate.

And beyond the campus, beyond the reach of cameras and committees, the stars remained. They shone as they had for centuries, but to those who had listened they no longer seemed indifferent. They seemed patient. Watching. Waiting.

The Seam would open again. Of this, Winston was certain. But it would not be for him alone. The witness had been passed on.

www.ingramcontent.com/pod-product-compliance
Lightning Source LLC
LaVergne TN
LVHW010636110826
845149LV00014B/2848

* 9 7 9 8 9 9 4 6 7 4 3 0 7 *